Praise for The Lock

'I'm a big fan of B P Walter. You should be, too … his novels are charged with darkness and plotted with watchmaker precision. And *The Locked Attic* is his sneakiest, snakiest thriller to date – a mind game in which the rules are ever-shifting'
A. J. FINN

'Genuinely compelling domestic noir'
CARA HUNTER

'Sinister and chilling, clever and gripping. *The Locked Attic* is the kind of just-one-more-page thriller that B P Walter is justly celebrated for'
CHRIS WHITAKER

'*The Locked Attic* is such an achievement. I was intrigued all the way and loved how it all came together'
SUSAN LEWIS

'The most compulsively readable, blistering, addictive mystery I've read all year'
GREG BUCHANAN

'I was completely hooked. Absolutely addictive'
JOHN MARRS

'An unusual book which is part thriller, part coming of age… I raced through this'
CATHERINE COOPER

'Sharp, intelligent and compelling, this dark thriller will captivate you from the very first page'
LESLEY KARA

'Hooks you from page one and never lets go. Unputdownable'
MELANIE BLAKE

'I flew through *The Locked Attic*. It is a real page turner'
PATRICIA GIBNEY

'Cleverly written with lots of twists I never expected'
HELEN PHIFER

'Sinister, expertly plotted and extremely moreish'
CAROLINE CORCORAN

'A dark and totally addictive read'
S.E. LYNES

'Shifting time frames and multiple narrations deliver a deliciously layered story about family secrets and tragic loss… A riveting read'
WENDY WALKER

'A masterful tale of lies, secrets and obsession'
GUY MORPUSS

'Thoroughly engrossing. I had NO idea where the twists and turns were going to take me'
LIZZY BARBER

'A complete thrill ride from the first page until the last… *The Locked Attic* will be your new obsession'
PAMELA CRANE

'Tense, gripping, and heartbreaking. And it comes with a shocking twist you'll never see coming'
TIM GLISTER

'Perpetually twisting and genuinely unputdownable, *The Locked Attic* is an up-all-night powerhouse of a novel'
LAURIE ELIZABETH FLYNN

'Wow! *The Locked Attic* completely sucked me in'
PHILIPPA EAST

B P Walter was born and raised in Essex. After spending his childhood and teenage years reading compulsively, he worked in bookshops then went to the University of Southampton to study Film and English followed by an MA in Film & Cultural Management. He is an alumnus of the Faber Academy and formerly worked in social media coordination for Waterstones in London.

twitter.com/barnabywalter
facebook.com/BPWalterAuthor
instagram.com/bpwalterauthor

Also by B P Walter

THE LOCKED ATTIC

B P WALTER

One More Chapter

a division of HarperCollins*Publishers*

1 London Bridge Street

London SE1 9GF

www.harpercollins.co.uk

HarperCollins*Publishers*

1st Floor, Watermarque Building, Ringsend Road

Dublin 4, Ireland

This paperback edition 2022

1

First published in Great Britain by

HarperCollins*Publishers* 2022

Copyright © B P Walter 2022

B P Walter asserts the moral right to

be identified as the author of this work

A catalogue record of this book is available from the British Library

ISBN: 978-0-00-844612-3

Printed and bound in the UK using 100% Renewable Electricity by CPI Group (UK) Ltd

For my wonderful agent Joanna and the amazing team at
Hardman & Swainson

The Bible tells us to love our neighbours, and also to love our enemies; probably because generally they are the same people.

– G. K. Chesterton

Stephanie

NOW

I am in hospital. Confused, in pain, broken.

Desperately, I try to find something about my situation that might calm me, and try to force my brain to focus on the ambient sound of nurses hurrying around and patients demanding food and medication – continuous white noise that's distracting, yes, but not exactly soothing.

Sinister shapes and sounds move through my mind, like a shifting fog, sometimes obscuring, sometimes revealing. I can remember snatches of what happened. Broken fragments that are never quite properly defined. It's like I'm behind a wall of glass of ever varying density and transparency.

How did I end up here?

I try to take myself back to the moment right before

the pain thudded through my body. Small details start to take hold. Fingernails scratching on wood. Some sort of scrabbling. Trying to pull myself up. Hunting for something. Searching for something.

I'm pulled away from my thoughts by a kind-sounding nurse, who asks me if I'm up to taking a sip of water. I do my best, but my throat feels horribly dry and there's a strange taste – something acidic, perhaps. Like orange juice past its prime. When I mention this to the nurse, she says it's quite normal – a mixture of the shock and the pain meds. I ask if she knows what happened to me, and she nods and says, 'Yes, I heard, dear, when you were brought in yesterday.'

I frown, causing a sore tugging sensation to spread across my forehead. 'Yesterday? I've been here…'

'You were kept overnight, dear, for monitoring. What a horrible thing to happen, especially… well, with everything that's been going on…'

I notice her eyes flick over to the window, but I don't trust myself to move enough to follow her gaze properly. She seems to think I'd know what she's talking about. That I'd have the same details to hand as her. In my disoriented state, that's the thing that seems the most incongruous right at that moment. Absurdly, my mind flicks to a scene in a movie – *The Matrix*, I think – of a man waking up in a pod filled with liquid, and he's one of thousands in a strange world he doesn't recognise. His whole sense of what's real and what's inside his head has been turned upside down. Like I've been shown two images in a spot-the-difference game, only I can't even tell what's the same. It makes me feel powerless.

But as I lie here, those vague memories start to take shape. Edges start to appear. Clarity begins to emerge. And the image of a house arrives, clear and fully formed at the front of my mind.

The Franklins' house.

54 Oak Tree Close.

I remember what my son said, the day he first visited that place. 'Something's not quite right.' It sent a prickle down the back of my neck at the time, and it does so again now. It's all to do with that house. The things that happened there. What's hidden in the attic.

I reach for another sip of water and realise my hands have started to shake.

ONE

Stephanie

SEVEN MONTHS BEFORE THE EXPLOSION

It's hard to really know where this all started.

When I first met my husband? When we had our boy? When we moved to Oak Tree Close? They all vaguely feel like beginnings in some way. But I think the day that properly set the wheels in motion was the late October night I picked up my sixteen-year-old son Danny from his band practice at his mate Scotty's. The band practice had actually become a sort of party to celebrate Scotty's seventeenth birthday, which was officially the following week, but Danny would be in America then and I think a few of the others couldn't make it. So the party was tacked on to the end of their normal Friday night band practice. My husband had dropped him off, and even though he said he didn't mind going back to get him, I could tell he didn't want to venture out in the cold again. So I said I'd go.

I hadn't really wanted Danny to go to the party, but Pete said it was harsh to make the boy miss out just because we were going away the next day. 'He won't be able to sleep. He'll be excited anyway, so he might as well be hanging out with his friends.' I told him teenagers grow out of that so-excited-I-can't-sleep routine before a holiday, and besides, him being awake and out partying means *we* have to be awake – something that, at the age of sixteen, he probably hadn't quite clocked.

The temperature was falling fast and the light in the car had gone off, making the street lamps along the road seem even brighter, glowing in a thin mist that was starting to spread through the night air. I noticed the house to my left had Halloween decorations strung through the trees – warm-white fairy lights intertwined with a sequence of pumpkins and fake orange leaves. They'd probably just remove the pumpkins once the 31st had passed; that way they'd already have their Christmas lights up, prepped and ready. They put them up early around here, probably because so many of the families jetted off to their holiday homes in December. We'd never done that – a proper British Christmas was what Pete liked and, over the years, I'd grown to like it too. It had never been that much fun with my parents, but I'd got into the swing of things when I had kids of my own. Watching Danny tear open his presents really had been that special kind of magic so many parents talk about, especially when he was younger.

I was drawn out of my seasonal nostalgia by a noise from over near Scotty's house. The front door had opened and two figures had started walking along the path through the front garden and over towards me.

'Hi, boys,' I said, as Danny and Jonathan got in. I'd completely forgotten we were giving Danny's bandmate and schoolfriend Jonathan Franklin a lift, although since he lived practically opposite us it didn't really make much of a difference. I was used to ferrying him about, and at least the Franklins often returned the favour.

'Good party?' I asked, when neither of them replied to my cheery greeting. I started driving, wondering what on earth was going on. I usually got a 'Hiya' at the very least from Danny, and Jonathan wasn't a rude, unfriendly boy, although he could be a little shy.

There was something else different too, something I realised as I manoeuvred the car out of the tight cul-de-sac and onto Elm Tree Road, which was just one of the many rabbit-warren-like streets that made up our neighbourhood. Danny was in the front with me, his guitar clutched between his legs. He didn't usually do this, not when we had Jonathan in the car. They'd always sit in the back and talk about things – trivial stuff, like the fact Scotty always played his guitar slightly flat, or something that had happened in maths class and why Mr Redmond was 'such a prick'. But nothing was said at all. Silent and separated, they just sat as I drove, an awkward tension seeming to radiate off both of them.

'Is everything OK?' I asked, and Danny finally stirred, jerking his head towards me as if he'd only just realised I was there. 'Oh fine, yeah… just tired.'

He wasn't just tired. I knew something was wrong. But it didn't look like he was going to elaborate, not while Jonathan was in the car. Nor did he seem keen to hang around when we got home, after his friend had sloped off to his own house over the road. He just disappeared upstairs, swiftly followed by his father, asking if he had everything packed for the flight tomorrow.

And that was that.

He behaved relatively normally the next day, was generally fine in America, if a tad quiet, while we stayed with Pete's brother. It was only once we returned and the days started to edge into winter that that odd night in the car with the two boys came back into my mind. And everything went spinning off in another direction. A direction that both changed my world and obliterated it.

TWO

Stephanie

THE DAY OF THE EXPLOSION

I was having a dream when the first explosion occurred. Something about my wedding day, but we couldn't find any flowers – someone had stolen them from the church, and then we ended up finding them in a Tesco bag-for-life out in the graveyard, swimming in blood. It was all rather horrible, especially when the vicar, who was the spitting image of Frank Sinatra, poured gasoline onto them, cackling as he did it, and created a mini blaze amongst the gravestones. Stranger still, my mother was there, looking delighted, which was a rarity in itself, and stood behind the burning flowers singing 'We Three Kings', the song she'd sung to me as a child, no matter what time of year it was. Desperate to take hold of her, I reached out my hand, stretching, trying to reach her.

But the explosion put an end to all that.

I was pulled into reality in an instant, flailing around in my duvet, looking about me, unsure where the noise was coming from. It was so loud, and deep, with a heavy bass resonance so strong it was almost as if I could still feel it vibrating within me.

I felt both alert and disorientated as I scrabbled around on the bedside table for my phone. I picked it up and looked at the time. 6.45am. I scrolled through the in-built news app, then BBC News, but couldn't find any reports. I opened up Twitter and typed in *Kent* and *Bang*. Someone called CassieLovesZayn had tweeted:

OMFG what the fuck was that? MASSIVE bang. Anyone else in Hangway in Kent hear it?

A guy simply called Gavin had replied:

Yeah, love. Massive. Definitely a bomb.

Although I wasn't any more of an expert than Gavin, I had to agree with him – a noise that loud certainly sounded like a bomb blast, or at least what I'd imagine one to sound like. But there wasn't anywhere around here someone would want to attack. We weren't near any tourist landmarks that would result in mass fatalities. I was continuing to scroll when I saw a woman named LexieStarSigns had tweeted:

The power station has gone up, it's on fire! I can see it from my house!

I rushed to the balcony. The trees were too high for me to see much, but there was something there that wasn't usually part of my morning view. A dark, ominous layer, getting larger, blossoming and growing and starting to fill the sky above the trees and the woodland my house backed onto.

I returned to my bed. Was I in danger? If the power station had gone up, was I at risk of shrapnel falling on my house or smoke inhalation or something? Whilst the thought of my own death no longer troubled me, I still didn't really like the idea of choking amidst the unfurling carpet of black smoke crawling its way across the horizon.

I spent the best part of the next half hour sitting on my bed, scrolling through social media, checking what people were saying and watching the news organisations steadily get pictures and reports up on their websites; some embedded tweets from the public amidst their reporting, including the ones I'd already read, along with a statement from Kent Police saying they were dealing with a 'major incident' and in the process of evacuating nearby residences within a two-mile radius of the power station. All other residents within the Hangway area must apparently stay inside their houses and keep away from windows.

In spite of the advice, I returned to the French windows of the bedroom and went out onto the balcony. The sky was growing darker with the smoke now and there was a strange scent in the air. Burning, yes, but something else, something nasty and chemical-smelling. I went back inside and started to wander through the dark house. Though the day wasn't especially chilly, it was cold out on the landing. Perhaps the chill came from how empty the place was. Large empty houses were sad things. All that space just felt so unnecessary. I never used the cinema room, or the home gym, or the swimming pool anymore. I kept mostly to my bedroom, interspersed with trips to the kitchen to get myself bowls of cereal or to the hallway to take in deliveries.

It was when I went down to the kitchen to make myself a coffee that I realised the power wasn't working. I glanced at my phone and saw that it had no connection to the house Wi-Fi. Instead of coffee, I had a glass of orange juice, congratulating myself for it still being fresh and drinkable. I wasn't a totally pathetic recluse, I thought to myself as I journeyed back upstairs. I didn't let food go off; I still ate reasonably well. But in spite of that, things were far from calm in my world. I was always teetering on the edge of reality and something else, something more dangerous but still strangely tempting. Madness, perhaps? I don't think I ever properly lost my grasp, not completely. There were nights when I thought I had literally gone mad with my grief and I'd never pull myself out. But then the spell would break and the dawn would come and I would be sitting there, clutching a pillow, realising I was both starving and thirsty and I would manage to pull myself up, take a shower and carry on with my day. My day inside, doing nothing much but existing. Reading books. Tidying. Watching TV without any real interest or enjoyment. It's a cruel irony that these are the things I never felt like I had the time to do when everything was how it was meant to be. I always wished I had more free time. I never expected to end up with too much of it.

Instead of going back to my room, I went to Danny's bedroom. It still showed evidence of his younger self, before he became a teenager. A large stack of boardgames remained at the bottom of his wardrobe that he hadn't touched since he was ten. Some plush cuddly toys from Disney movies like *Lilo & Stitch* and *Monsters, Inc.* were under the bed – too embarrassing for him to have had on show, but too loved to be discarded completely. On the surface level, some things had changed though. The posters of *Harry Potter* had been taken down and replaced with ones of video games that I knew next to nothing about. I didn't like them – they featured angry-looking men and overly sexualised women and cars. They gave the room an edge I didn't like. Something a bit hard and laddish, something I didn't want my son to turn into. I went over to his bed and sat down cross-legged on it. I was tempted to curl back up into the covers and breathe in his smell and get lost in a world of memories, but I knew I shouldn't do that. If I did that, I wouldn't leave for hours. Images of his childhood would flash before me, as if projected into the darkness of my mind by a beam of light both dim and vivid, flickering and ultra-sharp. Him splashing about in his paddling pool on the balcony garden when we had our London flat. Him running through the leaves in the park, kicking them into the air, laughing and shrieking. And more recent moments that I can't escape, no matter how much I want to. His change of behaviour. His moods. The secrets he wouldn't share. And the things he knew that I so wished he hadn't.

I stared out at my dead son's belongings and couldn't help but feel the crushing weight of everything in the room pressing down on me. All the things he'd owned, all the toys he'd played with, all the clothes he'd worn, all the books he'd read and the movies he'd watched. And mingled amongst them, all the things he'd never do, all the clothes he'd never wear again, all the books he'd never get around to reading, all the movies he'd never watch. All the secrets he'd never share. And there were a fair number of those in here, I was sure of that. Things I would probably never know. Things I'd been in the middle of uncovering just before it all happened. Before everything ended.

The day my husband and son were killed.

THREE

Stephanie

FOUR MONTHS BEFORE THE EXPLOSION

The last conversation with my husband before he died was a stupid spat about how he'd got the washing mixed up and seemed to have lost a number of my things and Danny's rugby shorts in the process. It wasn't the first time things had gone missing – a favourite dress of mine had vanished, one I'd wear for special occasions, like a rare evening out to a posh restaurant with Pete, along with some of my underwear and shorts. Pete had said they must be in my cupboard and I just wasn't looking properly. I took everything out and put it back again, just to prove him wrong.

'Whilst I love it when you try to be helpful, I think perhaps you should just leave the laundry to me,' I'd said bluntly as I flung my things back in, coat hangers scraping as metal hit metal.

'You're always saying I should do more myself while we find a new housekeeper,' he moaned as I rather dramatically swung the cupboard doors shut. I still had Danny's PE kit to sort out. Part of me wondered if Danny should be doing this himself, now that he was sixteen and it was his own choice to be playing football after school. I was also furious that, after what had happened the night before, this day – the penultimate day of the Christmas holidays – wasn't the calming, healing day we'd planned. Granted, Danny had seemed much better during the morning, trying to reassure us he was OK after what had happened the night before. He had given me such a fright.

The mention of a potential housekeeper led to another mini-argument, something I was trying to avoid. With something evidently on Danny's mind, I had hoped Pete and I could have avoided petty squabbles for one day at least, just whilst we tried to find out what was going on. It was stupid, the idea that we should have someone cleaning our house and washing our clothes and doing the ironing when we could easily do it ourselves. I only worked part-time at the local travel agent's in the high street, and Pete had started to take more of a backseat role in his company. It wasn't like we didn't have the time. Although time did still seem to run away with us, and, even though I hated to admit it, part of me did miss having someone doing everything for us when we'd lived in our house on Warwick Square in central London. Upon moving to Kent, I had been adamant that a luxury like that wasn't 'an essential' and although I relented and allowed Pete to employ a cleaner who came in once a week, a 'housekeeper' felt way too old-fashioned and more like something you'd find in *Downton Abbey* than in a house in the suburbs.

Pete and I had been so caught up in our disagreement, I'd forgotten the plan for the afternoon: that Danny was to go to the cinema with his dad to cheer him up, followed by a pizza together. Pete was going to get to the root of what had been wrong with him for the past few months. And what had caused the unsettling drama of the night before. But all this was thrown into disarray when Danny asked if he could go round his friend Scotty's for band practice. The request made me instantly anxious. 'But... you and the band haven't got together for months... and... are you sure you're feeling up to that? I don't think it's a good idea after what happened...'

I didn't know how to put into words what had happened mere hours previously. I was still shaken to the core with the fear of it and no matter how much Danny insisted the whole incident hadn't been as serious as I feared, I was still haunted by that feeling of complete and utter dread. The curtains swaying in the wind on the balcony. The sky lighting up with fireworks. That feeling of world-altering, unstoppable dread and panic lingering in the air around us.

But Pete told me it was a good sign that Danny wanted to be around his friends. He said it was good he wanted to see them and try to go back to normal. All talk of involving medical experts or therapists or medication could wait until the start of the new term, he assured me.

So I just went along with it.

My boy set off to his friend's house, Jonathan walking alongside him, with the plan that Pete would pick Danny up later to take him out for some dinner.

It was the last time I would ever see him alive.

I treated myself to a long bath that evening, before I knew anything was wrong, of course. I let the tension ebb away out of my body, the hot water gently lapping at my chin, the warm light complicated by a soothing silver-grey scented candle flickering on the little unit next to the bath. But any sense of calm I managed to achieve wasn't destined to last.

The hours went by and Pete and Danny didn't return.

I realised they would have a lot to talk about, which

worried me in and of itself. What was Danny saying to his father?

As the minutes ticked on, I became more and more worried and began to text them – short 'just checking everything's fine' messages at first, followed by more panicked demands they call me or at least confirm they were OK. I pulled on a comfy tracksuit and padded barefoot down the stairs, phone clutched in my hand, and sat next to the Christmas tree, hoping I would hear the car on the drive outside at any moment.

I got no reply to my messages. They didn't even come up as read. I then worried about what situation Pete might have had to deal with when he'd got there.

It was all going wrong. I'd hoped the band practice and dinner would help Danny relax. Get back to normal. Work his way through whatever was going on with his friends. And this weird atmosphere between us all would have dissipated.

But of course that never happened.

I got the call from the police a few minutes later.

I can't really remember what they said, but the key words had me running to the front door, forgetting to put on my shoes. I clung on to the fact that they were alive – they were still alive! – otherwise the police wouldn't have phoned; they'd have visited. I just needed to get to the hospital.

That's all, I told myself. Just get to the hospital and they'd be there – perhaps a bit bruised, maybe a broken arm or two, but they'd be alive; they'd mend.

It would all be OK.

As soon as I'd got out of the house and aimed the keys at my car, I saw her. Janet Franklin, walking her mother's enormous Newfoundland dog, Charlton. On normal days I found it funny how bored the dog always looked in Janet's company, as if he, like the rest of us, was tired of her smug superiority and snobbish jibes and endless stories about why her children are amazing at anything they do. But on that evening, I couldn't see the dog's face. In the light from the street lamps and the Christmas lights tastefully adorning her house, I could only make out Janet's face looking at me as if I were insane, dashing out of my house in the freezing cold without shoes or a coat. And I didn't wait for her to say anything. I just shouted at her. Shouted the only thing I had on my mind, that I needed to let out, to tell someone, otherwise my overwhelming panic might swallow me whole. 'A crash!' I said. 'They've been in a crash.'

Of course, I realise how it must have sounded to Janet. Saying *they* must have made her instantly fear for the life of her own son. Because her boy, Jonathan, so often got a lift home with us. And I could see it in her face, all the fear and disorientation and horror that were rushing up inside of me.

'But... I thought the boys were together? Jonathan's not come home... Is he...? Where...?'

Then it all changed. Within a second, the whole situation was reframed, for Janet at least. Because her boy came running up to her out of nowhere, and we both stared at him.

'Oh my God!' she shouted and ran to him, putting her arms around him. 'Where the hell have you been?'

'I decided to run back from Scotty's,' he said to his mum, pulling away from her. 'I had my gym stuff on already.'

She continued to just stare at him, then came the relief. Even in the dim light I could see it fill her face as she stepped forwards and clutched him in her arms once more, leaving me to turn away and get into the car, letting waves of white-hot fury rush across me – fury at her for delaying me, for wasting this past minute or so, a minute that could have been vital.

It could have been. But it wasn't. Because they were dead by the time I reached the hospital. They'd died even before I'd put the key in the ignition.

FOUR

Stephanie

THE DAY OF THE EXPLOSION

Months on, I could still picture her face, although I may have gone over it in my mind, filling in the details, the way you try to sharpen a photo on your phone that's a bit blurry. The obvious wave of relief. The relief her son hadn't been smashed up and killed, wasn't on the way to hospital, fighting for his life. As I sat in Danny's room, thinking back, I couldn't help but hate her. I understood, of course I did. But I hated her all the same. For being so obvious with her relief, and for being glad that it was my boy, and not hers. And for the fact that, if our roles were switched, I would have felt the same thing.

Janet wasn't the only person whom I'd hated during those long nights of darkness alone in the house, curled up in a ball under my duvet. There were times when I thought about Jonathan too. And there was a lot to think about there. I hadn't dealt with any of it.

A noise outside the bedroom made me jump. It was the sound of a police car – the electronic screech they sometimes make. Not a full nee-naw, but definitely an 'emergency services' sort of sound.

I got up and watched it through Danny's bedroom window, which looked out onto the front drive and Oak Tree Close.

Then the announcement began: *'This is an emergency announcement. There has been a major incident in the area. Please stay inside your home for the present time and stand away from all windows. You will be told when it is safe to leave your house. Stay inside.'*

The car then crawled off around the bend as Oak Tree Close snaked towards Tyler Way, and in the distance I could hear the same words being repeated. At this time of year, the road outside should be sunlit and bright, but today the sun had been smudged out with ever thickening smoke, now covering most of the visible sky above the houses and trees. It was like we were caught in the middle of a post-apocalyptic storm with no wind and rain but an eerie half-light that clearly told you danger was coming.

As I looked out, my gaze settled on the house across the street. The Franklins' residence.

And for a moment – a blink-and-you-miss-it moment – I was convinced I saw someone. Someone doing the same thing as me. Janet's husband, Richard, perhaps, looking out of one of the bedroom windows? Watching. Or was it Jonathan?

Although I wouldn't be able to swear it under oath, I had a feeling the figure had been male, but from this distance it was impossible to be sure. Were they just staring out at the street to see what wreckage and smoke the explosion had caused? Or had they been watching me?

I think back to the other occasions I've sworn I've seen someone at one of the windows of that house, looking over at mine. Then my mind turns to Danny's friendship with Jonathan. How he had turned up that day, just as I'd learned about the accident.

During my mad, tortured moments of grief, when my mind spiralled into cavernous pits that seemed never-ending, I'd wondered if that boy had caused Danny and Pete's deaths. Wondered if he had somehow tampered with the brakes, somehow made the car unsafe. I had seen him lingering by the house when I'd nipped out to put the recycling by the pavement the day before the crash. I'd presumed he'd been waiting to speak to Danny, and he'd ignored me when I called out to him. The events of that evening, and the horror of the day after, had temporarily driven it from my mind.

Steadily, as the devastation changed and I adapted as best I could to my terrible new world, I realised my fears were probably warped by grief rather than informed by fact. I think I was searching for blame where none existed.

Or perhaps blame *did* exist.

I was just looking in the wrong place, or thinking about it the wrong way.

Because Jonathan knew something. He still did. And he was living in that house, just a matter of metres away.

I turned back to the room I was in and switched my gaze to Danny's possessions. I'd carried out a full-scale search of this place about two weeks after he died, desperate to find out what had been going on in the lead-up to his death that had changed the child I loved from a happy, sprightly, cheery boy into someone sullen, harsh and withdrawn, as if the world was ending around him. But I'd found nothing. Nothing very much of interest. No discovery that helped make sense of any of it. No drugs. Nothing shocking like a weapon or a pile of blood-stained money. There was a packet of Durex thin-feel condoms pushed to the back of his sock drawer, but that wasn't very surprising. I just left them where they were. I could feel the box wasn't completely empty, which was something of a relief, although it had been opened. I hadn't been sure if he was sexually active, but he'd been on some dates with a couple of girls at school since he was fifteen. Nobody became a girlfriend as such, though.

Now, they never would.

There were no answers to my questions in his room. Even his laptop and phone had revealed nothing as far as I could find.

I turned back to the window, wondering if I should duck down or stand far away from it like the announcement suggested. Then, as my gaze settled on the house opposite, I thought about what I had heard during the past couple of months. I thought about what Danny had told me. The snatched parts of conversation. The worry burning within me.

In an instant, I knew what to do.

The answers to my questions lay within those walls. Within that house. And the family who lived inside it.

It didn't take me long to get ready. I pulled on some tracksuit bottoms, a T-shirt, and a zip-up hoody. I tied my hair back in a pony-tail. I went down to the hallway and pulled on the trainers I'd barely worn in the last four months. Then I opened the front door.

As soon as I stepped out, I could tell something was different. Not just the light. That was still low, like it was twilight and not an early morning in late spring. I noticed it on the cars first – a strange, fuzzy grey layer that was starting to build up over the roof, the bonnet, and on the ground and grass too, like dirty snow. And the air. It felt warm and thick to breathe, with that harsh, chemical smell.

Trying not to think about the danger I was putting myself in, I carried on, allowing the front door to close behind me. I made my way down the drive, and out into the road. I could hear some alarms going off in the distance, and the far-off screech of sirens. But the immediate space around me was oddly peaceful. No shriek of school kids. No cars zooming past. Just... silence.

After standing on the pavement for almost a full minute, I continued with my journey. A small journey, yes. But for me, at that moment, it felt momentous.

I tried to remind myself that there was nothing left to harm me. There was no hell I could bring about that I had not already inhabited in these months of white-hot despair.

Maybe that was why, while crossing the road with my sleeves up to my face to stop me inhaling the smoke, and observing the dreamlike world that used to be our neighbourhood, I felt like I'd slipped into another time and place altogether. Perhaps I'd come through my months of grief and entered a new world that looked the same as before but grimmer, dirtier, and covered in ash. A distortion of reality, as cruel as it was beautiful.

I arrived at the front door of 54 Oak Tree Close, an impressive-looking house, though slightly smaller than ours, and without waiting to think about what I was doing for any longer, I reached up and rang the doorbell.

I heard the Franklins before I saw any of them. Someone said 'Who is it? Is it the police?' then another voice said 'What's happening?'

Janet Franklin opened the door a few moments later. In her early fifties with slightly greying hair and of average height and build – and dressed today in a warm-looking pale-lilac dressing gown – she was like a stereotype of a comfortable, middle-class suburban woman.

'What... Stephanie? What are you doing out here?' She looked confused and, as her eyes scanned across me, a little irritated.

I was well aware that Janet liked to control everything, even down to preposterous details. From school fêtes to charity raffles, she liked to have a hand in steering the ship to make sure everything and everyone ended up at one destination: hers. It was likely the 'major incident' this morning had already thrown her into a frustrated mood (the thought of a serious situation happening that didn't require her input must be very trying for her) and me turning up at her door, standing in front of her for the first time in weeks, was the final straw.

'Is there some sort of... I don't know... crisis? Anything I can help with?'

I should have thought about my opening pitch for getting into her house, but standing there, with my mouth open in front of her, all I could think of saying was 'I... didn't want to be alone. Can I come in?'

She gaped at me for a good few seconds, then said, 'Well... oh... all right, come in.' She stood back, allowing me over the threshold. 'Perhaps... er... leave your shoes outside.'

Trying to resist the temptation to roll my eyes, I tugged off the trainers and left them just inside the door on the mat.

'We haven't seen you in so long, Stephanie. As you know, I tried to message, but after your text...'

This was true. Janet had, I suppose to her credit, reached out to me during the first few weeks of my grief. She'd sent me a few WhatsApp messages, asking if there was anything she could get for me at the shops and saying if I ever wanted to talk I could join her on one of her walks with Charlton. I suppose it was nice. Kind. The sort of thing a friend would do. But Janet had never really been a friend. And in the midst of my grief, all her previous slights and thinly veiled nasty comments were somehow magnified. Little things, like the time when she pulled a face at the school charity bake sale because I'd brought in my cupcakes in an Asda carrier bag, or when she'd presumed I wouldn't know what celeriac was. I'd never really worked out if it was because I'm a bit younger than her and her gaggle of other ultra-mums, or if she could just tell I came from a less moneyed background, or if it was the remnants of my Somerset accent, which was faint but still present on some words. Whatever the reason, a colder, more calculated side of Janet had very much made sure I didn't feel entirely welcome within her little community, and that she only tolerated my son because he was Jonathan's friend. I hadn't said all this in my response to her message. I'd just replied *No, thank you* and left it at that.

'I know… I've not really felt like doing much,' I said, straightening up to face Janet in the low light of the hallway.

Janet clearly felt embarrassed by this answer because she changed the subject and said, 'All the power is out. I suppose it's the same over at yours. Come through into the lounge and I'll make you some tea – the Aga's warm still.'

Wishing I'd paused to come up with some sort of plan of action, I walked along the narrow hallway and into the lounge. I didn't quite know how I was going to do it, but it was better than doing nothing.

It was time to get some answers.

FIVE

Stephanie

TWO YEARS BEFORE THE EXPLOSION

Naturally shy and quiet people are often called upon to excuse or explain their dislike of talking to strangers or wishing to avoid them completely, and this was certainly the case between Pete and me. When we were in London, he would often ask why I didn't just 'chat to some of the neighbours' in our apartment or see if Delores in the flat next to ours wanted to grab a coffee sometime.

'Because Delores is a high-powered businesswoman who co-manages a fashion and cosmetics brand. We have nothing in common.'

This wasn't entirely truthful – or at least, not the whole truth. Of course, it was definitely a factor, but I still would have felt squeamish about just starting up a conversation with her, even if she spent her days doing the things I did: shopping for food, taking my husband's clothes to the dry cleaner's, trying to match my son's socks and put them into drawers.

After I'd finished university, I'd fully planned to get a job and put my degree to use, but the more the years went by, the less attractive the idea became. Having to prove myself to bosses, get my annual leave signed off, trying to befriend and be polite to colleagues – all of it started to sound less like normal life and more like a nightmare. A nightmare others were fully able to cope with, whereas I would probably be reduced to a trembling wreck.

So when we moved to Oak Tree Close, I wasn't exactly in a hurry to start knocking on doors with muffin baskets saying, 'Hi, we've just moved in!' as they do in television shows. I might have got used to the comfortable way of life that Pete's money had brought me, but that didn't mean I could easily converse with those who had known nothing other than extreme wealth for their entire lives.

In some ways, London was more suited to me, as nobody really had much time for or interest in others. In Oak Tree Close, however, it became immediately clear we'd be expected to 'participate'. The word sounded like a threat when I first heard it in that context, falling from the lips of a woman named Drucilla, who lived five doors down, and arrived at our door a mere three hours after we'd said goodbye to the men from the moving firm.

'I've brought you some local organic honey that my brother-in-law produces over in Cheshawk Road,' she said, beaming, her eyes bright but slightly shifty, darting around the hallway at the boxes stacked along the corridor. She looked to be in her early forties, with a perfectly styled blonde haircut and earrings that reminded me of Camilla Parker-Bowles. I was a bit puzzled at first, before I realised it was some kind of welcome-to-the-neighbourhood offering. I tried to be polite and friendly, and she was too, in a way, but there was a definite edge to the way she said, 'We're all good friends along Oak Tree Close and welcome anyone and everyone to the fold, especially those who are ready to contribute and participate.' *Contribute and participate.* I felt myself going weak even at the thought of it. Bring-and-buy sales at the local church? Coffee mornings and book clubs? Nothing of this kind was ever expected of me when we lived amidst the busy streets of central London.

As it happened, Drucilla Maguire and her family didn't turn out to be the nosy neighbours that defined our time in Oak Tree Close. That honour, of course, fell to Janet and Richard Franklin.

I first met them five days after our arrival. I'd decided to return to my daily run – something I had done in London nearly every day without fail, whatever the weather, enjoying the familiarity of my route along Elisabeth Street and back to Warwick Square, stopping off for a strawberry-flavoured mineral water at the Sainsbury's near Victoria Coach Station. I knew if I didn't get back into the habit sooner or later, I'd end up losing one of my favourite hobbies. So, on a pleasant Thursday afternoon, I got into my running clothes and set off down the road, deciding against any listening material while I got used to the geography of the neighbourhoods. And it was on this first run, less than five minutes in, that I collided with a large metallic-blue Range Rover. Or rather, it collided with me, properly knocking me over onto the hard ground.

It was probably my fault, misjudging how far away the car was from me as I ran across the road.

I looked up to see a man and a boy in the front seats, both staring in shock. Then the man quickly got out of the car and came over to me.

'Are you all right?' he asked. His voice was low and well-spoken, with a clear note of worry in his words. I looked up at him, focusing on his face, still recovering from the shock of having been knocked over. It was lined with age – I guessed he was probably about sixty, with his hair transitioning from light-brown to grey. He was wearing thick squarish glasses, and behind them I could see the concern and alarm in his eyes. They widened a little when I didn't answer straightaway. Perhaps he feared I'd hit my head and could be concussed. Maybe he just envisaged a lengthy and costly lawsuit.

'I'm fine,' I said, taking his hand and getting shakily to my feet. 'It was my fault, I'm sorry.' I felt something wet on my leg and looking down was startled to see blood already staining the grey material of my leggings.

'You're injured. Get in the car and I'll give you a lift back.'

I looked up at him, frowning. He seemed to guess what I was thinking.

'I'm Richard Franklin at number 55. You've just moved in opposite us, haven't you? Number 42?'

'That's right,' I said, getting into the back seat of the car, nodding in both confirmation and thanks to him as he stood back with his hand on the door so I could gingerly bend my legs. I was quietly terrified of getting blood on the spotless seats, wincing as I went to close the car door. To my surprise, Richard took my hand instead, peering down to examine it.

'You've grazed your palms badly. Sorry, I should have noticed that before I pulled you up. It must have hurt.'

'Oh... er... I didn't notice...' I said, a little embarrassed. He didn't give back my hand straightaway, just stared at the scratches and granules of grit caught in my broken skin. Then his eyes came up to meet mine. An odd prickling sensation ran down my spine. He released my hand, gave me a thin smile and went to get back into the driver's seat. I looked ahead into the front of the car and could see the teenage boy watching me. As soon as he saw me notice him, his face snapped back to the road ahead.

The drive back only lasted a minute or two, but the silence made it feel like hours. When we got to the house, I turned to go back into mine, muttering some thanks about the lift, and was about to apologise again for all the bother when Richard cut across me. 'You can't just go home. You're bleeding. Come inside and we'll get you patched up.'

He didn't wait for a reply, instead walking purposefully to his front door, unlocking it and heading inside. His confidence and direct manner suggested he was a man used to having his orders obeyed, and I glanced over at his son, who was pulling a Nike sports bag out of the boot of the car. He didn't say anything, but met my gaze very briefly as he passed me by, following his father over the threshold of the house.

I didn't feel like I had much of an option.

Inside, I felt a sudden sense of going back in time to my childhood years, when I was a guest round a friend's house, viewing everything with a stranger's eyes. Back then I'd found houses like this both intimidating and exciting, with their many rooms and hidden places to explore – and explore I did, often through games of hide-and-seek, before going back home to my parents' much smaller and less grand house on the poorer side of our town. The Franklins' house looked well lived-in but also nicely cared for; a little untidy but still presentable. Tasteful creamy white wallpaper, hallway with a place for Joules-patterned wellington boots and trainers, a little table where post had been left (a new copy of the *Spectator* and a *RadioTimes* still in its delivery wrapping). I could hear the hum of voices – probably Radio 4 – coming from deeper into the house. Was someone else home? Or perhaps they left the radio on all day to dissuade burglars? I'd heard of people doing that.

I followed Richard through to the kitchen, which looked exactly how I expected – clean, but 'busy', with some books and magazines on the table at the end, a mug on the counter top and an Aga to the left of the window that looked out on a neatly manicured garden.

The warm, lived-in feel of the house would be welcoming to some, but to me it felt strangely alienating. I'd never experienced this. Not in my own home when I was young, nor in our London flat, which was too grand and imposing outside for my tastes, and too sleek and stylish and modern inside to ever feel like a proper home. But this, I thought looking around me, this was the type of house, the type of existence, people dreamed of. I wondered if they were happy here. If they felt as comfortable and as settled as the house suggested. I wondered if our home would be like this in a month, a year, a decade.

'Come over here and I'll put this on your grazes,' Richard said. His voice snapped me out of my thoughts. He'd conjured up a first-aid kit, as if from nowhere, and was taking the plastic off a pack of rolled-up bandages. 'And we should clean the wounds with one of these.' He picked up a small rectangle which I presumed to be an antiseptic wipe.

'Oh, I'm sorry, you don't have to go to all this trouble,' I said, feeling awkward having this much attention placed upon me by a stranger, when I just wanted to get home and sort out my cuts and scrapes myself.

Richard didn't offer me reassurance exactly, just shook his head and said, 'Come over here,' again. So I obeyed. He took out the wipe, took me by the wrist and gently brushed at my grazed hand, dislodging most of the grit with very slight streaks of blood coming off onto the material. Once again our eyes met, as they had done in the car. Then the moment was gone and he was starting to unwind the bandage and gently wrap it round my hand. That was when I heard a thud somewhere to my left, and within seconds a figure came into view through the archway that led into the lounge.

'Oh! What's going on here then?'

I turned to see a woman in her late forties or early fifties, with greying brown hair and a dark-red expensive-looking coat on, even though it was far from cold outside.

'Janet, you're... back early.' Richard said, drawing away from me quickly.

'My mother decided to go out with a friend without telling me, so I had a wasted journey. And I see you're spending time with a *friend*, too?' She gave the word *friend* the very slightest amount of emphasis – just enough for it to be awkward, but discreet enough for her to potentially deny it. She managed to give us both what appeared to be a warm smile anyway, as if she was genuinely happy to see me in her kitchen.

'This is Stephanie, from the house opposite. I hit her with the car. As in, she—'

'It was my fault,' I said, feeling I should come to his rescue. 'I was out on a run and completely in my own world and stepped out in front of the car without paying attention. But I'm fine, honestly. I really don't need all this fuss.' I clutched the slightly loose bandages around my hand. 'I should be going.'

'Oh my goodness, I won't hear of it. The least we can do is tend to your wounds. Let me see,' she said in a similarly authoritative voice to her husband's.

'It's fine, really,' I said again, stepping away and edging towards the doorway into the hall. 'Thank you so much for... everything.'

I knew I was sounding flustered and tried not to look at either of their faces as I turned and walked in the direction of the front door. I could hear my hosts following me, with Janet saying, 'Let me get the door for you.'

'I can manage!' I said, trying to sound bright and cheery but probably coming across as anything but.

Just as I stepped outside I heard car doors slam. Pete was home with Danny, but as he walked around the car he glanced in my direction and noticed me. He carried on into the house, but Danny let the front door swing close, jogged down the drive and crossed over the road to me.

'Mum?' he said, a note of confusion in his voice. The

bandages and the blood on my leg no doubt made the whole thing even more bizarre.

'I was just saying hello to our neighbours!' I said, still attempting to sound happy and carefree. I turned to introduce him. 'This is my son, Danny.'

'Oh, hello,' Janet said, distractedly.

'You look about Jonathan's age,' Richard said, more enthusiastically than I'd have expected. 'We should get him down so you can both meet properly.'

Janet looked at her husband, clearly puzzled by the suggestion, but before she could say anything he'd called up the stairs.

'Jonathan. Down here. *Now.*'

'Richard, what—?'

'He should meet his neighbour,' Richard said. 'It's only polite.'

I saw Danny's eyebrows rise, clearly feeling the awkwardness of the situation. Soon the thud of Jonathan coming down the stairs filled our ears, then the boy came into view.

'What?' he asked, bluntly.

'This is... Daniel, was it?' Richard said, gesturing at my son. Jonathan frowned, apparently unsure what was expected of him.

'Well, say hello,' Janet sighed at her son, seeming

keen to get this over and done with as quickly as possible.

'Er… hi,' Jonathan said, adolescent awkwardness writ large on his face.

'Hi,' Danny said, smiling, his hand lifting in a half-wave.

'Well, shake his hand,' Richard said through clenched teeth, sounding frustrated.

'Richard, really,' Janet protested.

Jonathan looked so embarrassed that I thought he might just bolt back upstairs at any moment. Danny, however, seemed to think the easiest way to get out of the situation was to go along with it. He stepped forward, the perfect model of old-fashioned politeness, and said, 'Great to meet you, Jonathan,' his hand outstretched.

For a moment, I wondered if Jonathan would decline just to spite his father, but after a few beats he stepped forward past his parents and shook Danny's hand.

'You two will probably become good friends,' Richard said.

I saw Janet's brow crease again. Maybe it was just the peculiar behaviour of her husband, or maybe she wasn't too sure about her son befriending mine. I had no way of knowing. But after we said goodbye and Danny and I headed back across the road towards the house, with me limping a little, I tried to put a positive spin on the whole thing. Perhaps it would be nice for Danny to already be acquainted with one of his classmates before the start of term.

If he was happy, I was happy.

That was how I'd always thought of motherhood. And aside from the more peculiar aspects to my first meeting with the Franklins, I hoped they would help play a part in us all feeling settled and welcome on Oak Tree Close.

SIX

Danny

TWO YEARS BEFORE THE EXPLOSION

I have to be honest with myself: the main reason for me trying to become friends with Jonathan is because of his sister.

Of course I know she'd never look at me. She and her friends hardly ever look up from their phones enough to notice boys staring at them. I sometimes watch her and the rest of them traipsing in and out of the house throughout that first summer in Oak Tree Close. My bedroom window gives me the perfect view across the road. It's like I have this burning need in me to see her in her natural habitat. It sounds a bit pervy or leery or just not very good, when I think about it, but I don't mean to be creepy. Mimi's just... well... amazing. She's sixteen. Nearly two years older than me. More confident. Seems totally sure of herself. Jonathan's more like me, though –

both in age and how he's slightly more awkward and quiet.

As well as the sister thing, it makes sense to get to know him. He's at the same school I'll be starting in September, and Mum and Dad keep encouraging me to be friendly if ever I see him in the street out for his evening run. I have asked how I'm supposed to be friendly when someone is dashing past you at God knows how many miles per hour.

But I know what they mean, and before long I get my chance to talk to him.

Earlier in the summer, I'd started to go swimming at the nearby leisure centre. It's a big, noisy place with three pools – one for teaching, one with a massive water slide thing, and another for lengths. I stick to the quieter pool with just lane swimming, which is apparently too boring for the shrieking kids. I quite often get a whole lane to myself and let the long summer days float past on a haze of chlorine and slow breaststroke. It feels weird, spending most of my time alone, when my main friends are back in London, but before long I realise I'm not missing them as much as I thought I would. I get the train in to London a few times to see them – it only takes thirty minutes to Charing Cross – but as the weeks go on I find I'm messaging them less on WhatsApp, not thinking about them as much throughout the days, and soon I have my own routine, my own life, and increasing nerves about starting the new school in September.

I'm thinking all the while I'm in the showers after doing my eighty lengths, then whilst getting dressed. It's close to closing time and the changing room is almost empty, apart from a dad with two young boys down the far end; he's chasing after one of them, who seems to be refusing to give up his brother's shoes. It takes me a while to realise I'm not the only other person: a guy my age is sitting around of the corner of the L-shaped room.

Once I see him, I realise who it is straightaway.

Jonathan Franklin.

He's pulling his trainers on and frowning a bit as if he's pissed off about something. I try to think back if I'd remembered seeing him in the pool. I'd been so caught up in my own thoughts I probably hadn't noticed him. But I notice him now, and within a split second a plan comes into my mind. This boy holds the key to my happiness. If I could just become friends with him, close enough to become a frequent visitor to his home, I might stand a chance of making her notice me. Making Mimi Franklin, the face that's haunted my dreams for weeks, aware of my existence for the first time. It's probably wrong of me to use him in this way, but at this very moment it all makes sense and seems perfectly reasonable to me.

'Hey mate,' I say, going over to him. I cringe a bit as I say it. I don't think I've ever called anyone *mate* in my entire life and it sounds fake, but it jolts Jonathan out of his daydream and makes him look up at me. I can tell he knows who I am – I'm not sure how, just in the way his face moves as his eyes meet mine.

'Oh… hi,' he says.

He looks awkward and embarrassed, as if he's been caught doing something he shouldn't. He gets up quickly, as if he felt I expected him to do something, almost like the way men stand up for women in those old-fashioned period dramas on TV. This causes his towel, trunks and bag to fall off the bench, leading to him hurriedly scrabbling around for them on the floor.

'You OK?' I ask, both a bit amused and puzzled by how oddly he's reacting. 'I'm Danny, by the way. We met a few weeks ago when I—'

'I know who you are,' Jonathan cuts in, a little bluntly.

'Of course, yeah, sorry,' I say, realising it was probably stupid of me to introduce myself again, especially considering how odd our first meeting was, with his dad suggesting we shake hands. A second or two passes with neither of us speaking, then he seems to regret his words and starts to apologise for interrupting me. 'Sorry, I just meant… I remember you…'

I laugh and he laughs too, and after that it isn't so awkward. I tell him I'm walking back home to Oak Tree Close and wonder if he wants to walk with me. He says he does and we leave the leisure centre together and start the trip back. Based on how the intro in the changing rooms had gone, I begin to worry the mile-long walk will be majorly awkward. But once we settle into our conversation, it's nice to listen to another guy my age talk about what it's like to live here and what to expect at Fletcher House School.

'It's not so bad, really,' Jonathan says. 'I mean, it's dull and stuff, but there aren't any scary teachers or awful school bullies or anything.'

The way he says 'scary teachers' makes me smile, as if we were eight-year-olds nervous about getting a terrifying character from a Roald Dahl book as a form tutor. As time goes on, little things like that make me realise how much I like Jonathan. He says things that made him seem both young and complicated at the same time. Or just in need of a hug.

'I hear they let girls into the sixth form,' I say, wondering if it's too early to bring up his sister.

'Yeah, but they get taught in the North Annex. They spend most of their time there, so we don't see them, really.'

He makes it sound like they're a rare breed of plant

being grown in a greenhouse. I try again. 'Is your sister in sixth form?'

He nodded. 'From September. But she won't be going to Fletcher's; she's staying at her school. They have sixth form anyway so there's no point her changing.'

Damn, I think to myself. I decide it might be too obvious to bring up Mimi specifically again, so I opt for a more general approach. 'Shame to hear we can't mix with the girls much. Though I'm sure you guys find ways.'

I laugh a bit and wait to hear if Jonathan and his friends do 'find ways', but he just shrugs and says 'I suppose.'

I laugh again and say, 'Well, if you didn't, all the Fletcher House boys would still be virgins when they went off to uni.'

I know it probably isn't that unusual to be a virgin when you go off to university. For all I know, most people are. But I thought if I sound more experienced than I am, Jonathan might find my company more appealing. It certainly raises his interest.

'What, you saying you've... you've already...?'

I make the agonising decision to be honest with him. 'No, I haven't. But that's kind of why I've been hoping we get to mix with the girls a bit at school.'

I glance at Jonathan in time to see him frown. 'So… you're after a girlfriend?'

It's my turn to shrug. 'No, not necessarily a girlfriend. I'm happy to play the field a bit. Nothing wrong with sleeping around, is there? Unless a particular girl comes along I want to get close to. Someone I, like, *really* fancy.' I make the sentence sound as casual as I can as an image of Mimi doing her warm-down stretches at the side of the road after a jog with a friend floats into my mind.

'I'm not really fussed about all that,' Jonathan says. He sounds almost revolted, like the idea of getting laid seems completely alien to him. 'I don't think it's good to shag around.'

This surprises me and I don't really know how to react to it. 'You mean, you get nervous chatting to girls?'

He's silent for a moment. We turn onto the far end of Oak Tree Close and I'm conscious we'll be at our houses in a couple of minutes. Perhaps I shouldn't have got onto this subject so soon, and with such little time.

Eventually, Jonathan says, 'A bit. But that's not what I mean. I just don't like the idea of men chasing after women as if they can't control themselves. As if that's all that matters.' His voice gets louder, as if this is something he clearly feels strongly about. 'It's pathetic, as if their entire lives are just a hunt for sex, and women are just these things to give it to them. I'm not going to be like that. I'm not going to be like—'

He stops himself suddenly, before he can finish his sentence.

'Like... like what?' I prompt, looking at him, noticing how his face is even more tense than before.

'Nothing,' he mutters. 'I just... nothing.'

I want to question him more, but he looks so upset with himself that I keep quiet as we get closer to our homes. When we part, he seems to have gone back to the embarrassed, awkward boy I'd spoken to in the changing rooms, not able to meet my eye and stumbling over his words. 'Thanks for walking me— I mean, walking with me. I'm sorry I... I mean. Yeah, sorry.'

I ignore all this, finding his awkward tumbling words too painful to acknowledge, and just say, 'Let's do it again some time. I mean, actually go swimming, or maybe for a run. Or maybe I could come round yours for tea.'

I'm afraid I sound desperate or weirdly keen, or even rude for inviting myself round, but he seems so relieved he hasn't spooked me with his strange little outburst it doesn't seem to matter. 'Yeah, let's do that. That would be great.'

He puts his number in my phone and I say I'll message him. Pleased the whole thing hadn't been a total disaster, I cross the street and let myself into the house. Inside, Mum is making tea and she calls out – something about getting the table ready.

'Did you have a good swim?' she asks.

I tell her I did and then mention I'd bumped into Jonathan Franklin from across the street.

'Oh that's lovely,' she says. 'It'll be good for you to have a friend when you start school.'

I wince at how she words it, as if I'm off to playschool aged four rather than fifteen.

'What's he like?' she says as she chops some onions, dabbing at her eyes with the back of her sleeve.

'Er... he's... he's fine.' I don't know what else to say, and she laughs and rolls her eyes.

I start to get the plates out and take them through to the dining room. Mum chats away about something, but I'm not really paying attention. I'm thinking about what Jonathan said. And the sentence he'd stopped himself from saying just in time.

SEVEN

Stephanie

NOW

L ying in hospital like this reminds me of when I had my appendix out, back when Danny was five and I was in my twenties.

I'd been dashing to pick our son up from his reception class in primary school just off Cadogan Square. I was running late, having been to a boutique furniture store in St James's to take a look at two different tables Pete had selected for our kitchen (neither were appropriate). I was furious with myself for running late, even though it wasn't entirely my fault – a bus had broken down near Piccadilly, causing a lot of commotion involving hooting horns and police trying to wave drivers around the great red mass stopping the flow of traffic. I'd finally reached the school, stressed and exhausted, skidding into what was definitely not a parking space, and was almost at the doors to the school when a shooting, stabbing pain in my torso caused me to double up in pain. I must have cried out, because I heard someone nearby say, 'What was that?' and then from around the corner a man and a woman rushed over to my side. I was helped into the school, where the secretary fussed around me for a while until my screams drove her to call an ambulance.

There was a lot of debate about whether poor little Danny, sitting on one of the uncomfortable wooden chairs in the small foyer, should come with me or remain at the school. In the end, I told them to call my husband to come and get the boy, and I went off in the ambulance alone.

Even though city life couldn't be held responsible, it was the thing that planted the seed in my mind to one day escape it all. All the noise. The mad rush. Go somewhere quiet and green and normal, with nice neighbours and an actual house and a garden that was ours, rather than one we shared with a number of people on a square. It had all occurred a week after I had told Pete I was finding London suffocating, finding my life difficult in ways I couldn't pin down, in ways I forever struggled to articulate properly. He'd found me chopping mushrooms in the kitchen, tears running down my face. He asked what was wrong and I told him I felt stressed and I didn't know why. And in that week he'd tried so hard to make things easier. He would bring home pre-made food from restaurants, increase the number of times the cleaner visited, sometimes arrive home in the middle of the day to take me on a lunchtime stroll around St James's Park, his hand in mine, or an arm slung around my shoulder. My security. My foundation of rock that I could depend on.

He didn't realise that taking away the cleaning and cooking meant I felt cast adrift, aimless and unfocused. I didn't have the heart to tell him. After my surgery, as Pete held my hand in bed, he'd said that he didn't think stress was a known cause of appendicitis, but I told him I didn't care. I just asked him to promise that one day we'd leave London and move somewhere else. And even though it took us nearly a decade to get around to it, I eventually got my wish. To an extent. Nice house. Garden. Quiet, green, normal.

But of course, the bit about nice neighbours didn't work out so well.

Perhaps it's the memories of feeling trapped and suffocated that make me want to get out of bed. Or a part of me suspects it's the lying here, slipping in and out of sleep, that's making me feel worse rather than even slightly better. Whatever the reason, I slowly ease myself up onto my elbows, and then the palms of my hands, taking note of the odd swaying sensation as I slide my legs out of the bed and try to stand. I manage a couple of steps, then I lose my balance as I stumble towards the wall and have to reach out and steady myself.

A woman with long red hair in the bed opposite me says, 'Hey, you all right, hun?' She reminds me of someone, but I can't quite put my finger on who.

'No,' I reply, bluntly. I manage to steady myself, still holding on to the wall. Then I turn and look out of the window. I can see it. Smoke rising up from a building in the distance.

'Is it still burning?' the woman asks.

I keep my eyes on the horizon. 'Yes, it's still burning.'

Silence falls between us for a little while, and then I become aware of a quiet tune. The woman's humming – something familiar. A children's nursery rhyme, perhaps. No, something else. But before I can make it out, she stops and speaks again, as if our conversation had never paused. 'I wonder if they'll ever figure out what went on. The truth doesn't always come out, does it? Can't trust what people say, these days.'

I let a few seconds pass, my thoughts starting to weigh heavy on me again. Then I reply, 'You're right. You can't.'

EIGHT

Stephanie

THE DAY OF THE EXPLOSION

The Franklins' lounge was a large, slightly curved room, with two big, comfortable-looking deep-purple sofas, a grey carpet, and matching grey throws. It would have been showroom neat if it weren't for some scattered magazines, a half-read novel with a bookmark sticking out of it, and a large Orvis dog bed in the corner, housing a partially shredded cuddly toy – presumably there for when Charlton the Newfoundland paid them a visit. An enormous bookshelf, tall and wide and crammed full with hardbacks, was on one side, showcasing a certain kind of fiction – the sort of thing that gets reviewed a lot on *Front Row* – I suspected Janet and Richard liked people to think they read, rather than actually spent time enjoying themselves. A lot of the volumes looked tellingly pristine, as did the tall candles on the mantlepiece, clearly there for décor rather than function.

Janet apparently had seen me looking at the candles because she moved over to them, saying, 'I rather think we'll need to light these, what with the power down and everything so dark outside. Really this is all a bit of a palaver.' She began looking for something along the mantelpiece and around near the fireplace.

'Where's everyone else?' I asked, taking a seat on one of the sofas, setting aside a *Waitrose Weekend* magazine as it poked out from behind a cushion.

'Oh, I think Mimi's floating around down here somewhere. Jonathan *might* have gone back to bed, although I'll be going to drag him out of it if that's the case. I think lying-in is one of the worst habits a teenager can acquire. He's got an essay on Kafka to finish and this disrupted day will be the perfect time to get it fine-tuned and ready for handing in next Monday. Don't want him to start slipping a grade.'

'And Richard?' I prompted, trying not to sound too interested.

'Dad's in his weird little attic recording one of his lectures.'

I looked round to see Mimi, the Franklins' blonde, startlingly photogenic daughter, standing in the archway leading through to the kitchen. Unlike her mother, she had opted for clothes rather than a dressing gown. Her top (a peach-coloured jumper) was oversized, causing it to hang on her wafer-thin frame. There was something slightly shimmery about it, causing its threads to twinkle in the low light, and it came down so low it almost covered her small denim shorts. I had occasionally seen Mimi going for a brief – and very slow – jog around the neighbourhood or, less frequently, accompanying her mother on a dog walk, and for those occasions her hair had been held back tightly out of her eyes. On this day, however, it had been untidily scooped up and bunched so that long golden strips floated around her ears and face. She brushed one of these strands from her eyes as her gaze turned to me.

'Hi,' I said, as she chewed her lip a little as if deep in thought, perhaps trying to place me or work out why I was sitting in the lounge on this unusual day.

'Hi,' she replied, still watching me. Then she turned her eyes to her mother, who answered her word-free question with a barely concealed shrug.

'Stephanie's... she's paying us a visit, aren't you, Stephanie? Needed a bit of company, didn't you?'

I was reminded a little of how some people talk to the elderly, spoon-feeding them sentences, chivvying them along with their stories or explanations.

'Yes,' I replied, simply.

Janet looked as if she wanted to say something more to her daughter, perhaps to remind the girl who I was and the tragic details of my backstory, but she clearly didn't feel she could elaborate in my presence.

'Have you seen the matches, Mimi?'

The girl looked thoroughly confused. 'What would I do with matches?'

'I don't know... burn things? Isn't that what teenagers do?' Janet laughed a bit, but I didn't find it very funny. She quickly seemed to realise jokes about raising teens were unlikely to sit well with me, so hurriedly changed tack and made out she was clearing her throat and coughing instead.

'What sort of lecture is Richard recording?' I asked, keen to change the subject.

'Oh gosh, it's *dreadfully* silly,' Mimi said, walking into the room properly and dropping herself onto the sofa. She spoke in a low, overly posh drawl which she must have worked on consciously. Although Janet and Richard were no cockneys, their accents seemed far more natural and, well, normal compared to their daughter's. Perhaps it was that girls' school she attended. Maybe you had to talk that way to fit in with the nieces of aristocrats and minor royalty. I knew full well Mimi had got in on a music scholarship, something Janet always boasted about where possible.

'His lectures are not silly, Mimi,' Janet said tersely, disappearing off into the kitchen. I could hear the sound of drawers being opened and closed followed by an 'Aha!' She returned seconds later brandishing a box of matches as if they were a trophy, and started to light the two large candles in their stands on the mantlepiece.

'It's all about *seduction* and *primal impulses*,' Mimi said, rolling her eyes and stretching herself out lazily on the sofa so that it became clear she wasn't wearing a bra under her baggy cashmere jumper. She let out a sigh, allowing it to inflate her cheeks a little, as if these subjects, for someone as wise and experienced as her (at the grand old age of eighteen), were tedious and dull.

'It isn't,' Janet corrected. 'It's about the representation of food and desire within art and culture across the centuries. From a philosophical perspective.'

Her daughter made a noise that suggested she wasn't convinced by this interpretation and carried on, apparently relishing the idea of making her mother uncomfortable. 'He's probably up there in his strange, dark den describing some naughty Bruegel painting and talking about ripe fruit and tensed flesh and—'

'OK, Mimi, that's enough. Stephanie isn't interested in your father's work.'

This wasn't entirely true – I wouldn't say I wasn't interested, I just had bigger fish to fry.

'I doubt it's even a proper seminar. I'm not quite sure what the point of an online university is, really, especially one started by some deeply dodgy tech billionaire in the US. I mean, where's the fun if you just log on to your laptop and sit and watch strange old men moan on about subjects only they care about?'

I could see Janet was close to flying off the handle, and while I was very tempted to let it happen, I decided raised tensions too early in the day might not make my job here any easier. I decided to cut in before she could.

'So neither you nor Jonathan have school today, then?' I asked Mimi, giving her a small smile. 'Must be nice that all this...' I vaguely waved my hand towards the window and the outside world, 'at least has one silver lining.'

Mimi raised a perfectly plucked eyebrow at me. 'Oh, school? Yeah. I suppose.' Like the subject of sex, school was apparently such a trivial part of her world that its cancelling apparently didn't warrant any cause for celebration.

The noise of movement up above was suddenly audible, followed by the steady thud on the stairs that I knew well: the sound of an unenthusiastic teenager just woken from their slumber. As predicted, Jonathan came into the room, his short hair – the same darkish-blonde as his sister's – sticking up at odd angles. He was in a slim-fitting white T-shirt that emphasised the fact he spent more time doing crunches at the gym than he did on his schoolwork, and tartan-patterned boxers. Even though I'd heard on the school grapevine that his grades weren't as startlingly good as the Franklins would wish, there was still something oddly academic about him. Perhaps it was his large, thick-rimmed round glasses, or the preppy way he dressed even when out of his school uniform, but I'd often found the general image of him as he got older full of contradictions.

It was clear at first that Jonathan hadn't seen me as he crossed the lounge floor in the direction of the kitchen, but as he turned to move around the sofa his eyes landed on my face. And the reaction was instant. A sudden, strained quality took over his features, causing an uncomfortable tension in his neck and jaw, and he backed away as if I'd just pulled a gun on him.

'Hello, Jonathan,' I said, holding his gaze, trying to communicate a sense of calm authority.

'Er... hi...' he said, his gaze now flicking between me and his mother, who had lit the candles and was busy moving photo frames and ornaments away from the flames, as if there was a realistic risk they would all be ablaze at any moment.

'Stephanie's just popped round,' Janet said, giving no more explanation than this, as if it was something I did regularly and my near four-month absence from their lives had never occurred.

Jonathan threw one terrified look my way and then walked quickly out through the archway towards the kitchen.

'He's been behaving very oddly of late,' Mimi said in her bored drawl.

'Well, he's been upset. He's—' Janet started, then stopped herself. I knew what she was going to say. That he'd lost a friend. That he was grieving for my son. That he was trying to come to terms with a loss that most people would never experience so early in life: the loss of a friend and confidante, something that probably felt very different to the grief other classmates may have gone through with a pet or even an elderly relative. But although I had sympathy for him – more sympathy than his mother or sister could ever have – I wasn't about to give the boy an easy ride. I wasn't going to let him duck his way out of this. His strange reaction proved a lot of what I had suspected.

Jonathan was hiding something. And I was here to find out what it was.

NINE

Stephanie

FIVE MONTHS BEFORE THE EXPLOSION

I was at the school to collect Danny from after-school maths club, which was less of a club and more of a way of improving the scores of the boys whose upcoming GCSEs might lower the school's overall average. Maths had never been Danny's strongest subject, and although his grades weren't dire, his teacher, Ms Prentice, felt they could be improved. She was an earnest, quietly terrifying woman, close to retirement age, who said everything in a chilling whisper whilst stroking the sleeves of whatever ancient cardigan she'd donned that day.

'You see, young Daniel just hasn't been applying himself to mathematics in the way we'd hope of a student of Fletcher House School,' she said during our autumn parents evening. 'I understand that, to a young man, the intricate beauty of algebra or divine perfection of fractions and equations may be hard to appreciate, but I think we're all agreed here that just about scraping a B isn't the sort of attitude we'd want to encourage.'

'Well, a B is better than I got!' I'd told Ms Prentice with a laugh, trying to dispel the strange, séance-like atmosphere she'd conjured.

She'd frowned at me and then offered up the details of her prescription: a night each week for Danny at the after-school club hosted by herself and another weird aging mathematician, Mr Withers. Danny was moody about the whole thing, but cheered up when, the next day, he'd discovered Jonathan had received the same sentence. I suspected this might mean he would spend most of the class chatting at the back of the room, but that was for them to police, not me, and I personally felt the poor boy was being worked too hard anyway. Part of me would have liked to tell Danny he didn't need to go to the maths club anyway, but Pete insisted he needed to get his grades up if he was going to try for Oxford or Cambridge. This always made me exasperated. Although Danny had passed the school's entrance exam, it had started to become clear as the years went on that he wasn't destined for the two most prestigious universities in the world. I'd hoped he would, as time progressed, be drawn to the prospectuses of some other institutions, perhaps Bristol, where I went, or Loughborough or Warwick. But Pete told me I was making him aim low rather than high and that he needed to develop a 'work ethic'.

The maths club was not a success. Danny and Jonathan did indeed mess around at the back of the class. Just before half-term, they had been found, rather mortifyingly, in possession of a condom filled with chewing gum, an item they swore had already been there, stapled to one of the desks, and they were just the unlucky souls to find it. All this nonsense had occurred before we'd gone on our trip to the US, but the discussion about it had had to be postponed when both Ms Prentice and Mr Withers had been struck down with a particularly aggressive strain of flu that had started to ravage the school's staff at an alarming rate. I had hoped the whole matter would be forgotten when the maths club had to be cancelled for two weeks then covered by someone else from then on, but this wasn't to be. Both teachers, now fully recovered, had requested a parent of each boy come in to discuss their behaviour at the end of one of the sessions.

My car had been blocked in during a gridlock situation in the Waitrose car park, resulting in my quick dash in to the shop for some milk taking twenty minutes rather than five. When I eventually reached the right block at the school, I was running very late and arrived at the classroom door to find Janet and Jonathan coming out of it and distinctly heard the words 'bad influence'. Were they talking about my son? I wondered as I walked into view, causing Janet to close her mouth and hurriedly do up her coat, clearly unwilling to look available for a chat.

Along the corridor I saw Danny leaning sullenly against the wall. He looked up at me and was about to come over when Ms Prentice materialised in the doorway without warning and told me that she felt it would be better if we had our conversation alone and that 'Daniel should remain outside'.

Just as I turned to go in, I heard Jonathan say to his mum, 'Going for a piss. Won't be long,' and slope off in the direction of the boys' toilets. Janet, looking displeased at his choice of words, shook her head crossly and said she would wait in the car. I shot Danny a sympathetic glance, then walked into the classroom.

The meeting with Ms Prentice and Mr Withers didn't take long.

Mr Withers told me in under a minute that if Danny was ever again seen 'throwing about a contraceptive item filled with polyisobutylene' he would be referred to the head teacher. He also remarked that further disruption to the class could have been avoided if the offending item hadn't been flicked across the room onto another boy's face. I told him I had spoken to Danny about this and I would again.

'The only positive note,' Ms Prentice said, 'is that Daniel and Jonathan seem to have settled down since Mr. Withers and I returned after recovering from influenza.' She let out a small cough and closed her eyes for a second before she continued, as if to imply recovery had been a close-run thing. 'I'm thankful that they no longer seem to be distracting each other. Indeed, the boys have even gone as far as sitting at opposite ends of the room. May I ask if this was something you advised Daniel to do?'

I frowned at her. 'No,' I said, shaking my head, but something about what she said made an odd sort of sense. Ever since that strange night when I picked up the unusually silent boys from Scotty's birthday party just before the half-term break, there had been something peculiar going on. They'd walked to school together sometimes, but it was quite a way and most of the time Pete or I dropped Danny off in the car. And, lately, Jonathan hadn't been with us. He often used to just turn up, invited by Danny without consulting us, and come in the car, but now I thought back I realised this hadn't happened for weeks. Had Jonathan been walking to school on his own? Had Danny rescinded the invitation to come in the car with us?

'Well, regardless,' Ms Prentice continued, 'it's been a positive step forward, I think, and we can now draw a line under this unfortunate business. Let's hope Daniel's grades continue to improve and we can all just move on. He has a lot of things to carry on with over the Christmas break, so that should keep him busy.'

I came out of the classroom moments later, feeling both irritated and curious. The whole conversation had been rather pointless, especially so long after the event, and Pete and I had already told him off at home for being silly in the class when he should be focusing on work. But I was concerned about Jonathan and Danny's sudden self-separation. Had they had an argument about something? Or a falling-out over the band? Maybe one of them was tired of letting Scotty sing and there'd been a disagreement about who should be on which instruments. I was thinking about this when, looking around the corridor, I realised Danny wasn't there. Annoyed he'd wandered off, I decided to go and check the car to see if he'd gone to wait by it. As I passed through the echoey, mostly empty maths and science block towards the exit I heard something that made me stop. The sound of crying, coming from the open doorway to my right. The boys' bathroom. And then another voice.

'Don't cry... We can... I don't know...'

It was Danny's voice. He was trying to comfort someone. And what that someone was became clear seconds later when another voice sounded out. 'Please, just leave me alone... I'm sorry, I'm really sorry...' The words were said through sobs, but I still recognised the voice. It was Jonathan. I moved closer to the doorway and heard Danny reply, sounding... scared? Frustrated? Angry?

'Just take it and... don't look inside. Just take it and pass it on and then that's the end of it, for ever. You promise?'

There was a rustle, as if something was being exchanged between the two of them. My curiosity was too strong. I threw caution to the wind and walked inside.

The two boys were standing in the middle of the bathroom's floor, the sinks and taps on one side, the urinals on the other. It may have been strange, but the thing that immediately hit me was how clean and pleasant the place was. The toilets meant for student use back in my old Somerset comprehensive had been in bad disrepair, with locks not working, doors falling off their hinges and drawings and charming little notes written on the walls, telling anyone who cared to read them that *Kelsey Granger is a fucking bitch slag who gives BJs for phone credit, the stupid fucking whore.* I'd visited the boys' bathroom once (I'd chased a hateful boy named Ryan Mathews in there when he'd stolen my homework diary and threatened to urinate on it) and it was even worse, with graffiti covering nearly every surface. But apparently this wasn't the case at Fletcher House School. It seemed our money was at least going somewhere.

'Mum?' Danny said, jolting my attention to him. I saw Jonathan move quickly, stuffing something into his bag – but not quick enough to stop me seeing it. A Waitrose carrier bag, scrunched up and wrapped around something.

'What are you two up to?' I asked, looking from one to the other.

'I need to be going,' Jonathan muttered, sniffing loudly then hurriedly wiping his eyes with his hand and nudging at his glasses. He left me and my son facing each other, the harsh fluorescent lighting making him look washed-out, pale, unwell even. Perhaps he was. Perhaps he was actually in deep distress and something was seriously wrong. Nothing about the conversation I'd overheard seemed normal.

He made movements to go, as if we'd naturally be on our way, pulling his bag over his shoulder, but I stayed where I was. 'What were you and Jonathan talking about?'

'You shouldn't be listening in on things in boys' bathrooms,' he said, now looking cross. 'It's… weird.'

'No, what's weird is Jonathan sobbing and you giving him something in a plastic bag. I saw you. So tell me, what's going on between you two?'

'Nothing!' he shouted, his voice echoing impressively around the bathroom walls. He tightened the shoulder-straps on his bag with one aggressive motion and then shoved past me to get out of the door.

I followed a few steps behind him, not saying anything as we headed towards the car. Neither Jonathan nor his mother were anywhere to be seen. I waited until we were on the road and winding back towards home, then restarted my questioning. 'What was in the bag you gave Jonathan?'

Silence greeted this, so I tried again. 'Danny, tell me – are you involved in drugs?'

He let out a laugh at this, although he didn't look very happy. It was a cold, mirthless sound, very different from his naturally cheery self. 'No.'

'Then tell me what all that was about. Does this have anything to do with that party before half-term? The one where you and Jonathan were all moody and silent afterwards?'

I saw his hands, which had been resting on his knees, clench the material of his grey school trousers into fists. This was confirmation enough, even without him answering.

'What happened there? Did you two get into a fight or something?'

'No!'

'What was in the bag?' I was conscious this probably wasn't the right way of getting a response, bombarding him with question after question, riling him up, but I couldn't help it. It was painful, being kept in the dark about something clearly bothering him so much.

'It was… condoms.'

This took me by surprise. '*Condoms*?' I repeated, 'Why would…? Does this have anything to do with that silliness in the class? Was it you who stapled it to the desk?'

'What? No!'

'Then why are you smuggling in condoms for Jonathan Franklin?'

Danny looked very uncomfortable.

'Because… because he doesn't want to buy them himself. He's embarrassed.'

I digested this for a second, then asked, 'So why was he crying? Gratitude? Was the apparently bulging bag of condoms so moving he just had to sob like a wounded child as you handed them over?' I shouldn't have got sarcastic, but nothing about this added up.

'He was upset because... the girl he fancies, Sylvia, she's the sister of one of his football mates. She's now going out with someone else, so...'

This explanation wasn't helping matters. It just made me angry.

'But he still needed the condoms? No girlfriend, no chance of using them. But you still did a tear-filled little exchange?'

'You asked! Now I've told you. I got them for him to be nice. To help him out.'

'From *Waitrose*?' I said, half laughing. 'Lads your age don't go into Waitrose to buy condoms. I'm sorry, I just don't believe it.'

We'd reached the house by this point and the car had barely come to a stop when Danny leapt out. Pete was just arriving too and was opening the boot. Inside was a large real Christmas tree. I'd completely forgotten it was Friday night and we'd said we'd put it up and decorate it after dinner.

'Hey, how did it all go?' Pete asked, but his son just walked straight past him and let himself into the house.

'That bad, huh?' he said, turning to me. 'Did they tell him off?'

'Erm... a little. It's fine,' I said. I didn't want to go into the whole thing with him there and then, especially not on the driveway, directly opposite the Franklins' house, so I said 'I'll just take the shopping in, then I'll come back to give you a hand with the tree.'

Pete smiled and gave me a quick kiss, then I grabbed the shopping bag from the back, the Waitrose bags-for-life now taking on a strange new significance. I didn't care what he said about buying condoms for Jonathan – I didn't believe a word of it. That meant my son had lied outright to me about something that clearly mattered to him.

It was a new sensation for me as a parent. And one I didn't want to get used to.

TEN

Danny

ONE YEAR, EIGHT MONTHS BEFORE THE EXPLOSION

The new school isn't that bad. It's bigger than the one I was at in London, with a very grand-looking manor house feel to it. Fitting in to a year group that already knows each other made me a bit nervous at first, but I'm glad I sort of know Jonathan by the time term begins. He and I saw each other at the leisure centre a few more times before the holidays finished, and I'm relieved when I find out he's in some of my classes and can show me where to go.

At lunchtime, a few weeks into the new term, he tells me his mum had said to ask me if our families fancied sharing lifts. 'She says it's silly, us going in the same direction each day, so if your mum was OK with it, we could do one way and your mum or dad could do the other.'

I'm not really sure what to reply since this is very much my mum's area of things rather than mine. Part of me wonders why Jonathan's mum hasn't just spoken to my mum about it herself, considering they live opposite. But I like the idea, so I just tell him it sounds great. There are some mornings I choose to walk, if I'm up early enough, although I've become more exhausted as term's gone on and decide a definite lift would be a good thing to rely on, especially when it starts to get properly cold. I'm about to turn back to go down the science corridor and wait outside my next class, but Jonathan isn't finished.

'Also… do you want to come over? Tomorrow night? To watch a movie and have tea?'

Once again, his words make me think of a child, as if we're both still in primary school. But there isn't much else to do around here, and the idea of finally setting foot in the Franklins' house makes my heart leap a little. Perhaps Mimi will be there, having dinner with us, keen to start up a conversation with me, the boy next door. Well, the boy opposite.

'Yeah… er, what's tomorrow? Friday? Yeah, I think that's fine. I'll check tonight and message you.'

The meal is tense. Awkward doesn't even begin to cover it. I'd become used to Janet Franklin talking away, mostly to herself, when it was her day to pick me and Jonathan up from school, and I thought she seemed nice-ish, if a bit, well, bonkers. I started to wonder if the things she said were chosen so I would mention them to my parents – like them planning a big new conservatory extension, or a new fridge-freezer arriving. Things like that. I honestly couldn't care less, but I nod along politely. I assumed dinner would be the same sort of thing, only with (I hoped) more Mimi. And Mimi is present. But so is Jonathan's father. And that's when things become tense.

Jonathan and I watch a film in his room first. It's smaller than mine, but has a homely, warm feel to it, as if it is well lived in. I'm still getting used to living in a different place, after spending years in our London flat. Halfway into the movie, a loud bell sounds and Jonathan starts to get up. 'Dinner,' he mutters, then adds, 'I wish she wouldn't ring that thing.'

I laugh. 'I'm impressed you have a dinner bell. My parents just shout up the stairs.'

'My mum does too,' he says. 'She only rings that when guests are round. It's embarrassing.'

I don't comment on this. I can understand why it would be embarrassing, but it doesn't exactly surprise me based on my experience of Janet Franklin so far.

At the table, Mimi is already seated, typing on her phone. I hadn't seen her upon my entry to the house so it's a bit of a jolt to find her there, in the flesh, looking as stunning as ever. She looks up at me, gives me the most fleeting of looks, says, 'Hey,' with a soul-crushing sense of boredom, then returns to her phone. I feel myself going red.

'Take a seat, boys!' Janet calls out from the kitchen in a dramatic sort of way, as if she were in a pantomime. 'Dinner is served.'

I think I hear Mimi tut as I take the vacant place next to her. For a second, I wonder if it was aimed at me, then realise it has something to do with her mother. A split second later, Janet swoops into the dining room and sets a large baking dish onto a collection of table mats in the middle.

'Lasagne,' she says, as if it were a grand statement.

Mimi tuts again and leans forwards, picks up the large serving spoon next to the dish of still bubbling lasagne, and begins to hack into it, dropping some onto her plate, all the while looking at the mixture of meat and pasta as if she can't believe she's about to eat it.

I see another spare space opposite Mimi. Jonathan's father isn't sitting with us. I've only ever been near him twice: the first during that strange meeting where he asked Jonathan and me to shake hands, and another when he had to pick me and Jonathan up from school, but he'd barely said anything in the car – just listened to some politics programme on Radio 4 the whole time.

Janet seems to guess what I'm thinking and says as she sits down, 'Richard's been delayed with a work call in his study.' Something about the way her lips go very thin after she says this suggests she isn't exactly happy about her husband being late for the meal she's cooked.

Mimi rolls her eyes. 'Up in his den. I swear, if any movie people come to make a horror film in Kent, we'd earn a tonne renting that place out. Dark, free from daylight...'

'Stop talking nonsense,' snaps Janet, 'it does have daylight.'

'Yes,' Jonathan says, 'a mirror. Facing the street.' There's something a little odd about the way he says this, as if he's making a point, but it's lost on me.

'Oh, come on. Regardless, there's a definite dodgy vibe to the place,' Mimi continues. 'I'm sure I could put it to much better use if the attic were mine.'

'Well, it isn't,' her mum says bluntly. 'And if you don't like the way your father keeps it, then don't go up there.'

Mimi makes a half-laugh, half-tutting sound, and sighs in a bored sort of way. 'Gosh, would I? None of us are allowed, are we?' To my delight and horror, she transfers her attention to me and says 'It's his lair. We're banned from it. That's what we'll tell the police when they find the bodies inside the walls. I saw a documentary about that once. About a man who killed all these people – ramblers, I think they were, somewhere foreign – took them home, wrapped them in polythene and bricked them up in the attic so that nobody would—'

'Stop showing off in front of our guest,' Janet says, her face now white with outrage.

'He's not *my* guest, Mother,' she says, putting her head on one side, examining me as if I'm a mildly interesting animal. 'Where have you come from again?' she asks before picking up a small forkful of lasagne and dropping it into her mouth.

Before I can answer, her mother cuts in once again. 'Mimi, that sounds a bit… I don't know… rude.'

'Why?' She shrugs.

'I don't mind,' I say, also shrugging, trying my best to seem carefree and interesting at the same time. 'I'm from across the street.'

Mimi rolls her eyes, which makes me think her mum may have a point about the rudeness. 'I *mean*, where did you come from before you moved *here*.' She emphasises her words as if she's dealing with a child. I feel myself going red again.

'Oh, er… Pimlico.'

'That's in London, Mimi,' Janet says.

'I know Pimlico's in fucking London, *Mother*,' she says, giving her biggest eye roll yet.

Janet drops her knife and fork with a clatter. 'Language, Mimi. That isn't appropriate.'

There's a noise of someone walking in from the hallway behind me, then Richard Franklin appears, tall and birdlike, with a fed-up expression on his face. 'Sorry,' he says, though he doesn't sound it. 'Meeting overran.'

'The food's in the centre of the table,' Janet says, stating the blindingly obvious. 'It will be cold now, but there we go.'

The steam that drifts up from the large spoonful Richard ladles onto his plate proves her wrong on this, although nothing is said about it. We all sit there, chewing away in silence, until Richard then says. 'What was inappropriate?'

Janet frowns at her husband. 'Sorry?'

'Before I walked in, you said something wasn't appropriate.'

'Oh,' she says. 'Mimi used some offensive language.'

'It wasn't *offensive*,' Mimi says, making a scoffing sound.

'Maybe she picked it up from her brother's room the other day,' Richard says, staring now at his son. 'I was walking past his door when I heard a burst of very foul language. It sounded like a bunch of louts shouting about something.'

I glance at Jonathan and see him looking outraged. 'I told you, that was a YouTube video.'

'Ah yes,' Richard says, nodding grimly. 'Your football obsession. Are you into football, Daniel?'

I'm impressed he's got my name right, even if he does still use the longer form. 'Er... it's all right. I'm not massively into it.'

'Jonathan here is,' Richard says, and there is something slightly sneering about the way he says it. I know Jonathan follows teams and matches with far more attention than I do, and I haven't really given it much thought, but by the way his father is talking about it anyone would think it's something to be ashamed of.

'Danny probably focuses more on his studies,' Janet says, now apparently keen to join in, 'unlike some I could mention.' She does a very obvious lean forwards to look at Jonathan, who now has his eyes on his plate, as if wishing he were anywhere else.

I look around at Richard and Janet, then back at Jonathan. I feel like saying something in his defence, but nothing comes to me, because what I see in the eyes of Richard and Janet scares me. That's the best word for it. I find it scary. Scary how two parents can so openly dislike their own children, and not be afraid to show it.

All of this becomes even stranger when I'm getting ready to go home. Jonathan had muttered something about going to put his shoes on to walk with me across the road. I tell him it's fine, I can easily walk across to my house myself, but I get the feeling he wants to talk to me away from his parents. But Jonathan leaves me waiting in the hallway for a long time, making me wonder if I should just leave or go and find him to tell him I'm not waiting any longer. After over ten minutes have gone by, I decide I might just go and say to whoever I could find that I'm leaving and thank them for tea. I pass through the empty lounge and the equally deserted dining room until I come to the door at the far end. From the sounds of it, there's some heated discussion being thrashed out inside. I step a little closer until I can hear the words quite plainly.

'And now on to the History homework, which reaches a new level of stupidity. I mean, I'm slightly shocked I have a son who has reached his mid-teens without knowing how capital letters work. Magna Carta. Capital M, Capital C.'

'I know,' replies a small voice. Jonathan's.

The other, apparently his father, carries on. 'You clearly don't know, otherwise the essay wouldn't be littered with errors. In fact, the only time you *have* capitalised the M is the instance where you referred to it as the *"Magnum Carter"*. But I'm sure I'm probably wasting my time telling you all this. In one ear and out the other.'

'I'm sorry,' Jonathan says, his voice so quiet I can barely here it. But even so (and perhaps I imagined it), I feel I can hear a whole lifetime of sorrow and resentment and sadness bottled up in those two words.

'Christ, you're pathetic,' his father says sneeringly. 'Just leave. And take this with you.'

I dash to the door and find my way back to the hallway, hoping my quick footsteps haven't been heard. If they were, Jonathan doesn't say anything when he steps into sight seconds later, with what appear to be some printed sheets of A4 clutched in his hand. He doesn't say anything about his conversation with his father about his homework, nor do I ask. In fact, he doesn't say anything at all as we walk across the street, the air chilling and misty, our footsteps the only sound in the quiet neighbourhood. 'I guess I'll see you on Monday,' I say, turning to him as we reach my drive. 'Thanks for tea.' He just nods and attempts a smile, but it doesn't really form properly on his face. Then he turns and walks back towards his home.

Later, Mum asks me what dinner at the Franklins' was like. I think about it all for a bit before I answer, then tell her that I don't think they're a very happy family. 'Not like us,' I say. 'We're a laugh compared to them.'

Mum tries to ask me what went on to make me think they weren't happy.

'I don't know,' I say. 'It just feels like something... something not quite right is going on there... The way Jonathan's dad talks to him... and the way Mimi speaks to her mother, and the way her mother looks at her...' I trail off. I don't want to go into it and I'm aware it will probably sound like nothing if I try to put it into words. Many families have squabbles at the dinner table. I know that. But there was something about the chill in the air at the Franklins' house that I really don't like.

Hatred – that's what it was. There was hatred there.

And it left a nasty taste.

ELEVEN

Stephanie

THE DAY OF THE EXPLOSION

The first part of the morning in the Franklins' house went by without any sign of the man of the house, Richard. As the minutes ticked on, it became clear that Janet was trying to avoid sustained periods of time in my company, but at least she bothered to show some effort. Along with two mugs of tea, I was also treated to some (seriously good) homemade sourdough with chickpeas and extra virgin olive oil. I should start getting more creative with my breakfast choices, I thought to myself, thinking guiltily of the sugary cereal I had in the cupboard. Although I didn't feel exactly comfortable in my surroundings, I found just being in the company of others did have a rejuvenating effect on me. There was something comforting about being amidst the bustle, the comings and goings, with Janet carrying piles of towels upstairs or Mimi moaning about a missing bracelet. Even Jonathan returned, eventually, although he still looked wary of me. He still hadn't bothered to get properly dressed, and was still in the T-shirt he must have slept in, although now with the addition of some loungewear or pyjama trousers of a similar burgundy tartan design to his boxer shorts.

Even when he did make an appearance he didn't linger long, and would disappear into the kitchen, calling out things like 'Where are the cornflakes?'

After his mother responded, and he shuffled off, I heard more words coming from somewhere out of sight: a whispered conversation that sounded as if it was in full flow before Jonathan had interrupted them. He must have left the door open to whatever room Janet was in, and it quickly became obvious she was talking about me.

'I mean, I don't want to appear heartless. It's all tragic – nobody would say it isn't. But she's just... well... settled herself in the lounge and shows no sign of going.'

'Maybe you could offer to walk her back to her house?' said a man's voice. Richard. They must have been in his study, having a quiet summit about me. I had no idea his work office was downstairs. I presumed it would be one of the unused bedrooms above.

'Oh, that's so lovely to hear you'd happily send your

wife out into some apocalyptic disaster—' Janet snapped, forgetting to whisper.

Richard mumbled something about having forgotten about the situation outside.

'Forgot? People have *died*. It said so on the *Guardian* website just now. I saw it on my phone. Two people who worked at the power station.'

More mumbling from Richard. I think he may have said the words *miles away*, perhaps implying that the imminent threat to ourselves here in Oak Tree Close was being exaggerated. After this, further eavesdropping had to be abandoned because Jonathan came wandering back in, cereal bowl in hand. He showed signs of heading straight for the door at the side of the lounge which led back out to the stairs and up to his safe haven, but I stopped him.

'Jonathan, is there any chance you could join me for a moment?' I patted the seat next to me and smiled, then regretted it since it probably looked creepy.

It was instantly obvious he didn't want to, as his eyes shot around the room as if looking for an escape route.

'Just for a moment,' I said, now sounding a bit pleading and desperate. He seemed to take pity on me and came to take a seat, opting for the sofa opposite.

'I've been wanting to have a word with you, Jonathan, about...' I took a deep breath. '...about Danny.'

This seemed to confirm his worst fears. His eyes widened, then he looked quickly at the floor, as if afraid he'd give something away through merely looking at me.

'I'm sorry,' he said in a small voice.

I leant forwards. 'What are you sorry about?' I tried to meet the boy's gaze, but he was staring resolutely at the carpet, his mouth clenched, both hands gripping the cereal bowl tightly in his lap.

'That he died,' he said, in little more than a whisper.

I blinked back some tears that were threatening to spill over. 'I'm… I'm sorry too. I know you lost a friend. And you've got nothing to be sorry about with all that. His death wasn't your fault.'

Jonathan also seemed to be fighting the need to cry, and I heard his breathing coming out slow and heavy, his eyes blinking rapidly. 'The guy who smashed into their car… he… he deserved to die,' he said, a harder, harsher look taking over his face. 'I mean, I'm glad… What he did was terrible. He was a drunk, wasn't he? Something like that. He deserved what happened to him.'

This isn't a subject I wanted to get into, although I was moved by the force of his words. 'It wasn't alcohol. He'd been smoking cannabis, but, well, that wasn't what I wanted to talk about.' It was my turn to take some steady deep breaths. Now I had what I wanted – an audience with Jonathan, alone – I was finding it much harder than I'd expected. 'You see, the thing is, Danny was... not himself just before his death. I think something had been bothering him for a while.'

Jonathan clenched his eyes, as if trying to rid himself of this situation, or perhaps push back a bad memory that had swum to the surface. Whatever it was, I didn't have a chance to find out, because at that moment someone walked in from the archway behind him and said, 'What's going on?'

Mimi was standing there, looking quizzically over at us both. Jonathan still had his eyes closed, and she turned her gaze to me as if to say, *What have you done to him?*

'Jonathan and I were just having a chat. About... my son. Danny.'

The reference to my deceased child either didn't register with Mimi or she decided it was best to ignore it, because she just prodded the boy until he opened his eyes. 'What?' he said, looking up, annoyed.

'Mother just said that there still seems to be hot water, but it might not last. So you should be quick if you want to shower.'

He gave a half-shrug in response to this.

She then looked over at me. 'He showers every day just to make sure his hair doesn't go curly, you know. He combs it and everything.'

She said this fact conversationally, as if we were two friends sharing quirky details about our families.

'Fuck off,' Jonathan muttered and got up.

Mimi let herself drop onto the sofa seat he'd just vacated. 'Oh shush. Just because you're ashamed of being *ginger*.'

This was clearly a sensitive subject as Jonathan threw an angry glance towards his sister and thudded out of the room and up the stairs. The whole thing was, of course, more than a little ludicrous, since Jonathan was clearly blonde, albeit the darker of the two.

'Now, now, Mimi,' I heard Janet's voice say in light admonishment. She came strolling into the lounge, carrying a large stack of what looked like magazines. 'It isn't nice to tease your brother. People of minority hair pigmentation shouldn't be made to feel ashamed about their natural colouring.'

The phrase *people of minority hair pigmentation* would normally have made me laugh – the sort of thing Pete and I would have giggled over together when I relayed it back to him. To anyone else, the unbearably clunky and jargonistic choice of language might be confusing, but for me it was just a reminder of one of Janet Franklin's less endearing qualities. The policing of language, and the phrases we should all stick to, was an obsession of hers. For the first couple of school terms when we moved to

Oak Tree Close, I decided to go along to a few of the PAFOF meetings (Parents and Friends of Fletcher House School). I thought showing an interest in the way my son's school was run was a good, productive thing to do and I even hoped – though I was unwilling to admit it at the time – that I would make some friends with the other mums. These meetings were never officially hosted by Janet. That unhappy task fell to a largely silent, ineffectual woman named Cynthia, a retired bookbinder from Cleethorpes who wasn't very interested in discussing anything other than the amount of swearing and violence in some of the 'more modern fiction' on the curriculum. But Janet seemed to think she should be chair, and regularly held court in such a boldly confident way that all the other attendees (five mums, two dads and Mrs Murray, a science teacher, representing the staffing body) seemed too terrified to nudge her out of the spotlight, especially given Janet's favourite subject: diversity.

She championed the cause with the vehemence of a prosecutor persuading the jury of a serial killer's wickedness, although in this case it wasn't clear if we were all meant to be the jury or the serial killer. We were told we were 'inherently sexist' because the English Literature classes studied two works by women and three by men. The school was 'endemically anti-gay' because the History GCSE syllabus was populated exclusively by 'heterosexual dictators or oppressors, like Winston Churchill', something not helped by 'the lack of an after-school club for LGBTQI+ pupils'. When asked politely by one timid parent named Annie what all those letters stood for, Janet pointed a severe finger at the scared-looking woman and proclaimed her to be 'the embodiment of the problem we're facing'. On the subject of race, Janet repeatedly mentioned how guilty she felt about the actions of her ancestors, and in one particularly embarrassing moment, apologised to 'the attendees of colour at the meeting' for how overwhelmingly white the school was. When it was suggested by Mrs Murray, whose parents were from Nigeria, that her little speech could be regarded as 'somewhat patronising', Janet quickly moved the subject on to the school's lack of gender-neutral bathrooms.

It was a curious phenomenon, all this, since at the end of one of the PAFOF gatherings, Annie walked with me to the car park and shared some details of the Janet of yesteryear.

'She wasn't always like this,' Annie said. 'She actually used to be quite the opposite.'

Interested in this rare nugget of gossip, I listened to how Annie's two kids had gone to the same playgroup as Jonathan and Mimi back in the 2000s, and how Janet was one of the types who moaned about how 'political correctness had gone mad'. Apparently, she had liked nothing better than to complain to the other parents about how the children weren't allowed to sing 'Baa Baa Black Sheep' anymore, how the word 'Christmas' would probably be banned in schools and nurseries any second because of 'the Muslims', and how they should hold on tight to terms like 'Mum and Dad' even if it 'offended the gays'.

I found this insight fascinating, and it led me to wonder why she had flipped so far the other way. Was it, perhaps, that having spent past years of her adult life spreading racist and homophobic untruths and mocking those trying to be sensitive to others, she was now doing penance by fighting performatively for equality? Maybe she felt guilty about the people and groups she had casually slandered and sneered at? Or it could, rather depressingly, just be Janet gravitating towards her two favourite things: to be the one in control, and the one with the loudest voice in the room.

Part of me was tempted to ask her about all this outright, as I sat opposite her in her lounge. But I decided riling her wouldn't be an effective way of getting what I wanted.

She had settled the large stack of magazines down next to her daughter, who shifted aside, looking irritated at the intrusion. 'I thought I'd go through these now to see if any of them could be donated to the school's charity sale in the summer,' Janet explained as she flapped about with the pages, 'but I think some have been stained with tea – Richard can be awfully clumsy.'

She flicked through the pages of *Waitrose Food* and *Country Living*, pausing occasionally to read the odd article or flash me an image of a stately home, remarking, 'Richard and I had dinner there once – the veal was terribly overdone.' Perhaps she found my clear lack of interest in her excursions rather difficult, because after a while she suggested putting the radio on. 'I think we have a battery one somewhere,' she said, laying a hand lovingly on an off-white Bose sound system that sat on a table near the bookshelves, clearly sad she couldn't put it to good use. An old, slightly tatty battery-powered radio was produced from somewhere beyond the kitchen and placed on the mantlepiece. I noticed how its grilled front was flecked with what looked like white paint. 'The builders used it a lot when they came to extend the conservatory,' Janet explained, after seeing me staring at it. A loud blast of what sounded like Rhianna's song 'S&M' immediately filled the room, leaving Janet looking scandalised, and she hurriedly tried to tune it to Radio 4. Mimi, who had been watching her mother with a look of bored semi-interest, got up and tried to help, but only succeeded in finding Heart FM. Eventually Janet settled for Radio 3, and some music started to fill the room, low and seductive, growing into a melody I knew well. Far too well.

'Oh I love this,' said Janet, settling herself down on the sofa with the remaining magazines, 'although I can't quite remember the name... Oh, it will come to me.'

'It's Mahler,' I said, keeping my eyes on the floor in front of me.

'Oh yes, so it is.' I could tell Janet was put out I'd got there first, '"The Quartet for Strings and Piano in A Minor", I believe.' She probably thought it would be out of my range of cultural appreciation, but I couldn't let that bother me now. There was a scent in the room that was growing stronger: cinnamon candles... and red wine. And a touch on my left hand. The feel of flesh against flesh. Pete's fingers interweaving with mine, nudging against the plates of the dinner we'd just had. One of our first at his London apartment.

I was vaguely aware of a far-off voice. A woman maybe.

It was Janet. Asking if I was all right. If everything was OK. But it wasn't OK. Because the room was growing very dark.

Then I felt a softness and stillness carry me off. And nothing but silence followed.

TWELVE

Stephanie

SEVENTEEN YEARS BEFORE THE EXPLOSION

I f I hadn't injured my leg in PE when I was sixteen, there's a chance I never would have met my husband.

It's weird to think that – how something so trivial, so seemingly minor could completely change the direction of your life. I suppose we've all got things like that in our lives. They're especially compelling when you hear of things like 'My great-grandma was just five minutes late to the Southampton docks and missed her voyage on the *Titanic*'. Mine was a double-edged sword. If Mikaela Jutt hadn't whacked me with the end of a badminton racket as punishment for losing count of the score (I hadn't lost score, she just didn't like the fact that she wasn't winning), I wouldn't have got married, had my child, or built our lovely family unit.

But then, of course, I wouldn't have lost them both, either. I wouldn't know grief so profound I'd worry I'd tear in two.

So, in the end, I'm glad Mikaela lashed out in her fit of rage, because even though losing Pete and Danny would become the worst thing in my life, having them for those years was so precious, so much a fabric of who I'd become, I wouldn't wish them away or want to erase the past. Never.

The cut and large bruise I sustained from the almighty whack from Mikaela made me scream in agony, causing the rest of the class to look over in alarm as my shouts echoed round the large school sports hall. Mrs Joyce, the PE teacher, ran over, blowing her whistle to stop everyone playing and supervised my trip to the medical room. I didn't see a doctor right away, just had PE lessons off for a few weeks, but eventually I told my mum I wanted to see the doctor as I was tired of the constant pain.

'Are you sure, love?' she asked when I spoke to her one evening whilst we were watching TV. 'Because now the health centre has moved to that ugly new building, it's a right pain to get to and either me or your father would have to take you.'

I waited for a moment before I responded, tempted to snap back that taking one's only child to the doctor's was the least a parent could do – in fact, many would regard it as a basic part of a parent's duty. But instead I just said, 'It wouldn't take long.'

'Well, you say that, love, but last time I was there it was a ninety-minute round trip – they make you wait for ages. And I'm decorating the tree tomorrow and I can't miss that. I promised Argento I'd be there.'

It took me a moment to realise what my mum was talking about, since 'decorating the tree' was something I normally associated with Christmas, and this was June. Then I remembered she was referring to the bonkers activity that she and her loopy group of friends were doing in the churchyard a few miles away. They draped cloth and other materials of different colours around the trees, apparently to encourage wandering spirits into their flowing, rippling folds. Argento was the leader of their group. I told her it sounded like something little kids would do – pretend they were in some special club and make someone the boss who told them which trees to decorate. Mum glared at me, disappointed at me for embarrassing her in front of this strange man who she was clearly in awe of. Argento was a tall, stick-thin man, hard to place in age, with slightly greying hair and dark beady eyes. He came to the house once to pick Mum up and I remember finding him quite frightening. My fear quickly decreased, however, when I overheard him having a phone call with someone in the street and discovered his real name was Gary, rather than Argento, and the odd Eastern-European accent he normally spoke with was actually completely fake. The fact my own mum would rather hang cotton sheets from tree branches with a group of hippie weirdos than take her daughter to a medical appointment would have upset me if it wasn't so depressingly predictable. We'd had rows about things like this before and they never went anywhere. 'I could walk to where Dad's working after school, if you could get me a late-afternoon appointment. That would be part of the way there. Then Dad could either finish early or nip out for a bit.'

During this conversation, Dad had been trying to get a splinter out of his thumb with a toothpick, a sight which made me feel a bit ill. He looked up, 'Er... what?'

'The doctor's, dear. Stephanie needs to go get her leg injury looked at. You need to take her.' My mum, who would be described by many as a floaty, vague, almost ethereal being, always suddenly became very brisk and to the point when addressing my dad, having learned from experience that the older he got the more confused he became at even the simplest of plans.

So a few days later, ready to attend my appointment at the health centre, I walked the two miles to Staplehay to the building site my dad was working on, walked all that way on the injured leg, exacerbating the pain further. The project was about halfway done, and he had been employed on it for a number of months, building a row of pristine-looking new houses on the site where once had stood a quaint little library and community centre. I was supposed to meet him at the entrance gates, since random people were not supposed to just wander into building sites, but I knew he wouldn't remember or would get sidetracked, so I just marched in.

I hoped, if I guilt-tripped him well enough, he'd take me for a burger at the McDonald's on the way back for tea. The other option was some tasteless vegan concoction my mother would likely serve up. Once inside, I walked around the edge, hoping I wouldn't be flagged down, and luckily spotted him fairly quickly. He was puffing on a cigarette (probably illegally) and chatting to a younger man. I noticed how good-looking he was immediately and was shocked that my dad would know or even be in the same square mile as someone that, well, that gorgeous. He looked like he had stepped off a catwalk or the pages of some glossy magazine. Designer stubble, short but slightly ruffled hair with natural highlights. He was smiling warmly and when I went up to make my dad aware of my presence he seemed unbothered by the appearance of a schoolgirl on a live construction site. In fact, he smiled even more warmly when he saw me and asked if he could help me at all. My dad explained that I was his daughter and then slapped his hand to his head when he remembered he was supposed to be taking me to the doctor's. We then departed, saying goodbye to the tall, gorgeous man without me getting time to discover who he was until we were in the car. 'He's the boss,' my dad explained. 'He owns the firm. Came to have a look at how we're doing. He's all right, a bit posh though; comes from Chelsea.'

The doctor told me in a cold, unfeeling way that I was risking causing lasting damage to my injured leg by walking on it and standing up every day, and my option was to stay at home and rest it for a week or get a wheelchair. The first option seemed the most attractive to me, so it was the one I told my dad about whilst eating the Big Mac he bought me. On the journey home I couldn't stop thinking about him: the gorgeous man with that perfectly ruffled hair, the stubble, the warm smile. I fell asleep that night imagining him next to me in bed; not exactly in a sexual way, just in a sense that I wanted him to be close to me, for me to feel him, smell him, to sense his warmth. I was seventeen. These feelings weren't new in themselves, but for me he felt particularly special.

When I returned to the building site a week later, after my prescribed rest, it wasn't to meet my dad (I knew he would have left by the time I arrived because he always went home a bit earlier on Fridays) but to see *him*. I couldn't help myself. I was drawn to him. My entrance to the site was more difficult this time around: I was stopped when I tried to walk in, but after pleading (and slightly flirting) with the guy near the gate, explaining that my father was a builder at the site and I was coming in to meet him, he relented. Trying to look like I knew what I was doing, I walked towards the little cluster of demountable buildings assembled in the corner of the first part of the space of land. I dawdled around the entrance to one of them, regretting coming and certain someone in a position of authority would throw me out any second. Then I saw him. He came out from one of the other buildings and no sooner had he put his foot down on the first step than he glanced up and saw me. He looked confused for a split second, then that warm smile spread across his face once again. 'Stephanie, isn't it?'

It was like I had been noticed for the first time. I'd never been properly noticed, either at home or at school, where I was well-behaved enough not to get into trouble, but not show-offy or conscientious enough to be one of the teachers' favourites. But staring at this vision of a man made me realise what I had been missing. How it felt to be looked at and truly seen. As if you really mattered in the world. As if your existence actually had a purpose, a reason, some deeply buried foundation you could hold on to. I must have been stunned into silence, all my bold intentions in going to the building site suddenly driven from my mind, because after a few seconds of silence he said 'Stephanie? Are you all right?'

I don't think I'd introduced myself when we had first met, but I presumed my father had spoken about me. I smiled at him tentatively. 'I was just looking for my dad,' I said, trying to sound more confident than I was feeling. All my instincts told me to leave then and there. Well, almost all of them. There was, of course, a part of me that wanted to stay, to see him, to make this trip worth it in some way. Perhaps a psychiatrist would have said I had an obsession developing, but I didn't care.

'I think you've missed him,' he said amiably. 'Do you have a mobile on you? If you don't you can use the phone in the office, if you like?' He reopened the door he had just come out of and stepped back inside. I did have a mobile but I followed anyway. I even called my dad using the office landline, making up some story about thinking I was supposed to meet him at work.

'Well, it'd take me another forty-five minutes to get back to you, with the traffic like it is on a Friday night. Can't ya just hop on the school bus?' he said down the crackly line. I told him the school bus would have gone ages ago. He then took the phone from me – not roughly but with a gentle firmness that took me by surprise.

'Hi, Kevin, this is Pete. No, don't worry at all, I'm not busy. Yes, she's here. No, it's fine, I have to go that way anyway. Yes, it's fine, honestly. OK, see you later.' He put the phone down and looked at me expectantly, as if he thought he should be congratulated on turning this situation around. I didn't know what to say. At least now I knew his name, I thought.

Probably just to fill the silence, he said, 'I'm taking you home.'

I recovered my voice. 'Yes,' I said, wondering how I should feel about what was happening. Excited? Worried? Nervous? All of them seemed viable options. I picked my school bag up off the floor and got up off the uncomfortable office seat where I had been sitting throughout the call.

'Oh, we won't leave yet,' he said. 'The traffic will still be bad at this time. It won't ease up for a while. You make yourself at home.' His voice was like listening to liquid chocolate. It had a warm, hypnotic quality, a well-spoken edge that was inviting rather than alienating or pretentious. I wanted to hear him say things. If he'd started reading out one of the health and safety manuals on the desk in front of me, I wouldn't have protested. He sounded almost edible.

We talked for a whole hour. We weren't disturbed once ('They think I've left for the day,' he explained). He asked me about my schoolwork, my family, my hopes for the future, and he volunteered details of his life in return. His family weren't pleased when he had used his trust fund to start a building company. They barely spoke anymore. Money wasn't a problem. He had made back everything he had gambled and a lot more besides. They still resented him though. I struggled to think how anyone could possibly resent a man so beautiful, friendly, kind, and open. He told me about his brother, the only member of his family he still really got on with, who met a woman whilst at university in Denmark; they had married, started a business together, and then settled in America. Pete had gone out there for the wedding but due to work commitments he only managed to visit two or three times a year now if he was lucky. His parents lived on Park Crescent in Marylebone, although they spent a lot of their time in a large house in the south of France. I found this idea of a family spread across countries fascinating. It had only ever been me, my mum, and my dad, living in a small two-bedroom house, worrying about money or where my dad's next contract was coming from. No sisters or brothers or aunts or grandparents. Just us. I told him this and he said, 'Trust me, I'm very envious of some aspects of your life.' He didn't expand much further, but I took what he said to be an expression of loss for the family unit he had grown up with. Although we had never been especially close or even very happy, I couldn't imagine not having Mum and Dad around me. They were just *there*. Always, whether I wanted them or not. Right then, at that point in my life, they were the only compass I had.

All this changed very quickly. It was only years later that I realised how incredible it was that all of life could have been turned upside down like that in a flash. The first big thing to move everything along happened as he dropped me off at my house. I turned to thank him and, spurred on by a sudden thought that I might never see him again, put a hand on his leg. I kept it there as I said my thanks and he smiled and looked at me very steadily and said, 'You're welcome.' He didn't remove my hand, so I just let it sit there, hoping it would be able to say all the things I didn't feel I could. It was like I'd suddenly become another person, ready to do things I wouldn't dare do under normal circumstances. Not for the first time that evening I was stuck for words. Then, at last, one question seemed more pressing than anything else.

'Can I see you again?' It came out in barely a whisper but he smiled his big, warm smile, and it was as if it lit up the whole car.

'Yes, yes, of course.' He sounded so relieved, so

happy, that for a second I thought he was going to cry. I looked at his kind, eager face, knowing, deep down, that we were inseparable now. I got out of the car and started to climb the stairs into my flat.

I didn't know then, of course, that we would start to meet up in secret, for walks in the park, for lunch at weekends when my parents were busy with their own thing. It never really crossed my mind to wonder if it was odd that a seventeen-year-old schoolgirl was spending so much time with a twenty-seven-year-old man. It just all felt right. And it continued to feel right, even when things became awkward. When difficulties or obstacles arrived in our path, including me getting pregnant with his child before I was even eighteen. But with him, although things were never perfect, my life always seemed to flow, regardless of what was put in its way. And after his death, I lost that flow completely, leaving me to navigate a strange, rocky terrain of the rest of my life alone.

THIRTEEN

Stephanie

THE DAY OF THE EXPLOSION

'Stephanie?'

I heard a panicky voice saying my name before I saw who was speaking. I couldn't properly tell where it was coming from. My name was repeated, louder and more worried. Or impatient, perhaps.

'Stephanie?'

Yes, that is my name, I thought dully to myself. Why did they keep saying it as a question? I turned over in bed to ask Pete to tell them to go away. But I wasn't in bed. The thing beneath me was a cushion, not a pillow. There was no duvet either. I was lying on a sofa and it didn't feel like my own. I opened my eyes and instantly remembered.

Janet.

She was standing over me, one hand nudging my

shoulder, looking slightly apprehensive as if I were a rare breed of spider she hadn't before encountered in her dust-free home.

'I'm fine,' I said, trying to sit up, but I felt dizzy again and abandoned the attempt for fear I would be sick.

'You fainted,' Janet said, still looking slightly wary of me.

'I'm sorry,' I replied quietly. I wasn't sure what she wanted me to do. Beg her for forgiveness?

'Were you feeling quite well this morning?'

'It was the music,' I explained groggily, realising it had stopped.

Janet looked even more puzzled. She turned to Mimi and told the girl to go and get me some water and a bowl of cereal. I didn't have the energy to tell her I didn't need any more food after the sourdough earlier.

I heard Mimi move off slowly into the kitchen and Janet moved away from me and settled onto the sofa opposite.

'Don't worry. Just lie there for a bit. Mimi is getting you something to eat.'

I was about to murmur that I didn't want anything but decided it was probably best not to argue with Janet. She was looking stressed already. I tried to sit up slowly, moving myself into more of a sitting position.

'Don't do anything that will make you feel worse,' warned Janet. 'You should just stay still for a moment.'

'It's OK,' I said, breathing slowly and looking around the room. 'How long was… was I out for?'

'Less than a minute. Any more than that and I would have called an ambulance.'

I wondered if an ambulance would still come as normal, what with the carnage outside, but again I chose to hold my tongue. I sensed movement behind me and turned to see that Jonathan had returned. He was peering through the front window of the living room, looking out onto the street.

'There was another explosion,' Janet explained, 'just after you collapsed. Not as big as the previous one, but it still made the house tremble a bit. It was then that you started to come to. I thought it might have woken you up a bit; dragged you back to the land of the living!' She gave a short bark of a laugh at that then went very still and sombre, probably realising that the concept of the *land of the living* was perhaps an insensitive one.

'I didn't hear it,' I said, still feeling a bit out of it. A noise did start to fill the lounge though, and one I certainly could hear: a helicopter was flying low, directly over our neighbourhood by the sound of it. Janet glanced up, as if the machine were visible through her ceiling.

'They've been circling for a couple of minutes. I

wonder if it's police. Or medical people. Or a news crew, even. You see that in films, don't you? Journalists and broadcasters dangling out of helicopters to get that perfect shot of some disaster. Of course, it's frustrating the power's still out, otherwise we could have the news on and really get to grips with what's happening.'

Her words were becoming like a background hum to me. I couldn't decide if I wanted to leave this place and give up on my whole aim of being there and wait for another day, or if now, having inserted myself into their lives on this strange day, I should just carry on.

Janet had now joined her son at the window and was remarking on how dark the sky was. When the cereal and water arrived, Mimi offered it to me with all the charm and warmth of a stern school matron, then disappeared upstairs without a word, followed not long after by Jonathan. Richard, it seemed, hadn't been moved enough by my collapse to come and see if I was OK, although I imagine Janet had already consulted him on whether they should call an ambulance or not.

'Eat up, Stephanie. We don't want you passing out on the floor again,' Janet said, returning to her seat opposite me, seemingly trying and failing to keep the annoyance from her voice. I was just about to ask about her husband – whether he had finished recording his university lecture – when I became aware of a tall, thin figure standing by the archway leading into the kitchen. He was standing right there, watching.

'I hear you had a bit of a turn,' Richard Franklin said, looking me up and down, as if searching for evidence of injury or instability. I just blinked at him. The phrase *bit of a turn* made me sound like a character in a Jane Austen novel who comes over faint whilst practising her needlework.

'Stephanie's fine now, apparently,' Janet said, giving the word *apparently* slightly too much emphasis, making it sound like she doubted my word, even though I hadn't strictly told her I was either fine nor that I was feeling better.

'Can we get you anything?' Richard offered, coming into the lounge properly now 'Some water, perhaps? Or something stronger.'

Janet sighed. 'Can you not start offering our guests alcohol at barely ten o'clock in the morning.' She looked over at me and rolled her eyes, inviting me to share in her disapproval. I kept my face blank. I found that the more I kept my reactions muted, the more the Franklins tried to fill the gaps. This could work to my advantage.

Richard strode forward, working his slim frame between the long, dark wood coffee table and his wife's knees, and sat down where Mimi had been earlier. After his prolonged absence, it was odd to have him in the midst of us, and I could see his eyes flicking around the lounge for something to settle on, some piece of inspiration for conversation now that he was here. He clearly found none, since he finally rested his eyes on the coffee table in front of us. Janet had returned to her magazines, though I suspected this was more performance than anything else, giving her something to do to avoid the awkwardness. Richard leant forwards and nudged the remaining stack of them on the table. 'Do we need all these?' he asked, frowning.

'That,' his wife said through thin lips and clenched teeth, 'is exactly why I'm looking through them.'

He looked annoyed by the response, but didn't complain, and sat back a little on the sofa. He took his phone out of his pocket and spent a couple of minutes staring at it, then remarked, 'They've evacuated more streets, apparently. Worried there'll be another bang.'

Janet looked up, an expression of mock surprise on her face. 'What's that? You mean you care what's happening, now?'

His lip curled into an expression of disdain. 'Don't be ridiculous,' he muttered.

'Sorry, my mistake,' Janet continued in her slightly false-sounding voice. 'It's just that from the way you spoke earlier, it sounded as though you didn't think the huge explosion nearby was much of a concern.' She had climbed in pitch with every few words until she sounded more than a little rattled. Catching me staring, she immediately relaxed her face into a calmer, more neutral expression and moved her eyes back to her lap. Her husband, on the other hand, turned his attention to me.

'So, Stephanie, if we're all supposed to be staying in our houses, how come you're here?'

This was very typical of Richard – to be all silent or quietly polite, and then suddenly come out with something blunt and borderline rude.

'I just... didn't want to be alone today,' I said, knowing full well this probably made me sound like I was after pity and sympathy, but I didn't really care. If pity was the only thing stopping them chucking me out, I had no problem using it. Richard seemed ill at ease with this answer, and a pained expression flickered across his rather gaunt-looking face.

'No, of course not. What a terrible thing... that... How awful it must have been.' His words were jerky, like a CD that's started to skip, and his mouth twisted uncomfortably as he tried to find the words.

I didn't bail him out. I didn't offer him any 'thank you's or 'It's OK's. I just let him squirm, unsure of how to treat the widowed, grieving woman in front of him. The cereal Mimi brought me was steadily getting softer, soaking up the milk. I took a mouthful of it and the dull crunches of the flakes sounded like earthquakes in the silent room.

'You all finished with your lecture?' Janet asked.

'Evidently,' Richard replied in a low monotone.

'Young people these days, learning online… video seminars and stuff,' Janet said. 'It's all so different to when I was a student.' I saw her eyes flick up to me, as if expecting a prompt for something, or at least a sign that I was listening. I gave her neither and took another mouthful of frosted flakes. 'I was at Exeter,' she added, apparently deciding it was best to just pretend I'd asked the question.

'Bristol,' I replied.

Janet, who had just opened a new magazine, paused, clearly a little thrown by the word. 'What? Sorry?'

'Bristol. I was at Bristol. You said you were at Exeter, so I thought I'd say where I went. I went to Bristol.'

Janet nodded slowly. 'Oh, I see. Right, yes. As in UWE? The University of the West of England?'

Over our years of living here, this sort of snobbery from Janet had become rather funny. Similar to her faux social-justice-warrior stuff (or, perhaps, in contradiction to it), Janet was fond of making sweeping statements and condescending presumptions about those she suspected belonged to a different social class than herself. At another time, I'd have wound her up a bit – told her that no, I actually just went to a nail bar in Bristol city centre that handed out BTECs to anyone with a pulse. But I wasn't in the mood, so I just opted for the plain truth. 'No, not UWE, although I hear it's also a terrific uni. But I went to the University of Bristol.'

Although I was fairly sure Janet knew I'd been to uni and had a degree – I must have spoken about it at some point – there was a fair chance I may not have specified which institution I'd been to. It probably seemed the most natural thing in the world for her to presume the new 'young mother' at the school gates with the Somerset accent went to a former polytechnic or did an Open University course whilst working as a checkout girl. And it riled me that those two potentials could be seen as *less than* or not as worthy as her days swanning around Exeter.

'I studied English Lit,' I added, which made Janet's eyes grow wider still.

'Well,' she said, turning her gaze back to the magazine, trying to recover herself. 'I'm sure that was… convenient. Being relatively close to you. You're from Somerset originally, aren't you?'

This Janet definitely knew. 'Yes. Bridgwater.'

'I went to Bridgwater once,' Richard said, unenthusiastically, but Janet didn't seem interested.

'Mimi did look at Bristol, but it didn't really offer her

the flexibility she wanted, and I think she'd rather prefer Cambridge, or Guildhall.'

Richard let out something between a laugh and a cough, which Janet ignored.

'Doesn't she want to go to the university where her father teaches?' I asked, strongly suspecting neither Mimi nor Janet would want anything of the kind.

'Oh no, definitely not,' Janet said, looking horrified.

'Or Canterbury Christ Church?' I offered, guessing the reaction this would invoke.

'What? No! She wants to study *music*, as in proper music with performance, not *entertainment journalism*.' She laughed a little, both at her own joke and, it seemed, how preposterous the whole suggestion was anyway.

'Well, I believe they do have a music department,' I thought I'd add, both to keep some sense of balance and to wind her up a little further.

'Jonathan, however…' she cut across me '… is less of a dead cert. He needs to pull his socks up when it comes to his grades. But he's got a bit more time. But you know what teenage boys are like…' She shook her head, tutting, and this time didn't seem to twig how insensitive her words were.

I stood up. All this talk about her offspring and their futures was making me feel faint again and I'd become dimly aware of how full my bladder was feeling since I'd drunk the tea and the glass of water. 'I need to use the loo,' I explained.

'Out in the hallway and turn right,' Janet said, not looking up from her magazine-rifling.

I followed her instructions and came to a little downstairs bathroom. I'd been in it once or twice before when we'd infrequently attended the odd Christmas drinks or garden party. It was decorated in a tasteful plain cream with a framed photo of a seaside view at dusk on the wall. I wondered if it was somewhere the family had actually visited, or if it was one of those stock images pre-framed that Janet had added to her basket when she was drifting round John Lewis. A small jar candle had been placed on the ledge above the taps – Jo Malone's Pomegranate Noir – and although it wasn't burning it still gave off a rich, heavily perfumed aroma, adding to my already dizzy state.

As I sat down, I saw to my left that there was a little pile of magazines, similar to the ones Janet was pretending to sort through in the lounge. I picked some of them up. A lot of recipes for 'Beetroot and Guava Cake' and articles about how 'Pistachios will be the next big thing'. In between a copy of a John Lewis catalogue and an old *Sunday Times* weekend supplement, I discovered something else: a small pile of A4 paper. It looked fresh, newly printed, although from a quick glance I saw that the pages were Christmas themed, with a border of holly and berries around the side. Then I realised what they were: copies of the Franklins' Christmas Round Robin. Either Janet felt her guests would welcome the opportunity to brush up on the family's adventures over the previous calendar year or – and perhaps more likely – spare sheets of it had inadvertently got collected together with the rest of the downstairs loo reading material. The paper felt expensive, of course. Janet wouldn't settle for any recycled rubbish. For all her empty chatter about saving the planet and climate change, she didn't really alter her own life to suit her much-voiced principles. She still drove around in one of those huge polar-bear-killing cars.

I perused the opening paragraph of the round robin, remembering it well, having received it myself.

Upon our second Christmas in this town we had been promoted to the Franklins' list of involuntary subscribers to this excruciating yearly ritual. I had encountered round robins once before in my life – my mum had a friend from her schooldays who had 'come up in the world' and always sent her one. But nothing could have prepared me for a round robin from the House of Franklin.

I could practically recite them from memory, or at

least make an educated guess at what each one would contain when it arrived.

One year Pete and I, helped along with a bottle of Christmassy Baileys, had spent the evening sitting at the kitchen table making our own annotations on the first one we had received whilst screaming with laughter. It was probably a cruel waste of time; time I could have spent wrapping up more of Danny's stocking-filler presents individually rather than grouping them into twos and threes to save time. But it was fun. Poking fun at posh people was a laugh, as if by doing so we were avoiding the uncomfortable truth: we were gradually becoming the people that we mocked. The house, the car, the private school – all paid for by Pete, who could never completely hide his own roots. But we had always considered ourselves different from the likes of Janet and the other parents at the school.

We were from the real world.

We were more unconventional.

We were special.

Or, maybe, we were just hypocrites.

I brushed this uneasy notion aside and began to the read the whole thing properly.

Merry Christmas, all!

My goodness what a year it has been! Not only have we had amazing adventures, we all feel and agree that we have developed and grown as people.

Both Jemima and Jonathan have learned valuable lessons in time management and academic discipline whilst remembering to enjoy their youth whilst they still have it. Jemima is currently studying for her first year of A Levels and is loving every second. It's so wonderful to have a daughter who was born with a natural hunger to learn. It has become impossible to separate her from her revision. Even her boyfriend, Kenneth (charming boy, son of a human rights lawyer), has found it difficult to make her pay attention to the smaller things in life, such as rehearsing their duet for the school concert. It all went fine in the end; they played the three movements of (Emanuel) Bach's 'Duet for Flute and Violin' and received a standing ovation. Jonathan is also currently beavering away at his studies and has likewise managed to cultivate some truly inspiring hobbies. He has learned three different languages outside of his compulsory studies and has even started to tutor children who are not fortunate enough to go to a school that places the same importance on academic rigour. I have no shame in saying it: my own children are an inspiration to me.

January started off grim and cold, with Richard having to deal with a lot of situations after taking on extra work at the university. He has now been promoted to Head of Education. When we heard the news we were over the moon! He had already booked time off for the children's half-term holiday and we were initially planning to spend it kicking off the year in the garden. However, to mark Richard's success we decided to hop on an impromptu cruise down the River Nile. The whole experience was utterly fantastic. Egypt is a wonderful country and very friendly to tourists, although we did have to contact the British Embassy when Richard's passport was stolen by a man wearing a turban. Apart from this little hiccup, we were able to return to the UK only a couple of days behind schedule. Two months in and we have only caused one diplomatic emergency! Not bad for us!

The spring passed quickly, though the highlight was Charlton, the Newfoundland, winning the local dog show. He was truly sublime and everyone came up individually and said he was the deserved winner. I must confess I welled up a little too to see him so happy with his success. We are hoping he will now be onto a winning streak and are even contemplating entering next year's Crufts!

We spent the Easter holidays going rambling as a family; we all enjoy discovering new places on foot and have drawn up a *list of gourmet pubs we found reviewed in The Observer's food supplement we wish to visit when going on our rambles. Our most successful trip was to the Lake District, although there was a small issue at the hotel which involved a drunken woman from Leamington Spa who did something very rude to Richard at dinner and we had to call both the management and then the police. The whole situation actually worked out rather well as the woman was wanted in several counties for sexual harassment and the authorities were most grateful to us for alerting them to her presence in the hotel. The managers also gave us vouchers for a free two-week stay, so we will definitely be returning, providing it is pervert-free next time!*

This is the first year that Richard and I were able to get away ourselves without the children, so in the summer when Jonathan was staying with some neighbours and Mimi went to visit Richard's mother in Hertfordshire, we decided to go and stay with our very dear friends the Marchendales in... and this was very exciting... their holiday apartment in Venice! What a treat! Richard and I had both visited Venice before of course, but never together, and to be let loose in the most romantic city in the world without the children was absolute heaven! It goes without saying we got up to a lot of exciting things, and thankfully didn't have any passport situations to distract us.

When we returned to the UK we were overjoyed to see the children; it was the first time we had properly been apart. I enjoyed the holiday but was starting to feel like we were one of those poor, fractured families you read about; the kind who have people dotted around the globe and don't talk to each other. I just wanted them all back in our warm nest. That first meal back in our home after three weeks of separation was one of the really special moments of the year. I am quite emotional even writing about it. We all reminded each other how lucky we were whilst we ate the lemon and herb partridge that Jemima had cooked up for our return. She is really becoming quite the domestic goddess in the kitchen! Delia Smith had better watch out!

As we reached late summer, I decided to start a book club in our small town. I have always been an avid reader and love engaging with people about the books they read. I got together with some of the mums at Mimi and Jonathan's schools and we decided to meet once every three weeks in one of the restaurants in the high street and discuss our chosen read. I insisted all our books had to be written by female writers of colour. It was the only sensible thing to do. Of course, I did make a few exceptions, like the new Jeffrey Archer, and a John Banville, and naturally the new Julian Barnes, and we've been loving going through Martin Amis's back catalogue. Next up: Philip Roth's entire oeuvre! Can't wait.

As the year draws to a close and I think about the upcoming couple of weeks I am reminded of what a joy Christmas with the family is. We have Richard's sister and mother coming to stay, and my parents and siblings will also be dropping in on Boxing Day. We had a spectacular game of Guess Who I Am last year and we are all very excited to try it again. If you haven't ever tried the game I suggest you do; it is immense fun! You write down a famous person on a piece of paper and attach it to the forehead of the person on your right, then one by one they have to guess who is written on the paper through asking questions, with everyone else only able to answer 'Yes' or 'No'. It's such a hoot! Though I have to admit it took me a shameful amount of time to guess that I was Sylvia Plath, whereas Jemima seemed to guess that she was Jane Seymour within two questions. This year we have agreed to raise the stakes by only picking leading LGBTQI+ figures from the twentieth century. I'm looking forward to it already!

Anyway, this leaves me and my fellow Franklins to wish all of you a wonderful Christmas and I hope you have a fulfilling and enjoyable New Year.

Festive wishes to one and all!

Janet Richmond, on behalf of the Franklin Family.

Five months after receiving it and reading it for the first time, its contents no longer made me laugh. What was the point of laughing, when I no longer had anyone to share it with? Phrases and sentences that I would have once read aloud to Pete flashed in front of my eyes, as if highlighted in fluorescent ink, then faded away into nothingness. All this didn't stop me cringing at the essay's contents. The insufferable presumption that the world cares what Janet and her preposterous family have been up to throughout the previous twelve months! Who cared if they'd had more holidays in a year than many children in Britain will have throughout their whole childhood? Did they think it made them more likeable or desirable or worthy of people's admiration?

I was pretty sure that if one posted this on Facebook as a spoof example of how ridiculous round robins could be, people wouldn't believe it. 'Nobody's round robins could be *that* bad!' they'd say. Janet had successfully cooked up a piece of writing that you just couldn't make up and nobody would believe it if you had. It was pretty clear to me she had exaggerated and embellished a number of events within the self-aggrandising essay. For one thing, Charlton wasn't even her bloody dog; it was her mother's, yet anyone reading it would think she had brought him up since he was a puppy. And they didn't cause a diplomatic incident in Egypt. Richard lost his passport, like hundreds of travellers each year. It probably wasn't even stolen, and Janet's need to mention that the alleged thief was wearing a turban was, for all her overtures about diversity and constant policing of language, just an example of her underlying racism.

Glancing again at their other vacation-based incident – the woman in a hotel in the Lake District – I wasn't sure whether to roll my eyes or be suspicious. Even if it had occurred how Janet described, it was still a pretty weird thing to put in a round robin. I couldn't shake off the nagging thought that Janet was over-compensating for something. Had the woman really been to blame? Or had she been tempted into an intimate situation by a womaniser, at some place more private than a restaurant, only to be caught by his wife? Because Richard Franklin *was* a womaniser. I knew this. And I suspected Janet knew it too.

I looked through the last part of the letter and I felt a pang of hurt at the book club situation. I remembered saying to Pete at the time that I was slightly upset that I hadn't been invited. 'Would you have actually wanted to join?' he'd asked, his eyebrows raised. Of course I wouldn't have actually wanted to hop off to Prezzo with Janet and the other mums and indulge in affected musings about books they were only pretending to read. But it would have been nice to have been asked. After all, I did have a first-class English degree. I wasn't in the habit of flaunting it, but the thought of Janet's group of school mums having book chats without me had made me feel a bit snubbed. I'd almost said something about it to Pete back when we'd read the letter the first time around, but had chosen not. I didn't want to look needy, like I wasn't settled and happy in Oak Tree Close. But now, I regretted not sharing that with Pete. I regretted trying to keep up a front, when he was always so good at comforting me when he needed to. He would fix his kind eyes on me, the eyes that made me feel like I was already in the warmth of his embrace even before he had moved to put his arms around me. He would tell me what I needed to hear, tell me I didn't need a group of snobbish mums to make me feel validated or needed.

I was about to put the sheet aside when another sheet of A4, this time folded in half, slipped out onto the floor. I picked it up and opened it out, frowning when I saw it was handwritten. I scanned it quickly, then re-read it more slowly. It didn't take long – it was very short.

Dear Alexa and Logan, I just wanted to include a little handwritten note inside this thanking you again for being so amazing this year. I'm so grateful to you for letting me stay back in the summer for that week. You made the whole thing much easier. Nobody suspected a thing. As I mentioned in my email back in the autumn, I'm healing well and everything seems to be fine so far. Hope you have a wonderful Christmas – we'll have to arrange another meet-up next year. Merry Christmas, Janet.

There were a number things particularly interesting about this.

The first thing clearly apparent was that it was a practice attempt. There were some crossings out and scribbles, and a little loopy doodle shape in the corner, suggesting Janet had been trying to get the ink flowing from the pen. This letter meant a lot to her, it seemed. She had been keen to get it right.

Then there were the contents. Why had Janet had to stay with Alexa and Logan, whoever they were? In what way was she 'healing well'? Had she had an operation? Or perhaps an injury? *Nobody suspected a thing.* So whatever it was, she seemed to have kept it a secret. All this puzzled me.

And then there was a feeling I hadn't expected. A feeling of pity. I wondered if Janet also had experience of what it was like to feel cut-off and so totally alone. For the first time, I think I saw her in a slightly new light.

After having a quick pee, I tore up one of the round robin sheets into little pieces, along with the handwritten letter, and dropped them into the toilet and flushed the chain. Seeing them swirling away, engulfed in the rush of water felt like I was erasing those last few minutes. As if I'd never read them.

The first noise that greeted me as I emerged from the bathroom was a small crash, as if someone had dropped something heavy on the coffee table. I walked into the living room with trepidation. Janet was standing, Richard was still seated, and the coffee table was loaded with a number of large hardback books. As I drew closer I realised they were recipe books; the collected works of Nigella Lawson.

'We don't have it!' Janet snapped suddenly. 'They are the only ones we have! As I have told you.' Richard peered at the books on the table and sniffed noisily.

'I need her one on Italian food. There's a paragraph in there I distinctly remember reading that would work well with my comment on the carnal connection between food and sex. I wanted to weave it into the discussion.'

'Well, you'll have to find it online,' Janet said, sounding very frustrated as she came away from the bookshelves. 'And anyway, I don't know which bit you're talking about at all. We've never even owned *Nigellissima*.' She sat down on the sofa next to him and started flicking through the pages of *Nigella Christmas*. 'There are some Italian-inspired recipes in here. Maybe you could *weave in* some of those?'

Richard sighed loudly. 'The fact they are Italian isn't the important point. For God's sake, I remember you reading the bloody book when you got it. It sat on the kitchen table for ages!'

'You're probably thinking of a different book altogether. Are you sure it was even Nigella?'

Richard looked like he was trying to stop himself losing his rag. 'Who else sexualises bloody linguine?' he said through gritted teeth.

'Well, I think you've got it wrong,' Janet muttered, though still loud enough for me to hear.

I decided to sit down, though neither of them paid the slightest bit of attention to me. Nigella Lawson had been one of my mum's favourites on TV. She had videoed all of *Nigella Bites* when it was first broadcast, even though my dad had referred to it as 'frying-pan porn'. When I was at university I had rewatched episodes with Pete; a piece of nostalgia for me while I adjusted to my new life with him and the baby in our apartment in Bristol.

'Once again, I think your imagination has run away

with you!' Janet was sounding close to hysterical and I wondered if she was always like this behind the scenes, or perhaps the combination of my sudden arrival and the explosions happening nearby had pushed her over the edge. Or maybe things were more tense with her husband than they appeared on the outside.

'I know what I read and I know what I saw. You've just lost the book. You could at least be brave enough to admit it.'

Janet slammed the Christmassy-coloured tome down on the table with a loud bang and stormed out of the living room, shoving past Richard and disappearing into the kitchen. Loud crashes started to emanate from the doorway. It sounded like she was taking out her anger on the crockery in the sink. Richard looked up at me quickly, probably checking my reaction. I looked back at him blankly. After a moment's pause he said, 'I think... I should probably go and see if she's OK,' and stood up. He didn't look embarrassed, just mildly annoyed by the situation. He too disappeared into the kitchen and I remained seated, listening. Their conversation continued out of sight through fierce but audible whispers and then built up once again into a shouting match.

'You just love making me seem like a fool, don't you? I think you're a sadist! You're obsessed with making me feel small and stupid!'

It sounded like Janet had a lot of built-up resentment. I wondered if their holiday in Venice together had been this tense. From the way she'd told it, it had been a romantic break for the two of them, but perhaps that was all nonsense. An image of them sitting in a gondola, glaring at each other, not speaking, floated into my mind.

I listened to their argument for a minute more then stood up. It was time to investigate upstairs. Mimi and Jonathan had been absent for a while, and I decided it would be stupid to waste a chance of catching Jonathan alone.

I walked out into the hallway and climbed the stairs as quietly as I could. The noise of water running from taps started up suddenly from the direction of the bathroom. Maybe Jonathan was in there? I walked to the door of what I presumed to be Janet and Richard's bedroom. I was very tempted to have a real nose around. I stepped in and opened one of the drawers at random. It contained perfectly folded jumpers and cardigans. Women's stuff, from what I could see. Apparently Janet has a penchant for John Lewis's own-brand knitwear and the Per Una range from M&S. I closed the drawer and headed back out onto the landing. The shower was running. I looked over at the open door of what was obviously Jonathan's room – the bedroom of a teenage boy. Such a thing used to be a daily part of my routine.

I'd either be in there picking his clothes up off the floor that hadn't made it to the laundry basket or taking down Coke cans to the recycling or hoovering up Oreo crumbs. Jonathan's room, though far from entirely orderly and neat, was a little tidier than Danny's had ever been. Perhaps Janet was more of a stickler than I ever was, or maybe their cleaner just came more often than ours used to.

I stopped myself going too far with my reminiscence and walked purposefully into Jonathan's room.

FOURTEEN

Stephanie

NOW

I drift in and out of sleep for much of the afternoon. I find hospitals aren't places for deep sleep. Not unless you've been deliberately put under. Instead, you get this nauseating semi-consciousness, forever doomed to be woken by a medication trolley knocking against your bed or staff members calling to each other across the ward in loud voices.

It sounds strange, but at times I get the feeling I'm not alone. That there's a figure standing by my bed. No, that's not right – sitting. Sitting by my bed, in the chair meant for visitors.

Watching me.

The mixture of drugs and pain must be affecting my mood. Or perhaps it's because of what's happened to me. Whatever the reason, I find the sense of someone being near me but indistinguishable extremely unnerving. It's like looking at a painting but knowing something's just not quite right about it.

Worst of all, I think I know who it is, sitting there. In the room with me. I know it. And she's the reason I'm here.

At one point, I wake up crying – not hysterically so, just with tears rolling out onto my pillow. A stressed-looking nurse passes my bed, then stops and turns back to look at me. I wonder if she's torn between getting on with her work and the feeling that she should comfort me in some way or at least ask if I'm OK. But it turns out my presumption is wrong: there's something specific she wants to ask me.

'The police want to talk to you. They've gone away now, but they'll be back, so long as you feel up to it.'

I tilt my head up a little, trying to focus on her. 'They were here? The police were here?'

The nurse nods. 'You were out of it then, but the nice officer I spoke to said they'd return. They need you to answer some questions about what happened.'

'Right,' I say, now trying to rub my eyes without moving my head too much. 'I'm not sure I'm ready now, but I will be soon. I definitely want to speak to them. I have things I want to say.'

FIFTEEN

Stephanie

FIVE MONTHS BEFORE THE EXPLOSION

'Danny, could you go and see if the cherry pie's done?'

I was in the middle of opening a forgotten stack of Christmas cards and putting them on the mantelpiece. They'd arrived earlier in December but had been tucked out of the way, and if I didn't open them today the entire purpose of their festive wishes would soon be irrelevant. Pete was glued to *Miracle on 34th Street*, with the rapt attention of someone trying to make sense of a play by Pinter. We were supposed to be having guests round – the Winters. They were Pete's friends, as usual, although these ones were normally quite fun to be around. Sadly, they'd both come down with some horrendous colds and had to cancel, saying they didn't want to give it to us in time for Christmas Day.

'Very considerate of them to warn us,' I said, although I was a little irritated that I had already bought the food we were going to cook for them.

'Either considerate, or they couldn't be bothered,' Pete mumbled as he started eating some of the nice crisps I'd planned to put in bowls.

So instead of a lively festive gathering, we'd settled down for Christmas Eve on our own, eaten our dinner without our guests and were now about to tuck into a warm cherry pie in front of the television and the roaring fire. It would have been idyllic and cosy, if it hadn't been for our main growing concern: Danny. He'd spent nearly all of the day in his room and when I tried to give him jobs to do – like pop out to the shops to get some cinnamon and ginger – he'd just grunted and trudged off without even saying goodbye. He only came down to watch a Christmas film with us because I went upstairs and guilt-tripped him into it, saying it would be nice to spend such a special evening with his parents rather than stare moodily at the walls of his room. It was almost like he'd reverted to being a child again – though a withdrawn, difficult child, quite different from the boy he used to be. This impression was amplified further when I consistently heard audiobooks of stories like *The Famous Five* and *The Chronicles of Narnia* coming from his bedroom rather than the usual thudding bass of a rock song or something he was streaming on Netflix. I got the feeling he was seeking comfort and solace from the familiarity of those childhood tales, although what he was trying to escape I still couldn't find out.

For all his determined concentration, Pete fell asleep at 9.25pm, just before the film ended. Considering it had been me who had done most of the work that day, I wasn't too impressed with this, although didn't complain when he said he might go to bed for an early night. This left Danny and me alone. I asked him if he wanted to choose something else to watch – perhaps another film?

'No,' he just said, barely looking up from his phone screen. He got to his feet and stretched, then mumbled something about going to bed too. I made a joke about how lucky it was we weren't one of those families who went to midnight mass, otherwise we'd all be falling asleep in the service. He didn't respond.

I decided I'd had enough. Taking a deep breath, I said, 'I wish you'd just tell me what's wrong.'

This was going against what Pete and I had agreed a few days before. We'd both been nagging Danny to explain why he was acting so strangely, with me maintaining it was something to do with that weird scene I'd witnessed in the boys' bathroom. But we never really got much of a response, just assurances he was fine and entreaties to stop pestering him. Pete decided we should just leave him to work through whatever it was. 'Teenagers have friendship problems, relationship issues, make-ups, break-ups, sexual experimentation, all that sort of stuff,' Pete said dismissively. 'You must remember what it was like when you were his age.' I told him I did, although I chose not to mention that the one big crush and sexual experience that had defined my later teenage years had all been down to him.

Although I had prepared myself for a cold response from Danny, when I asked him on that Christmas Eve night when we were alone in the lounge, I wasn't ready for what he actually said. He froze halfway to the door, then turned around slowly to look at me. There was something deeply unsettling about his face, like he was in severe pain or trying not to be sick. Then he said, 'Stop asking me. Please. Just stop.'

That was when I worried something really, really serious was going on. I took a step towards him and saw some tears escape his eyes. 'Danny, my love, please… what is it?'

He rubbed at his face, as if furious at himself for letting the tears fall, yet unable to stop them. 'It's all just… I can't… I don't know…'

'Just tell me what it's about. Please. Just a few words,

just give me a hint. I'll do anything to make whatever it is go away, or we can sort it out...'

'It's... photos...'

I frowned, confused, although even without any context, there was something in that word that made a chill sweep the length of my neck and back. 'What photos? Who has photos? Photos of what? Is this... is this to do with Jonathan?'

He winced at the sound of the name and wiped more tears away.

'Tell me, Danny, or I'll march over the road to that house right this second and demand that boy explain everything if you don't start talking—'

I shouldn't have made that threat. Perhaps, if I hadn't, he wouldn't have made his. Because the next words he said were the worst he'd ever spoken.

'If you do that... if you tell Dad about this, or try to ask me about it again, I'll tell everyone about what *you* did.'

If the cold ripple I'd felt earlier had been a chill, what I experienced then was an ice-cold tidal wave, cutting through me, ripping me to pieces. He couldn't have just said what I'd thought. How... how could he possibly...?

'Danny...' I said. It was the only word I could muster.

'You heard what I said. I know everything. Don't ask

me about it again and I'll keep your secret. Even though it makes me feel ill thinking about it.'

He looked at me as if I were a stranger – a terrifying, repulsive stranger. Then he left the room, leaving me standing there by the Christmas tree, as the strains of 'Silent Night' emanated from an advertisement on the television behind me.

SIXTEEN

Stephanie

THE DAY OF THE EXPLOSION

Jonathan's room smelled different to Danny's. Probably down to the aftershave Jonathan used, I thought, as I walked further inside. I'd always just thrown a Lynx spray into the trolley in the supermarket for Danny, something Pete thought tantamount to a crime. But Danny didn't seem to mind. Looking at the bedside table in Jonathan's room, it seemed he was partial to Ralph Lauren's Polo Eau de Toilette 'Natural' scent. I picked it up and sprayed a little on my hand. It was what I'd imagine a rich businessman in a suit to smell like, rather than a teenage boy. I put it back down and noticed the antiperspirant was from the Adidas sport range. That was more fitting. I briefly glanced in his drawers, taking in the expensive designer labels of his clothes, occasionally mixed in with something more ordinary, like the odd white T-shirt from H&M.

The whole room was dark. At first I thought it was because of the smoke outside, but then realised his blinds were down. There was a MacBook Pro on the desk at the end of the room. The screen was glowing invitingly so I sat down on the chair in front of it and opened up his documents folder, pausing to check I could still hear the shower still running. I scrolled down through the many homework assignments. I noticed one called *Trial Translation Draft 6*. It had taken him six drafts? And another essay titled *Cold Comfort Farm: A Discussion on What was Really in the Woodshed* which ran on to 12 different variations. All this was either a symptom of his mother's controlling hand in his homework, or Jonathan's language skills weren't as great as advertised. I left the documents and headed to the photos folder. I just hoped he had his iCloud set up so photos appeared on his laptop as well as his phone. There must be something. Some clue. Something to point me in the right direction. *Photos*, Danny had said. That one word was all I had. I scrolled through the different subfolders. 'Skiing 2013', 'Center Parcs 2016', 'Butlins 2017', which felt curiously off-brand for the Franklins. Another said 'Christmas gifts' and I was about to click on it to see what Jonathan had been asking Santa for when a voice from behind me said, 'What are you doing?'

I turned to see Jonathan himself standing behind me. He had a towel around his waist, and the rest of him was dripping wet. He'd clearly just got out of the shower and had come back to his room to find me so wrapped up in my nosing that I was unaware the noise of the water had stopped.

'Oh... er... sorry, I was... just looking.'

He frowned. 'On my laptop? Why are you looking on there?'

I felt myself going red as I stepped away from the computer to face him properly. I was annoyed at myself for acting like a naughty child. I needed to retain the role of authority here. Jonathan was the child, and I was the adult. And I was tired of being in the dark when it came to him. I wanted to know everything.

'Close the door now.' I said it in a commanding tone, the kind I used to use when Danny had opted for TV instead of homework.

To my relief, it worked on Jonathan and he came in and closed the door behind him.

'Why are you on my computer?' he asked, taking a step towards me.

'Because I want to know what was going on with my son before he died. What was going on between you two.

What you did or said that made him turn into a completely different person in the weeks leading up to his death. You see, I *know* something was wrong. And your evasion and refusal to talk isn't going to stop me. If you want, I'll go and get your parents in here right now and ask them what they think it could be, because I don't seem to be getting very far with just you.'

I went to stand up, but Jonathan put a hand out to stop me. 'Wait. Please.' He stood there, like a dripping statue, water running down his face, which looked different without his glasses on. Younger, more fragile. After a few seconds he moved to the side and let his frame drop onto the bed with a thud. He put his face in his palms, rubbing at his eyes. 'It's all... it's all just so fucked.'

I was desperate to chivvy him along, to ask what was fucked, what was going on, but I knew from experience that when a teenager starts to tell you something they're finding difficult, it's best to hold fire on the third-degree questioning until they've got it all out. So I sat still and silent, waiting for the boy to continue.

After almost a full minute, he did.

And his story astonished me.

SEVENTEEN

Danny

A YEAR BEFORE THE EXPLOSION

y crush thing on Mimi Franklin has started to fade. Back when we first moved here I didn't think it would, but as time has gone on I've started to look around at the girls more my age. Girls I might have more of a chance of falling into bed with than Mimi.

Although I do still think about Mimi in *that way*, I've kind of moved on from thinking she is a 'realistic prospect', as Jonathan would put it. He doesn't know I've been thinking about his sister like that – it's just the way he always speaks about the girls he fancies. Are they a 'realistic prospect', or out of our league. It doesn't help going to an all boys' school, with only the sixth form girls in the North Annex to look at from a distance as they play sports on the field we share.

Our friend Scotty always says 'What sort of girl

decides to go to an all boys' school for sixth form? A girl who wants to find the man of her dreams.' We always tell him he's a jerk, but I think we all secretly hope he's right. And when the girls started coming to our house parties or hanging out to listen to our band practice, I too began to think his generalisation might have some truth to it because some of them really have been all over us. Really quickly. Two weeks ago, I was both surprised and nervous when Sara Watkins told me to follow her upstairs at a party at Scotty's rugby friend Noah's house. But I followed and did what I was told, going into an upstairs games room where older boys were drunkenly playing pool, while the massive TV on the wall played a weird edit of *Game of Thrones* battle scenes set to rock music. Scotty was on the sofa already, getting friendly with Sara's friend Aoife. Sara just pushed me down and started kissing me and I went along with it. It was fun and exciting, and I felt myself going weak with pleasure as Sara kissed down my neck then started unbuckling my belt and unzipping my jeans.

I'd thought losing my virginity – even if it wasn't the full-on virginity – would be this big, huge thing, but it didn't really feel like that. At least, not until I tell Jonathan about it, two weeks after the party, when summer is getting ridiculously hot.

Jonathan and I decide to go swimming, hoping it will

cool us down. It does just about, but also leaves us tired and a bit aimless afterwards, not sure what else to do. We end up wandering through the nearby woods that back on to the far end of Oak Tree Close. Probably how the road got its name. I think I once heard Jonathan's mum saying the oak trees that lined the road used to be part of the wood back when it was a huge forest, before they chopped a lot of it down and built loads of houses. Even though the wood isn't that large now, it's still the sort of place where you can lose hours of the day without meaning to. And that's what we decide to do. We spend an hour just ambling around, the bags with our swim kits nudging our backs as we wander between the path and the wilder bits, our wet hair drying quickly in the heat. Eventually we get too hot and sit down by a fallen tree in one of the shadier parts and share a can of Coke Jonathan got from the vending machine at the pool. It's still cold and I only realise how thirsty I am when he passes it to me and I take a sip.

'Thanks,' I say and he smiles at me. We sit in silence for a bit. Jonathan and I often sit in silence. Silence with him is comfortable. Not awkward like it would be with some of the other people in my class. It doesn't feel like we have to worry about saving up things to say, trying to make conversation, scared of dropping the conversation ball and making the situation flatline.

Jonathan does break the silence though, eventually. And he wants to talk about the party from a couple of weeks previously. The one held at Scotty's mate's house.

'I heard that you and Sara talked a lot at the party,' he says.

I laugh, realising the news of me and Sara's activities had eventually reached him. 'Yeah... more than talked.'

A few moments of silence go by before he replies. 'Yeah. Yeah, Scotty said.'

I sigh. 'Yeah, well, I didn't think he could keep his mouth shut. But then neither could Sara.' I laugh again, but I feel him tense next to me.

'Don't... don't say stuff like that. You're not like that.'

I frown at him, suddenly confused. 'Not like *what*? It was only a joke.' I turn quickly to face him, my legs scraping the twig-covered ground as I move.

'Don't talk about girls like that, as if they're... I don't know. I know Scotty and Noah and his friends go on about girls like that, as if they're just there to do what they want for them, but you're better than that. You're better than all of them.'

This is coming completely out of the blue for me. Jonathan has never said anything like this. In fact, he doesn't normally talk much at all; it's usually me doing the talking, like moaning about my parents or homework or wanting a car as soon as I'm seventeen, and he just listens and says stuff now and then. Helpful stuff, in agreement, mostly. But this... this is new.

'Er... well... sorry. I didn't mean it badly. I was... Sorry. I was just embarrassed that Scotty's been telling everyone that I got off with Sara.'

Jonathan says nothing. He just sits there, now playing with a leaf in his hands, shredding it slowly.

'What... what do you mean... that I'm better than all of them?'

He's still facing forward, but when I glance at him I can see that his face has gone all tense. It's rigid, like he's clenching his jaw.

'I... Don't worry. It doesn't matter.'

'What? It obviously does. What's going on?'

Then he looks at me, and I'm completely shocked as I can clearly see tears in his eyes. They don't fall though. He stays calm. Doesn't burst into tears. And a couple of seconds later, I wonder if I've imagined them. And then everything goes out of my mind when he speaks.

'I love you, Dan.'

I feel something drop within me, like I've become a pebble that's been plunged into a deep pool.

'Are you...? Do you mean...?'

His lip starts to tremble a bit, but he bites it hard with his top teeth and takes in a slow breath through his nose.

Then he says, quite calmly, 'I've loved you for ages. I've just always been scared to say.'

I'm trying to digest what he's saying. If he'd just told me that he was gay, that would be simple and I wouldn't have thought much of it. But this is much bigger news. And I'm not sure how to take it.

'You mean… you like guys, not girls?' I don't know if this is the right question to ask, but I feel I need to get some firmer details on all this.

He shakes his head. 'I like girls. I still, like, fancy girls. But I also like you.'

I frown at this. 'Are you saying… you saying I'm like a girl?'

He makes a half-grunt, half-laugh sound. 'No, I'm not saying that. I just mean that's how I feel. I fancy girls. *And* I fancy— I love… *you.*'

Still frowning, I ask: 'Why are you telling me this?' It sounds harsher than I mean it to. I see his eyes crease at the sides, as if I've said something upsetting. 'I just mean… why?' I'm struggling for words. 'I just wondered… are you asking me out?' I decide to smile, to make all this a little bit lighter than it has become. I'm relieved when Jonathan smiles a bit too.

'I think I am. But I think you just like girls and only girls. That right?'

I nod automatically. Then I pause. I've never thought

about it. It hasn't crossed my mind that I would ever fancy or want to do stuff with anyone other than a girl. Over the past few years, they've become one of the main things I think about. It was like, when I got to thirteen, a switch had been flicked in my brain and I suddenly started noticing them everywhere and what they were wearing and how it made them – and especially certain parts of them – look and how that made my heart leap a bit. I think back to a horribly embarrassing time at our local pub restaurant when the waitress dropped her little notepad as she was walking away from our table and had bent down to pick it up and Dad said, 'Eyes back on the table, Danny.' I realised I'd been staring at her obviously and felt cross with them all for noticing, and cross with myself for not being at all subtle. Whereas if it had been a guy who had dropped his notepad, there's no way I'd have thought to stare in the same way. So that's why I pause when Jonathan asks me. I don't feel like I've had time to think it through to give a definite 'no'.

I decide to speak out loud what I'm thinking and just be honest. 'I've never thought about it. I mean… the idea of guys together doesn't freak me out or anything. I just haven't ever thought about it… like… to do with me. Does that make sense?'

Jonathan nods. He sits up a bit and seems to be relieved I am at least OK to talk about this unexpected subject he's brought up. 'Yeah, it does. Because I'd never thought about it... about anything to do with guys until we became friends.'

I smile again. 'You trying to flatter me?' I mean it playfully, but it probably sounds a bit forced. Jonathan just shrugs.

'I just... think you're amazing. You talk just... so easily about so many things. You're confident about *everything*. You're good at everything. Everyone likes you at school. Anyone would be your friend, but you've... you chose me.'

I am about to say that with us being opposite neighbours, I haven't exactly chosen him, but then I remember his sister and why I'd originally started to hang out with Jonathan in the first place. I close my mouth. That bit probably wouldn't sound very good to him.

'Stop with the... I don't know, the praise. It's embarrassing. I mean, I'm not amazing—'

'Sorry, I know. I shouldn't have said all that. It's cringe.'

I laugh a bit at that. 'Yeah, it is cringe. But I don't really mind. It's OK.'

He turns to face me properly. 'Really? You... don't want to stop being friends or anything?'

I shake my head. 'No, definitely not.'

We keep eye contact after I say that. He smiles and keeps looking at me. And I keep looking at him and his deep hazel-coloured eyes, still a bit red at the edges from the chlorine in the swimming pool.

We seem to slip into some parallel universe at that moment. Right there, in the woods, it's like we've found a door to another world. Both of us together are thrown into something strange and exciting and extraordinary. Something we will always remember. And before I know it I've leaned towards him and he's leaned towards me and we are kissing, my lips on his, his face touching mine. I can feel the prickle of stubble on his chin. I can taste the Coke Zero, and the Polos he crunched earlier when we'd set out to the pool on what I thought would be a normal day. I can smell his shower gel that I'd seen him rub on his body in the shower moments earlier. It's odd. All of it is odd. But it isn't bad. And the more it carries on, the less odd it feels. I lean in further and his hands move around me, inviting me into his embrace and I become aware of his palm moving down my back to my shorts, clasping on to me, exploring, and then I'm suddenly very aware of how into it I'm getting, and at that exact moment Jonathan's hand moves round the front to my waist and he finds what he's looking for. Pleasure rushes through me so fast I gasp and draw back.

'I'm sorry,' he says straightaway, pulling his hand back. 'I got a bit… carried away…'

I'm panting as if I've run a mile without stopping, my heart beating a furious rhythm in my chest. 'It's… it's fine. I just… I need to stop for a bit. All of this… it's just…' I laugh then, and the act feels like a relief, as if I'm either going to laugh or cry and I've chosen the more enjoyable option. Jonathan is still looking absolutely terrified, so I move back over to him and kiss him again. It feels like the most natural thing in the world from that point on. From the moment I decide to go back for more, to allow his hands to continue their journey across the top of my clothes, I realise I don't mind it at all. After what feels like a thousand dizzying years, but what can only have been a minute or two, we stop kissing and break apart and sit there, side by side against the fallen tree in silence. The non-awkward, comfortable silence we've had before, only now it feels even more comfortable and nice.

When we start walking, Jonathan starts talking. He has questions, and so do I. But whereas before, these questions would have astonished me, they now seem just part of this new thing between us. The answers I have to give – and I know I have to give them – aren't entirely the ones he's been hoping for. I know that. But I also know it's better than a flat-out no. So I tell him I'm not gay and don't really know if I'm bi, and I'm also fairly sure I wouldn't be up for having sex, not full-on sex at least – especially since I haven't yet gone all the way with a girl yet. I tell him that I don't mean it as anything bad towards him, just that I don't feel comfortable with *that*, at least not right now. But what I am up for takes him by surprise. It's him that suggests it. As a compromise, maybe. Would I be up for sleeping with him? Not shagging, actually *sleeping*. He says we'd fallen asleep together once on the same bed last year when I'd slept over and we were watching movies late. He's been thinking about that time ever since, and wants to be in a bed with me again, the two of us falling asleep together. And in this new parallel world we now seem to be living in, this as an idea doesn't seem that bad. In fact, part of me even thinks it sounds quite nice.

Instead of finding it weird and strange, I too find myself looking forward to the coming weekend, when Jonathan will come to mine for a sleepover on Saturday night, and instead of sleeping in the guest room or on a camp bed, he'll actually be in my bed with me. The thought of it makes me smile. And when I tell him I'm cool with it, he smiles too.

EIGHTEEN

Stephanie

THE DAY OF THE EXPLOSION

'It all happened at that party – the one where you picked us up. At Scotty's house before Christmas.'

I nodded but didn't say anything more, glad my instincts had been correct. I hadn't been going mad. Something did happen that night.

'It was all fine, but then some of them started doing… started doing coke. I don't think it would have got weird, if that hadn't happened. Well, maybe it would… I don't know.'

I felt my heart beat hard in my chest. 'Did Danny… Did he try the cocaine?'

I waited, desperate to know the truth and suddenly utterly terrified of it. But then Jonathan shook his head. 'No, he wouldn't do that. And neither did I. But I don't think Scotty would have got so stupid if he hadn't been on it.'

'What did Scotty do?' I prompted, forgetting my commitment to silence.

I saw Jonathan's hand tremble as he raised it to wipe his face again, and as he did I realised it wasn't just water from his hair he was brushing away. Tears were now running down his face. I thought about going over to put an arm round him, but I didn't want to interrupt his flow, and he may have found it odd to have his mum's friend hugging him while he sits there, naked beneath a towel and sobbing on his bed.

'Scotty took the photos.'

A chill ran down me with these words. It was the way Jonathan said the last two words. *The photos.* As if they were a known quantity, already famous in their own right. Is that what all this was about? Just as I had guessed, some photos did hold the riddle to this strange mess, connecting all these dots together? The key missing piece of the puzzle? And there were just two words I needed to say now. Two words that could unlock everything I didn't know: 'Show me.'

I didn't expect him to refuse, not after he'd begun his tearful story, but that's what he did. I felt sorry for him. I didn't want to distress him further, but when he started shaking his head and said 'No... no, I can't,' I didn't hesitate. I got up and moved towards the door, knowing what would make him do anything I asked.

'It's time to involve your parents.' I said it confidently, not looking at him.

He got to the door first, his large fist on the handle, his tall, muscular frame, a fair way along the transition from boy to man, blocking my exit. If he fought me, he would win. I didn't feel threatened physically by him, exactly, but as I met his eyes I became aware of something strange and disturbing in his face. A building mass of desperation, like an animal caught in a trap.

'There's no point. The whole thing's finished. It's not a problem anymore. I told Danny it was all over before... before he...'

He didn't finished the sentence. He didn't need to. Then somewhere, not far away, a sound cut through our staring contest. A light, reedy sound that fluttered and fell, then came up loud and high again. It took me few seconds to realise what it was, then it clicked. It was music – the sound of an instrument. Mimi must be practising her flute in her room. The sound seemed to bring us both down to earth.

'Jonathan, either let me out or do what I ask,' I said firmly. He moved straightaway, stepping out of the way of the door. He went back to his bed, where he sat down and returned his head to his hands. 'OK.' He said it quietly, his face still hidden, so that I almost didn't hear him.

I walked over to the desk and sat on the desk chair. After a few moments of silence, Jonathan took a deep breath and leaned over to his bedside table to pick up his phone. He tapped about on it, flicking and scrolling, for what felt like an age. Then, at last, he held it out to me in a trembling hand.

I snatched it from him and held it close to me. At first, I wasn't sure what I was looking at. Then it became clear. And I realised the shapes in the shot were people. Two people. I swiped along to see if there was another shot, and sure enough, an even more explicit image came into view.

'The second one's a screenshot. From the video.'

I felt my heart lurch and my chest grow tight. There was a *video*? With trepidation, I swiped again. Sure enough, the next thing to slide onto the screen was a moving image. It was quite fuzzy and dim, but then the screen blared with white, which then dimmed down again. Someone had turned the lights on in whatever room it had been shot in, the brightness flooding the sensor of the camera, obscuring everything. Then, when the focus returned, everything became instantly obvious. I watched the whole thing with mounting nausea, which quickly gave way to anger. Fury. Proper white-hot fury. 'What sort of sick… nasty, sick…'

'You think it's sick?' Jonathan looked up at me properly now, tears once again obvious in his eyes. 'You think what we did was sick? *Why* is it sick? Because we're both guys?'

I looked back at him in confusion. 'What? No, I don't mean *that*.' I flapped my hand at him, hurrying to correct the misunderstanding, even though I wasn't in the right frame of mind to express myself properly. 'I meant, what sick, nasty person videos people like this and laughs at them while they're— I mean, I never liked that boy Scotty – he always seemed a bit sneery and too self-satisfied, but this is… this is cruel.'

Jonathan shook his head. 'Scotty's not nasty, honestly… He didn't mean it badly. It's because he'd taken the coke that he got over-the-top and silly.'

My mind was spinning. There was too much to cope with here. Too much to compute. '*How* can he not be cruel? He burst in on you and… and Danny while you were… together and starts pointing his camera at you. And I presume that's how the blackmail started? Has he been holding this over you both all this time?'

Even as I said this, desperate for a eureka moment to solve all the weirdness and mystery and put an end to the secrets, I knew it didn't really fit. It didn't explain the conversation I'd overheard between Jonathan and Danny. Nor did it explain Jonathan's defence of the boy who, with his insensitive videoing, had the power to do so much damage.

'He hasn't been blackmailing us. Really, it isn't him. Scotty's all right, really.'

I shook my head. 'How can you defend him? I can hear him shouting and laughing on the video. It's like he's shaming you.'

Jonathan's eyes were wide, his head turning from side to side. 'That's just what he does. He's an idiot, but he didn't mean it badly. He was just having a laugh. And the shouting was because he was just surprised because it was me and Danny together, not Danny and Sara or me and some other girl.'

I thought about this for a moment. 'You mean, he didn't know you two were...'

He shook his head. 'Nobody did. But he was completely cool about it. He handed the phone over to Danny to show him he'd deleted everything. But before he did that, he sent everything to both of us. I think he thought that was funny or something. He can be a bit of a twat.'

I closed my eyes, thinking about what to ask next. 'So... the two of you were a couple? Boyfriends? And everyone knew except...?'

Except me. I found I couldn't say the final two words out loud, but I didn't need to, as Jonathan was already rushing to correct me.

'No, no, honestly, we weren't… We just… It was only that night, really… Although a few times before, we'd…'

I nodded. 'OK, I get the picture.' I was going to move on to my next question, but Jonathan didn't seem to think I'd properly understood.

'No, really, it wasn't like that… not before that night. We'd never had sex. We just… slept together.'

I blinked at him. 'Slept together?'

He gave a little nod, and looked pained, as if something about this was harder for him to confront than the video of him with his pants down.

'It's a bit hard to explain,' he said, quietly.

'Try me,' I said.

NINETEEN

Danny

ELEVEN MONTHS BEFORE THE EXPLOSION

The sleepover is easy to arrange. Mum says yes straightaway when I ask if Jonathan can come over for tea on Saturday night. She even says we can order a pizza and take it up to my room if we want to sit and watch films. She says something about getting the main guest bedroom ready, but I say no, Jonathan can sleep on the floor on the camp bed. She laughs at that.

'You boys – it's like you're still ten and excited for midnight feasts! Reminds me of *Malory Towers*.'

I don't know what that is, and I don't ask.

I feel a bit nervous on the Saturday morning when Mum and Dad are shopping. I wash and tumble dry all my bed sheets then put them all back on (something that's *a lot* more difficult than I'd expected). I tidy my room in a way I never normally do when Jonathan comes round, then hoover the carpet of both my room and the landing, even though our cleaner, Yvon, has only just been two days before. I don't fully understand why I'm going to all this trouble. I just want it all to be nice for the evening. It's like I'm going to meet someone for the first time. My mind keeps wandering onto what it will be like later when it gets to the moment to settle down to go to sleep. Will it be weird and awkward? Will he expect anything more, hoping that I've changed my mind and I'd be open to... other stuff? Even if he hopes it, I know Jonathan will take my lead. So I decide to wait and see how I feel about it all when we get there.

The day drags by, feeling like years rather than hours. Something happens in the afternoon when I go downstairs to get a drink that makes me even more uneasy. Dad's in the middle of unboxing a new toaster and breaking up the box for the recycling, and Mum's sitting at the kitchen table scrolling through the Mail Online website on her iPad. She pauses on a headline about two actors who started an affair with each other after years of friendship and acting together, despite the fact they both have their own partners. The woman is really stunning, even though she's old – about forty – and a big covert photo of her caught kissing the man on a beach somewhere fills the screen.

'Everyone thought this would happen,' Mum says vaguely to the room in general, probably aware Dad isn't listening. 'Things always get messy when friends become more than friends.' She shakes her head, begins to scroll on, then sees me standing there. 'Everything OK, love?' she asks.

It takes me a few seconds to respond, causing both of them to turn to look at me properly.

'You all right?' my dad asks.

'You coming down with something? You look a bit pale.' Mum gets up and goes to feel the temperature of my forehead. I duck out of her reach, tell her I'm fine, and go back upstairs.

Even when Jonathan arrives, followed an hour after by the Domino's, time still seems to crawl. Because Mum and Dad are around, I greet him as I would normally and try to be as natural as possible. We watch *Fast & Furious 8* in my room whilst eating the pizza, just the same as we ever would, with me sharing my views on the film as it goes along, him nodding and occasionally agreeing out loud (although, for probably the first time ever, I find myself avoiding commenting on the hot women). Finally it gets to around 11pm and I can hear Mum and Dad going to their room. Jonathan and I are sitting on my bed already, with our backs to the wall and our legs stretched out, facing the TV across the room. Silence falls as the credits come to an end and I turn the screen off. 'So...' I say, looking at him.

'So...' he replies, then gives me a small smile, which makes me smile and laugh a bit nervously.

'Shall we... er... get ready for bed then?' I ask. He nods.

I tell him he can go and use the bathroom first, so he goes off with his toothbrush from his little overnight bag and I sit there on the bed. My heart starts to pound a little. I'm suddenly aware I haven't planned what to wear in bed. I normally sleep in just boxers for most of the year, or naked during the summer. Should I find some proper pyjamas, I wonder? Just keep my pants on? I'm thinking about this all when it's my turn to go and brush my teeth. When I get back to my room, Jonathan is still fully dressed, so I can't even go with what he's doing.

'Shall we get into bed then?' I say, a little awkwardly. He nods, and takes off his top. I do the same. It's clear we're both watching each other as we move to unzipping our jeans. We tug them off, followed by our socks, until we're both standing in just our underwear, unsure of what to do next. I go over to turn the main light off, to give me something to do, although the desk light is still on, so when I turned back to him I can see quite clearly that underneath his white Tommy Hilfiger boxers, Jonathan is standing very much to attention. I freeze as soon as I realise this, and then Jonathan must have realised too as he turns around and walks towards the bed.

'Go ahead… er… get in,' I say, if only to stop him standing there awkwardly, obviously embarrassed. He gets in under the duvet, and I do the same. The temperature is a lot cooler today, so getting into bed next to another warm body feels instantly comfortable and relaxing. It's like the awkwardness has eased slightly now that we're both in here together and we're over the first bit. Now all I realistically have to do is sleep, and I do that practically every night without issue. Or is that all? Even though I'm still fairly sure I'm not up for doing anything too major with Jonathan, all this lead-up to tonight – whatever tonight is – has made the thought of just drifting off to sleep a bit of an anti-climax.

As if reading my mind, Jonathan says, 'So, do we… just go to sleep now?'

I take a deep breath. 'Yeah, I think so…' It's clear to me that Jonathan has been hoping it isn't just sleep that's on the cards, and after our kissing incident in the woods, I can't blame him. That whole experience certainly felt like the start of something, not a one-off thing in itself. I turn onto my side to face him. He does the same, so we're both looking at each other, like we were when we were sitting up against that fallen tree. We stare into each other's eyes. I shift myself a bit closer to him until I feel my foot brush up against his leg. He moves a little too, so that we meet in the middle, our faces almost touching, our bodies close together.

After some minutes like this, Jonathan says, 'Can we kiss again?'

I think about it, the question reverberating around my head. Do I want to kiss him again? Or shall I just turn over onto my side and tell him we need to sleep. I feel a pang of pain, realising I don't want to reject him in this way after he's shared so much of himself with me, after he's shown me something that he's clearly been freaking out about for these past couple of years. I don't want to hurt him like that. I want to make things OK. Make him happy. And then I realise that there's quite a simple way of looking at all this. It means a lot to him, and it doesn't really ask for a lot from me. So I just say yes.

'Yeah, OK.' I roll towards him a little.

It isn't as disorienting as our time in the woods, when it felt like my heart was about to beat out of my chest with the surprise of it all. This time it feels quite calm, once I get used to the rhythm of it, the spearmint flavour toothpaste both of us have just used, the weight of his arms and legs as they mingle with mine. Although I keep my hands around his back and shoulders, Jonathan's start to roam along me, like they did in the woods. I don't stop him. I find the whole thing oddly interesting, like I'm going on an unusual safari. I wonder, as his hands start to get more adventurous, if what we're doing will just eventually make him more upset when he wants to go further and I reach a point where I say no. But all of that feels like a future problem and I let my mind grow blank as Jonathan continues.

What if my parents hear us? Will they think we're watching porn?

Afterwards, Jonathan comes back up to lie next to me. 'You all right?' he asks, a little breathlessly as he lies back next to me, our bodies touching.

'Yeah,' I say, also breathless.

'Yeah… me too,' he says.

I don't know what to say to this, so I just keep quiet. I became aware Jonathan is looking at me, so I turn my head to look at him. 'You sure you're OK?' I ask.

He smiles, looking a bit shy. 'Best day of my life.'

I laugh, though not in a nasty way or laughing *at* him, just because it surprised me.

'This won't make things weird between us, will it?' he asks, sounding a bit worried.

I shake my head. 'No.'

He seems satisfied with this answer, and then rolls forward a little so he can rest his head on my shoulder, with an arm entwined in mine. We're just like any other teenage couple in bed together. After a few minutes of silence go by, I wonder if he's gone to sleep. Then he says something I really hadn't expected.

'I think my dad has a thing for your mum.'

It takes a moment for these words to sink in. 'What? You mean… what, like, he fancies her or something?'

I feel Jonathan nod slightly. 'Yeah. I caught him watching her from the window as she was going on her run. Then he went back to the window a bit later to watch her finishing the run and going inside. Like he knew how long it would take her to do a lap around the streets. Like he does it often.'

Why, of all times, Jonathan has decided to talk about my mum now, when we're cuddled up in bed together, I have no clue. The idea of his dad, who I've always found a bit stuck-up and rude, having the hots for my mum makes me feel a bit sick. 'I… haven't noticed anything, but, well, I suppose if all he's doing is looking from the window… I mean, it's a free country.'

Jonathan doesn't reply to this straightaway, just makes a little grunt as if to say 'yeah' and sighs. Then, after a pause, he says, 'I just noticed it… then, and some

186

other times too. Because it's like…' He stops halfway through the sentence, like he doesn't know how to finish it.

'Like what?' I prompt.

'It's like… how I sometimes watch you. When you're going for a run, or doing your exercises on a Sunday morning in the lounge if it's raining.'

This makes my brain spin a bit. 'But… how? The running machine's in the room at the back. How do you…?'

'You do some stretches and cool-down stuff in the lounge while watching TV. I can see across the street.'

He's right. I do. And I don't quite know if I like the idea of being spied on. Then I find I can't stop thinking about my mum, off for her run, not thinking about someone watching her. An older man like Richard Franklin, staring at her from an upstairs window across the road.

'Sorry, I don't mean I spy on you…' Jonathan's body has become tense, and he tries to sit up.

'It's fine,' I say, encouraging him back down with my arm, and bringing him closer to me. I'm not sure why I keep trying to comfort him, to make the world better for him, but it just feels like the best thing to do. The only thing to do. 'I think… I think we should sleep now.'

He gives a small nod. If he expected us to do anything more that night, he doesn't say. And although my world has been rocked and turned, I find falling asleep with him held close next to me even easier than when I'm alone.

TWENTY

Stephanie

THE DAY OF THE EXPLOSION

'We would just… just *sleep* together. That's it. When I stayed round your house or he stayed round mine. We wouldn't do anything, really. I mean, we kissed a few times, but, well… nothing like *that*.' He gestured at the phone in my hand. 'We'd just… sleep together.'

He made it sound curiously innocent and tame, especially after I'd just seen something a lot more grown-up on his phone.

'Were the two of you in love?' I asked. Even as I asked it, I regretted it. What could two teenage boys know of love, at such a young age? Then I thought back to when I was seventeen – just eight months older than Danny had been – and how I'd fallen so passionately in love with his father so quickly. Of course teenagers could fall in love.

And if Danny had a chance to experience the swirling, fluttering, deranging, heady excitement of all that, however briefly, before he died… well, that should be seen as a blessing.

Jonathan's reply, however, didn't offer such an optimistic framing of their relationship. 'No. I loved him. I don't know if he loved me like *that*. He wanted to try, but… I'm not sure. I think he mainly just fancied girls.'

I frowned, then looked back at the phone in my hands. Its screen had gone blank now, but my mind still played back the footage I'd just watched. 'But… how come you both ended up…'

Jonathan shrugged. 'I think he was just doing it to be nice. To make me happy. It's weird, but I think he *wished* we could be together, but also knew it wasn't ever going to work. Although the last time… the last time we spoke, it sounded like he wanted to try and see if we could be. But yeah, that night at the party was the only time things went properly further like that. It was all because I'd told him some good news about an internship I was trying to get on to. It was late in the evening and we'd both gone to one of the empty bedrooms upstairs at Scotty's house to chat, to get away from the loud music and the other people smoking weed and doing coke and stuff. Anyway, I told him I'd got an internship – a work experience place during this summer at *Goal King*.'

I felt my brow crease with confusion and Jonathan clarified.

'It's like a sports magazine, but online. It's huge. Well, for football and rugby fans it is. They do loads of sports and have people write all about the players and follow their careers. It's not gossipy or anything; it's like proper sports journalism.'

'Is that what you want to do?' I asked.

He nodded, looking eager and excited, as if he'd momentarily forgotten the weirdness of our conversation. 'Definitely. It's really hard to get an internship there too, especially if you're still at school, but they take sixteen-year-olds for a two-week summer one each year, and I applied and got it.'

'That's really good,' I said, trying to smile, to sound encouraging. But the light was fading from his face, and he began to look pained and on the verge of tears again.

'My mum doesn't think so. She thinks writing about "a bunch of louts kicking a ball around" isn't proper journalism.'

I bit back a sharp retort about Janet. It didn't surprise me that she wasn't jumping for joy at her boy's passion for sports writing. If the internship had been at *The Guardian* or *The Times*, I'm sure half the neighbourhood would have heard about it. In fact, it probably would have made the headline of her round robin that

Christmas. But writing about the dramas of the football pitch? I couldn't see her settling for that.

'So you told Danny about this news?' I said, keen to return to the main part of his explanation.

'Yes. I was so happy about it and I didn't want to tell him in front of the others. They wouldn't care or understand how important it was. So when we were alone, I told him and he hugged me. And I... I kissed him.' He dropped his gaze to the floor when he said this, seemingly embarrassed. 'It wasn't the first time we'd... that we'd kissed, but it was different to the other times. It became more... I don't know... We just got carried away. And then we ended up in the bed.'

I took in a deep breath. 'Well then, if it was all rather sweet and happy between you two, and the other boys weren't being nasty, then what went wrong? *Why* did Danny end up looking like a ghost of his former self for the weeks after that party? Because it must have been something awful for him to change like that. Did you, I don't know, treat him badly or something? Did you try to blackmail him with the photos?'

Jonathan shook his head fervently. 'No, I told you, I would never, *never* have done that – anything like that. I... I loved him.'

'Then what *happened*?'

The boy was crying properly now, big tears falling

down his smooth, handsome face, making him look even younger and more vulnerable than I'd ever appreciated. But I didn't let that stop me. I had come so close to finding out what was going on there that I wasn't about to pause for his tears or wait for him to backtrack and fall silent. I stood up and nudged his shoulder roughly. 'Jonathan, I need to know. You haven't told me everything. What was in the bag Danny gave you? There *must* be something more to this.'

He wouldn't look at me. He just continued staring resolutely at the floor.

'Jonathan!' I said loudly again, giving him another push.

Something had flipped inside me. For all the sympathy I felt for him, it was nothing compared to the pain I felt for my boy – my poor, darling boy, who had died during what was clearly the most agonising time in his life. I grabbed at his shoulders again, this time with both hands and shook him. I continued to yell at him, trying to get him to look at me, to tell me what I needed to know, but he just shook his head, maddeningly stubborn.

I'm not sure what it was in that moment that did it. It was like I'd reached some cerebral threshold that was suddenly surpassed – too many things crammed into the hellish vortex of my mind, creating a weird fusion of anger and desperation. The anxiety I'd felt when I realised Danny knew my secret. The pressure that had put upon me, the sleepless nights when I'd felt like I was going mad, then the soul-destroying grief when my family was ripped away from me. And, if I'm honest, my hatred of Jonathan for surviving. For declining the lift that would have killed him too. How dare he sit here, keeping things from me, hiding important details from me, when he shouldn't even be fucking breathing. So I shoved him, hard, catching him by surprise and he fell backward onto the bed. I didn't care if I was hurting him – I got up on top of him and pinned his arm down, trying to stop him wriggling out of my grasp. Finally he spoke, but it wasn't anything helpful.

'Get off!' he sobbed. 'Please. I'm sorry. Just… please, get off me.'

He could have overpowered me. Could have used all that muscle he'd built up swimming and playing rugby and working out at the gym – things he used to do with my son – but it was like he'd lost his strength. Lost his resolve to fight. He'd been wrung out by baring his heart to me and didn't have any energy left to keep up his defences. I looked down at his tear-stained face, noticing the way the dim grey light from the landing's skylight made him look paler than his usual naturally tanned colour. Then I realised, with a jolt of horror, that he hadn't let me open the door earlier and that the light from the landing shouldn't be able to be seen from the room.

I turned around, knowing there could only be one explanation and yet praying it wasn't true. But it was. Someone was standing at the door. Someone was watching me.

I stared from the doorway, then back to the bed – to Jonathan, lying there, with the towel he had once been clutching now open, his nakedness now starkly apparent, and me sitting astride him. I tried to say something. To offer some sort of explanation. But I could see the whole thing had been horribly misinterpreted.

It was all there, in the shock on Jemima's face.

TWENTY-ONE

Stephanie

NOW

'Would you like us to call someone for you?'

A young nurse asks me this while I'm staring at the empty seat next to my bed.

'No,' I say. I barely look at her before she walks away. I can't face explaining to another person my family tragedy. How I have no one. Nobody to call.

The recollection of their deaths comes to me as I'm lying there. Piece by piece, memories of the funeral start to dawn. Memories of the terrible day of me arriving at the hospital – the very hospital I'm sitting in now – and realising I was too late.

It's monstrous, the way your mind forces you to relive things. How it remembers and amplifies the cruel details that forever haunt you. Like the mounting sense of panic I felt as Danny's coffin disappeared from view. I had to grip my chair to stop myself rushing up there and clutching on to it, as if there was still something that could be done to save him.

I remember Pete's brother taking my hand, asking if I was OK. He was always kind, but I wasn't in the right frame of mind for kindness. Kindness hurt, almost as much as the grief. It made it all seem so much more real. I declined his offers of help as politely as I could. Told him he need not stay in the UK on my account. So he went back to America. Pete's parents went back to their home. No socialising. No hugging. No network of support. Just me, left to cry alone.

I knew, in that moment of loneliness, that the only person who could comfort me had vanished, had turned into a pot of ashes I didn't have a clue what to do with. I kept the urns in the wardrobe for a long time, then eventually scattered Pete's in the garden a month after his death, on the spot of the lawn where he used to sit in a deck chair on warm days reading *The Telegraph*. Danny's ashes, however, remain in the wardrobe. I don't feel ready to let them go. Whilst I felt the small, solitary ceremony I'd held for Pete by myself, standing on the patio, was in some small way freeing, I wasn't able to go through with it when it came to my son. At the time, I decided I'd keep them until what would have been his eighteenth birthday. Or perhaps on the day he would have gone off to university, when I would have had to let him go anyway, to some extent, to explore the big wide world without me.

I don't know if it's helpful for me to remember all these things now and risk getting swallowed up by the grief all over again. Or if it would have been better to keep them all packed away.

It's only once I see the old woman in the bed opposite staring at me across the ward that I realise my tears have started to flow once more.

TWENTY-TWO

Danny

SEVEN MONTHS BEFORE THE EXPLOSION

S cotty isn't the one who starts with the drugs, but he certainly doesn't stop it. If this was a party at my house, I'd have been traumatised to see both spliffs and white powder being passed around in my parents' home. They'd be shocked. I remember hearing my dad once talk to my mum about how he'd changed rooms at university because someone in his halls was doing coke.

'They think it's only themselves they're doing damage to, but it isn't,' he'd said. 'Gang violence, street crime, gangs controlling impoverished women and making them bring the stuff into the country, organised crime groups who deal in people trafficking – if they use the stuff, those are the sort of people they're funding.'

His words have stayed in my mind. I've never thought of drugs in the same way since – not that I've ever been tempted to use them before that. So at Scotty's party, when one of his mates whose name I don't know starts doing lines off the coffee table, I'm appalled. And to my relief, Jonathan looks horrified too. He's in the same room as me, next to one of the speakers pounding out some never-ending beat. We wouldn't be able to hear each other if we tried to speak, but we don't need words. His eyes tell me everything I need to know, and silently we agree to get away for a bit. We head upstairs, hoping to find a quiet empty room. I think we need a break from the music and the people. Part of me wonders if I should call my mum to come and get us early, but I also don't want to look like a child.

'Shall we go in here?' I say, opening one of the doors at random. Jonathan nods and follows me in. When I turn the light on, I instantly recognise it as Scotty's bedroom. I've been in here once, over a year ago, when we'd been round for a movie night and Scotty had sent me up to grab his phone charger. I'd been tempted to tell him to fuck off and get his own charger, but Scotty was like that: quick to give orders that somehow you felt obliged to follow.

The rest of the house is always spotless, but Scotty's bedroom is a mess. The floor is dotted with scattered pages, apparently schoolwork, along with exercise books, study guides, car magazines, trainers, socks, his Fletcher

House school uniform, including a blazer that has a large bright-green paint-stain on, probably from art class. I nudge a folder of papers aside with my foot to clear a path over to the bed. I instinctively sit down on it. Jonathan sits next to me.

I don't notice at first how close he's sitting, but after we chat for a bit about something pointless and forgettable, I feel his leg brush against mine. We've been having occasional sleepovers similar to the first one we'd had in the summer. Usually on a Friday night, Jonathan comes over to mine, we do our usual routine of movie and pizza, and then we both get into bed and drift off to sleep together. Sometimes we kiss, if Jonathan initiates it. I even quite enjoy it – I find myself looking forward to the sense of closeness and intimacy I've never found anywhere else before, even though I'd be lying if I said there aren't times when I imagine what it would be like to do it with a girl. To hold her in my arms as her hands move over me like Jonathan's do.

My brief moment of fooling around with Sara earlier in the year is still my only claim to any sort of experience at all. And I've been starting to wonder, perhaps, if my nights spent with Jonathan are getting in the way of me finding a girlfriend, or at least getting some proper action from somewhere – action that doesn't end with kissing and two people feeling very sexually frustrated. Because that's what it's become. That thrill of the new, back when Jonathan and I started our sleepover arrangement, has been replaced with a mounting sense of anti-climax. A feeling that we're constantly pulling away from what is clearly supposed to be the main event. The more we leave it, the more apparent this becomes to me. Each time we stop kissing and say goodnight, I feel Jonathan's hand remain on my back or my hip or my neck just that little bit longer, before letting me go, as if praying and hoping this will be the time I'll let him carry on. Venture into the unknown.

But that journey into uncharted territory ends up happening tonight, in Scotty's bed, at his birthday party, while the others enjoy their drugs and their drink. It's one of those experiences that seems vivid and electric when it's happening, then vague and hard to define once it's over. It all starts with him telling me about his internship writing for the sports website he's a fan of. He's anxious about telling his parents. He knows his dad won't approve and his mum will be dismissive – perhaps they'll even stop him going, telling him it will take too much time out of his Easter break the following year when he should be working on exam revision. I try to tell him it's amazing that he's got the place, full stop, no matter what his parents think. He says that he's sick of the fact that the only people in the world who care about him make him so unhappy.

'That's if they do care, and I'm beginning to doubt even that. I don't think they love me. I don't think they even like me. They just care about getting the grades, ticking off the exams, rather than *me* and what I want.'

In others, this sort of my-life's-so-terrible talk could come across as the opposite of attractive, but in Jonathan it brings out that instinct in me to hug him and tell him everything's going to be OK. I'm not sure what it is about him that does that to me, that makes me feel like I need to be his defender and protector. Perhaps it's that tense first meal I had back when we first moved to Kent, when I sensed that cold feeling of hatred running through the family. Maybe I just feel sorry for him – that he's been dealt a bad hand where family is concerned. Or maybe, a little voice says in my head, it's because I like feeling needed. Needed in a way none of the girls I fancy have ever needed me.

'I care about you,' I say, looking at him. It's a simple sentence, said quietly, but it seems to echo around the room, seems to drown out the pounding music from downstairs. And all of a sudden I'm kissing him, and he's kissing me, and I'm pushing him back down on the bed, rolling on top of him, then him on top of me, our mouths together, our minds working as one. Within seconds, our hands are on each other's belts and zippers, tugging down our jeans and underwear, and then we're holding each other in a way neither of us has ever quite dared until now. We spend ages enjoying discovering each other's bodies, as if for the first time – well, it feels like ages, but it may just be a matter of minutes. It's both gentle and rough all at the same time, both of us frenzied and greedy for what we've been denied before. It's all so perfect. Or at least it would have been, if the door to the bedroom hadn't opened.

And then the shouting starts.

'Caught in the act!' Scotty yells as soon as he bursts in. I recognise his voice straightaway, even before I see his face, and what he's holding. But once I've climbed off Jonathan and turned to face the doorway, I realise immediately what's going on. Scotty has a phone in his hand, and he's obviously using it to video or take pictures. At the same moment I clock what he's doing, I see the surprise dawn in his face as he realises who he's discovered shagging in his room. Evidently, he didn't expect it to be me and Jonathan.

'What the FUCK?! Oh my fucking God, this is *gold*!'

'Put the camera away!' I shout at him as I leap off the bed. I hear Jonathan swearing to my left as he scrabbles around for his clothes. I make a swipe at Scotty and the phone, but he leaps out of reach.

'Sorry, Daniel, old bro, this is too much of a beautiful moment not to capture!'

I make another dive for him, but he leaps aside.

'What's going on?' I hear a girl's voice from the door and I look over to see Sara. I've barely spoken to her since our brief moment together in the summer, but of all the people to be present at a moment so embarrassing, I wouldn't have picked her. Catching sight of me standing there, naked, and Jonathan hurriedly pulling on his clothes, is enough for Sara to put two and two together. 'Oh my GOD!' she exclaims, looking shocked. Scotty, on the other hand, looks gleeful.

'Lads, *lads*, there's nothing to be ashamed of,' he says, walking over to me and tapping me on the shoulder. 'We're all friends here. Only next time, would you mind not going at it in my fucking bed, OK?' He winks at me and smiles. He looks almost impressed, as if I've suddenly become a lot more interesting in his eyes. I'm no longer just 'Danny' – indecipherable from nearly every guy at school. I'm 'Danny who gets with other boys at parties'. Before I can digest all this, I need to get one thing sorted out. Immediately.

'The phone, Scotty. Please… just… delete it all.'

He had lowered the camera when Sara had walked in, but he lifts it back up now and starts to tap away. 'You sure you guys don't want me to hang on to it? It would make for a lovely addition to the best man speech on a big screen behind me at your wedding – *obviously* you'd pick me to be your best man, I should hope—'

'Scotty, I'm not joking. Please…' I'm close to tears all of a sudden. I think it's the disorientation of being so excited by Jonathan and me actually having sex for the first time mixed with the embarrassment of Scotty's arrival, followed swiftly by the rising panic of realising some of it's been caught on camera. Part of me knows, even then in my anxious state, that Scotty wouldn't ever try to use the footage maliciously, but his joke about the best man speech wasn't out of character – he's likely to consider it a hilarious addition to his endless repertoire of 'banter' and practical jokes. And I know I don't want it to become something as cheap as that. It's too personal. Scotty can apparently see how worried I am because he changes tack. 'Mate, calm down. I'm only having a laugh, honestly. I'll delete it – but first…'

I don't have to wait long before I discover what 'but first' means. A second later a ping sounds from the pocket of my jeans on the floor. Then another identical ping comes from across the room, over near Jonathan. 'There you go. You've both got it for posterity.' He gives me a wink and grins, then comes closer and holds his phone up so I can see the screen, showing his camera roll. He selects the most recent file. 'Here we go – delete.' The item drops into the bin symbol at the bottom. Before I need to prompt him, he then goes straight to his deleted items folder and performs the same task. Then he goes to WhatsApp, and clicks 'Delete for Me' in the chats where he's sent us the video. 'Happy?' he asks, holding out the phone. 'Want to check?'

I shake my head, saying nothing. I'm just desperate for these unwanted visitors to leave.

'Right, well, in that case, Sara and I have similar business of our own to, er, get down to, and since you've already claimed my room for your own, I suppose I might as well leave you guys to it and we'll go to the guest room. Just don't cum on my duvet.' He laughs, as if what he'd said was really funny, then walks out, holding the door open for Sara to follow. Sara looks unsure, and looks back over to me and then Jonathan, as if she feels she should say something but doesn't know what. After an impatient huff from Scotty by the door, she exits, leaving me and Jonathan alone again.

I kind of know I'll probably go on to regret what I do next. So much. Or rather, what I don't do. Jonathan comes over to stand by my side and hands me my clothes. I take them from him, silently, and start to pull them on. He's already dressed and standing a little awkwardly.

Eventually, he says, 'I suppose… I suppose you don't

need to put them on. We could just… carry on?' He takes a step towards me, putting his hand on my arm, but I flinch away from him.

'What? No. I'm going home.'

As soon as I say it, I know it's the thing I need desperately. To be at home with Mum and Dad, acting like nothing like this has ever happened. I feel shaken, humiliated, although I know nobody's done me any actual harm; there's a part of me that feels wounded too. It's like the world has kicked me when I was at my most vulnerable, just at the moment I've let my guard down, when I was trying out a new side of me. It's all gone wrong. And all I can hear is my mum's voice in my ear, speaking words of caution I ignored. *Things always get messy when friends become more than friends.* Words I would normally have dismissed or had no interest in now seem thuddingly relevant, as if they could only ever be about me and how I've fucked everything up.

'Oh. OK…' Jonathan sits down on the bed and watches me as I pull my trousers up. Something has changed now. Something I can't unchange, or am not brave enough to try.

After a minute or two of silence, he speaks again. 'Can I… can I still get a lift back?'

I shrug. 'I suppose. We're going the same way, so it

shouldn't be a problem.' I feel the stab of how formal and distant those words sound.

Shouldn't be a problem.

As if we'd never been in the same car before, never shared a moment more intimate than holding the door open for each other. I can't even imagine how hurtful my words must be in that moment. I've already arranged for us to drop him back home, so of course it won't be a problem. I should have the decency to look him in the eye, to respond in at least a semi-friendly way, but at that moment it's impossible. I can barely look at him. My eyes are glued to the floor, and it's only in my peripheral vision that I see how upset he looks. A brief glimpse of his face as I straighten up after doing my shoe laces is all I need to see. Tonight marks a 'first time' for both of us. First time having sex. First time our friendship has made that leap. But it's also another first time for me. It's the first time I've really let him down.

I walk towards the door, muttering, 'You coming?'

He stands there, staring, and whereas before I'd have found this endearing, at that moment it infuriates me.

'In a sec,' he says. He's dabbing at his eyes.

'I'll wait for you at the front door. Don't be long.' I turn to go, then pause. It probably gives him hope. Hope that I've snapped out of my cold, distant mood and returned to the warmth and kindness we'd both experienced just minutes earlier. But instead of making everything better, I just say, with a hard edge to my voice, 'Make sure you delete that video. From WhatsApp. I don't want that floating around online. Do it now.'

It's blunt and cruel and said as an instruction rather than a request or a plead. And as I leave him alone in that room and start my journey down the stairs, I've never hated myself more.

TWENTY-THREE

Stephanie

FOUR MONTHS BEFORE THE EXPLOSION

The last full month of Danny's life ended with one of the scariest moments I had ever lived through.

For New Year's Eve, we'd accepted an invitation to a grand country manor house in Oxfordshire from one of Pete's family friends – posh, aristocratic people I had never felt comfortable being around, but endured for the sake of my husband. I was grateful he hadn't bothered to keep up much of his 'old life' in which he mixed with high society; he had lost contact with most of the people he'd been at Eton and St Andrew's with and thrown his efforts into forming connections more in the corporate world that would assist his building company. Of course he'd relied on introductions from some of his rich friends, so he had kept some relationships alive. One of these was Rupert Ashton, a good-looking aristocrat of around Pete's age whom he had been friends with since school. Rupert was in the business of electric cars, something that bored me to the core, but which Pete found endlessly fascinating. And it was at his sprawling country estate that we were destined to spend our New Year's Eve celebrations. It wasn't too bad really. Rupert was always friendly and very easy to talk to. He had a remarkable way of putting people at ease, although I didn't much care for his parents – there was something stiff and chilly about his father, Lord Ashton, and I was convinced I could see Lady Ashton judging me each time she said 'Oh Stephanie, how... charming you look.' That little pause was everything.

There was some fuss during the day about whether or not Danny should be allowed to remain at home. Usually he would have happily come with us, but I had wondered if this year he would prefer to go to some sort of New Year's Eve party with his mates. But him choosing not to come and just sit in his room, alone and unhappy, wasn't an option I was willing to consider.

'If Danny doesn't want to come, maybe... well, maybe I should stay home with him,' I'd said to Pete at about 5pm, close to when we should have been leaving.

'That's not very polite to Rupert, is it, or Lord and Lady Ashton. And Titus and Pippa would like to see Danny, I'm sure,' Pete said.

I tutted. Titus and Pippa were two charming though slightly stuck-up teenagers that had some relation to the Ashtons – I think Pippa was Rupert's niece, and Titus was dating Pippa, though he was also the adopted son of some guy Rupert had been seeing or was seeing. To tell you the truth, I couldn't keep track of their family arrangements, nor did I really try.

'Can you please refer to Rupert's parents by their first names,' I said, exasperated, 'as if they're normal people? Any more of this Lord and Lady business and I'll be the one refusing to come.'

Pete got angry at this. He was always sensitive about his upper-class upbringing and would get shirty if I made digs about it. 'Right, I'm going to tell Danny he needs to buck his ideas up and snap out of this self-indulgent moody-teenager act, because I'm getting sick of it.' He moved towards the stairs, to go and find the boy in his room, but I got in front of him.

'Don't go blazing in there,' I said, putting a hand on his shoulder. 'I'm sorry, I didn't mean to snap at you, but... let's just tread carefully with him, OK?'

Pete gave me an odd look. 'Tread carefully? What's that supposed to mean?'

I cursed myself for my choice of words. But the truth of the matter was, my conversation with Danny less than a week previously had continued to haunt me.

If you tell Dad, I'll tell him what you did.

'I just meant,' I said, trying to keep my voice steady and at a lower volume, 'that if we go in there and piss him off further, none of us will get to the party.'

After some cajoling, Danny agreed to come as planned, although he sat in stony silence in the back of the car, not even bothering to put his headphones in as we drove through the streets of Christmas lights and onto the motorway, heading for Oxfordshire. Pete tried to fill the silence by giving us the lowdown on Rupert's current domestic situation.

'Rupert's only recently moved back into Marwood Manor as his main home with his new partner – a recent widower named Charles, Titus's adopted father. They've been living in the manor only for a few weeks whilst Lord and Lady Ashton transition to living in one of the annex buildings on the estate.'

The word *transition* made me roll my eyes. Only Pete could make the process of an elderly couple downsizing their home sound like a corporate restructuring.

'What's Rupert's new partner like?' I asked.

Pete considered for a moment, indicating to turn off the main road and taking us deeper into the countryside. 'He's an interesting fellow. I've only met him a couple of times. He's a bit younger than me. Went to Eton after Rupert and I had left, although I remember seeing him at the Ashtons' from time to time. I read all about his husband dying in the papers a little while ago. Tragic business.' I remembered Pete speaking about it at the time and found myself nervous that I'd now say the wrong thing to the widower.

We arrived at Marwood Manor – an impressive nineteenth-century Gothic mansion of the kind you'd read about in children's storybooks or romantic melodramas – at about 8.30pm. I stared up at its imposing front as we climbed the stairs. I'd visited before a few times, but I never grew used to it. The idea of living somewhere so vast actually made me shudder. Rupert was just inside the doorway, ready to welcome us, hugging Pete and slapping him on the back, and kissing me on the cheek. He shook Danny's hand and made all the usual comments about how quickly he was growing up, and I was relieved to see Danny smiling and responding almost normally. I'd been afraid he'd be rude and unfriendly all evening.

Lady Ashton, spotting us from just inside the library, came over and gave me her usual up-and-down glance, but I refused to let it bother me, and instead allowed Rupert a chance to introduce me to his new partner, Charles Allerton, and his son Titus, a smart, good-looking boy with dark-blonde hair, aged around fifteen or sixteen. I saw him and Danny eyeing each other, with a mixture of suspicion and empathy, in the way of teenage boys who didn't know each other well enough to be instantly familiar. Charles suggested Titus take Danny off and give him a tour. Titus instantly sprang into action, saying, 'Righty-ho – come on, Daniel!', and took my son by the arm as if he'd known him for years, apparently all awkwardness forgotten. I saw Danny looking a tad disconcerted as he was led away, and I felt the need to cling to him rise up within me. I didn't like being separated from him when I knew something was bothering him – something so upsetting it had caused him to threaten me, his own mother, with a terrible secret. A secret I'd kept hidden for years.

It was during the countdown to midnight that I became worried. We'd always been together during this bit, ever since Danny had been old enough to stay up. But at that moment, I found myself surrounded by strangers, my husband across the other side of the patio, as we waited for the fireworks in the grounds of the manor to be lit to mark the arrival of the new year. Eventually, Pete picked his way through the crowd over to me and said 'Happy New Year!' and gave me a quick kiss. He was slightly tipsy, having agreed it was me who would be driving us home, and seeing him enjoying alcohol freely irritated me.

'Where's Danny?' I asked, not returning his festive greeting.

He frowned. 'I assumed he'd be with you.'

I stared back exasperated. 'You've seen me all evening and he obviously hasn't been with me. He went off with Titus earlier and I haven't seen him since and it's worrying me…'

Pete held up a hand. 'OK, OK,' he said. 'Let's just look around. There, by the French windows – Titus is talking to Rupert's niece. Let's ask them if they know where he's got to.'

We went over to interrogate the two other teenagers, but they shook their heads. 'I'm sorry. Danny went off earlier, saying he was headed for the bathroom,' Titus explained. 'I haven't seen him since. I thought he'd found you both.'

'Is anything the matter?' Lady Ashton asked, wandering over to us, champagne glass in hand.

'Yes,' I said, at the same time as Pete was saying, 'No.'

I shot a frustrated look at my husband and explained we couldn't find our son.

'Oh, he'll be around,' Lady Ashton said. 'He can't have gone far.'

This was such a stupid thing to say, I would have

laughed if I hadn't been so worried. Across the whole estate there was, to my knowledge, a huge manor house, the annex, several out-buildings, stables, rolling fields, and a large maze-like garden behind a stone wall. He could be anywhere, and we could search all night and potentially fail to find him.

'Let's start with the kitchens – he may have gone down to find some food.'

I thought this unlikely, since his appetite had shrivelled up over the past week – he'd hardly touched anything of his Christmas dinner, and had survived mostly on Frosties since then. But just as I opened my mouth to respond, something caught my eye. A chill started to run down my back that had nothing to do with the cold winter breeze. At the window of the room in the top right-hand corner of the wall, on the little balcony below it, stood a figure, looking out into the distance.

'No!' I cried. I could see people turning to look at me now, but I ignored them. I had but one thing in my mind. 'Danny, please. Stop. Get away from the edge!'

I heard Pete gasp beside me, 'We need to go and get him.' He left my side, leaving me staring up at my son, my poor, sweet boy, just standing there, like a statue, not reacting to the gasps of the crowd below. Then I ran after Pete.

I could see him, moving against the tide of the other

guests, working his way back around towards the French windows leading into the house, apparently ready to run up to that room. Did he have the same fear in his heart as I did in mine? I didn't know. Perhaps he was just worried his son was going to embarrass him in front of his posh friends. But I knew that would be fraught with difficulty. It was likely much of the upstairs would be in darkness, and there would be room after room, corridor after corridor, passageway after passageway. It could take us an age to get to him, and by the time we did... I felt my stomach drop within me. Then I saw a flash of silver-blonde hair a few metres away and knew what we needed to do. I ran over to Lady Ashton, just as she turned to speak to me. I didn't let her get a word out.

'How do I get to that room?' I pointed above us.

'Oh my dear,' she said. 'Is that your boy—?'

I cut her off. 'Yes, and we need to get to him urgently. What room is that?'

She seemed to understand me at once. Perhaps mothers have a shared sense for the urgency in another's voice. An urgency that only comes out when you fear for your child.

'Follow me,' she said in a businesslike way.

I beckoned to Pete, and both of us followed as Lady Ashton marched quickly through the house towards the front, where the grand staircase led to the upper floors.

We began our ascent, moving quickly, but the whole time I was tempted to push past her and run ahead. As I predicted, the house was a rabbit-warren of rooms and corridors – seemingly hundreds of doorways, shrouded in darkness, and even when Lady Ashton hit the occasional switch to light our way, a menacing sense of gloom still pervaded.

'Through here,' she said eventually, slowing as she reached a dark-red door at the end of an especially dark corridor. I could see the door wasn't properly closed and Lady Ashton pulled it open and led us through. Inside was a fairly large room, though it was crammed full with a mass of what looked like old children's toys: puzzles, board games, a rocking horse – largely dust-covered and lit by a flickering warm yellow light in the centre of the ceiling. It was like a forgotten toyshop, with dust and cobwebs clinging to all the faded old belongings, along with several items of furniture and rolled-up carpets. Lady Ashton made no explanation of the room's curious contents, however, but just walked purposefully through the gap between all the stuff towards a winding metal staircase in the far corner. She began to climb. This was all so very odd, and the rising panic within me was growing stronger still. I was terrified of what I'd find in the room beyond that staircase. Terrified of what I wouldn't find. Terrified there would be nothing there but billowing curtains, floating in the night air, bordering an empty balcony, showing me nothing apart from the emptiness beyond and the screams from the people below.

But none of this was true, because when I made it up the staircase and walked into the room – which appeared to be a bedroom, and a lot emptier and tidier than the one we'd just left – I could see Lady Ashton standing in front of the window, looking out onto the balcony.

I marched forwards, calling out, 'Danny, come away from there right now.'

He didn't move. Didn't even turn to look at us.

Both Pete and I moved to go towards him, but she held a hand out to stop us. 'Can I just try and talk to him?' she asked. I wanted to say no, that this wasn't her son, that I was the one who should be talking him down, but she stepped away from me and carried on directing her words at Danny. And to my relief, I saw him turn slightly to look as this older woman approached him slowly, talking in a calm, measured voice.

'Do you know, Daniel, this room used to be where my son slept. Slept, lived, ate, played, as a child. He wasn't well, when he was very young, and couldn't go out and about like other children, so he spent a lot of his time up here. He used to desperately want to go out and play in the garden, but for a while we thought he couldn't until he got better. *One day*, that's what I used to say to him, *one day* everything will be well. And it really is true. Even when things seemed at their blackest. Even when he was in the middle of one of his darkest moments or couldn't see the point of life at all, I said, just wait, just be patient, and one day things will be better. That one day will come.'

If I had been anyone other than Danny's mum, I might have found the speech both interesting and moving. But at that moment, the only thing I cared about was whether it helped get my son away from that balcony and safely into the house. I watched as Danny stood still, half-turned towards us. It was like we were all frozen in time, waiting for something to happen. Then a massive boom reverberated around us as a gush of white and blue light flooded into the room. The fireworks had begun again – apparently there was a round two – and Danny's profile was framed with the explosion of sparks and stars. The bang seemed to jolt Pete into action. Marching past me and Lady Ashton, he walked out onto the balcony, seized Danny around the middle and pulled him into the room.

'Get off me!' Danny shouted, suddenly alive and writhing and kicking, trying to escape his father. This wasn't what I wanted – I wanted to talk him down calmly, to defuse his desperate state, but his father's actions seemed to ignite it. Pete wrestled with his son, pinning him to the floor as the boy's yells descended into tearful mumbles and then full-on sobs. He started to grow still, going limp like the energy had flowed out of him in a big rush, and he now had no more fight to give.

'Come on. We need to get him home,' I said to Pete, kneeling down next to them on the carpet. 'Danny, can you hear me? We're going to walk back downstairs slowly and get you into the car.'

Out of the corner of my eye, I saw Lady Ashton move. 'I'll go and make sure your car is ready and waiting for you,' she said briskly. 'Will you be able to find your way back down to the front door?'

I nodded. 'We'll manage.'

It took us some time to navigate our way back through the corridors, taking any turning and stairway we could find, simply aiming to go down and hoping we got where we wanted without too much delay. Danny came with us without protest, his father holding him by the hand as if he were five years old again, still crying quietly next to us. When we got to the main staircase, we found the hallway deserted, apart from Rupert and Lady Ashton, standing near the front door. I wondered how she'd managed it – to keep any other guests away to make sure Danny didn't have to endure all the enquiring faces, eager for the next part of the saga. Maybe she'd locked them out of the house, or had someone waiting by the doors to the library, stopping them venturing into the hallway. Whatever she'd done, I was grateful.

'Thank you,' I said to her and Rupert as we led Danny past them out through the large doorway and onto the front steps. I tried to show in my face that I really meant it, and Lady Ashton nodded at me, showing she understood my gratitude. Rupert laid a hand on Pete's arm and told him to call him if there was anything he could do, and they said goodnight to each other.

We drove home mostly in silence – a silence that remained when we got in and started to climb the stairs. Eventually, when Danny turned to go into his room, I told him to get into bed and I'd bring him a drink, not really knowing if this was the right thing. I was just going with my parental gut reaction to when anything seemed wrong. I didn't even really know if I should leave him at all.

But he seemed to sense my uncertainty and just said, 'Please, just leave me alone. I just want to sleep.' I nodded, and left the room.

Pete and I met on the stairs. He looked grey with the stress of the evening.

'Is he all right?'

I nodded. 'I think so. He says he just wants to sleep. I'm going to make him some hot blackcurrant.'

Pete seemed torn between going up to check on his son and following me to discuss the situation. He chose to come with me into the kitchen, allowing the breakfast bar to take his weight, letting out a long breath as if he'd been holding it all this time. I put the kettle on and turned to look at him.

'We can't let this go on,' he said. 'Acting up like this when we're out in public. I don't know what's happening but, well, it's like he's become a moody child again.'

I glared at him, enraged at how he was talking about this as if it was a behaviour issue. Like Danny just needed to be grounded or have his weekly pocket money stopped and that would sort him out. 'Pete, your son almost... almost did something... He almost...'

'What? You don't think—' I realise at that moment how differently two people can view the same situation. What I'd seen as a potential suicide attempt he'd seen as just a teenage boy acting up and embarrassing his parents. 'Oh come on, he's just been in a bit of a weird mood.'

I put my hands to my face, close to despairing at how unobservant he could be.

'Look, I don't think we need to get too dramatic about it, but fine, OK, I agree we need to talk to him. We need to get to the bottom of it, whatever it is that's been, I don't know, eating him up.'

I nodded, but didn't meet his eyes. I knew it would have to come to this eventually. And despite my fears of what would be dragged to the surface by confronting Danny and making him tell us everything, I knew Pete was right. This couldn't continue.

Some minutes later, I took the mug of warm blackcurrant into Danny's room. He'd removed his shoes and lain on top of the covers still in his black skinny trousers and light-blue shirt. He was fast asleep, clutching one of his pillows between his arms, his shoulders rising slightly after each steady, peaceful breath. Part of me wanted to wake him up, make him take a sip of the warming drink and tell him to get properly under the covers, but I didn't have the heart to take him out of his deep sleep. I hoped the rest would be healing, and he'd be able to wake up tomorrow and tell us everything without fear. Tell us whatever secret he was keeping. Mend whatever had broken between us. And if my secret came out in the process, so be it. I couldn't let my son destroy himself just to protect my marriage. Perhaps I'd misinterpreted the situation, seeing him up there on the balcony. And maybe I hadn't. It wasn't worth the risk. No marriage was.

But of course tomorrow never came.

Or rather it did come, just in a form so different from every other day I'd ever lived through before that it would render it incapable of ever being thought of as just 'a day'.

It was the day when everything fractured. When everything ended. And it made it impossible to ever discover Danny's secret.

Or so I thought.

TWENTY-FOUR

Stephanie

THE DAY OF THE EXPLOSION

'Get off him!'

By the way Mimi's face jerked and her body rocked forward, I could tell she'd meant to shout the words. But instead of a shriek, they came out as a broken half-squeak, the force knocked out of the words with shock.

I was momentarily frozen, unsure what to do or what to say. Then suddenly something clicked into place in my mind and I leapt backwards, causing me to smash the end of my elbow onto Jonathan's chest of drawers. Wincing through the fizzing pain in my right arm, I stumbled desperately towards Mimi, who was backing away from me as if I were a mad, dangerous animal caught in a trap.

'Please, Mimi, it's… it's not what it looks like.'

I looked over to Jonathan, hoping he would rush to corroborate my story, but he was too busy trying to reach the towel on the floor. When he found his voice he shouted at his sister to fuck off.

She shot an outraged look his way, then turned to me and yelled, 'You're sick! Just... sick!' Then she vanished from the doorway.

Jonathan had located some tracksuit bottoms and tugged them on, facing away from me. I was still wincing at the pain in my elbow, clutching at it with my other arm, blinking away my tears of pain. I mumbled something about going to find her and explaining, and stumbled towards the door. He didn't argue. He was probably just keen to see me leave. I didn't turn back as I headed out towards the landing and started treading cautiously down the stairs, but I was sure I heard the door close quietly followed by the sound of him crying.

I didn't know what to expect when I arrived in the lounge. I'd half expected to walk in on Mimi giving a thoroughly sexed-up retelling of what she'd discovered in her brother's bedroom, explaining to the shocked faces of her parents that the grieving widow was also a pervert who liked schoolboys. Thankfully, no such sight greeted me as I walked in. Instead, both Janet and Richard were seated on the same sofa, though at opposite ends, as pushed up against each arm rest as possible. Perhaps they had finished their argument like this and neither of them wanted to be the first to leave the room. I walked in gingerly, wondering if they'd mind me trespassing upon their silent stalemate, then decided I didn't really care and just sat down on the settee opposite them. I saw Richard's eyes flick over to me once, then return to the pages of his book. Janet had replaced her magazines with some papers, but seemed to be sorting through them in much the same way.

'We wondered where you'd got to,' Janet said, barely glancing up from the sheet of A4 in her hands.

'Oh I...' I had no clue what to use as an excuse, so veered off in another direction. 'I thought I should probably go home.'

Janet sighed in an impatient sort of way. 'Well, we won't stop you, of course, but apparently we're not allowed to go outside. They said so on the megaphone.'

I looked around, puzzled, as if I'd see some evidence of this announcement in the lounge. 'What do you mean?'

This caused another sigh. 'As I said, there was another explosion when you were asleep,' Janet said, as if going over a piece of maths homework with a difficult child.

'I wasn't asleep,' I corrected. 'I fainted.'

Janet ignored this. 'Apparently another part of the

power station has blown up or caught fire or something and they're worried about more smoke and falling bits and stuff. A police van was driving around telling everyone to stay inside and not leave. So, well...' She flung her hands in the air, briefly, as if silently saying, *We're stuck with you, whether we like it or not.*

I felt tiredness washing over me. I was upset, exhausted, and on the verge of giving up. After all, I'd come here to find out what was going on with Danny. And I'd got the gist. But even as I thought that, I knew it wasn't true. I was on the right path, certainly. I'd got a lot of the details. But there was still a lot left to discover. If the two boys had been happy and experimenting with each other, and their friends weren't being unkind to them, what had been causing Danny so much anguish? Why was Jonathan so het up about it upstairs and unwilling to tell the full story?

'Are you *still* reading that book?' Janet said, cutting through my thoughts. She was looking over at her husband, the disdain clear in her face. She turned back to me. 'My husband always picks these weighty Ken Follett-esque tomes and then spends almost the whole year trudging through them.'

'Oh,' I said, just to give me something to say. I didn't really care what Richard read, nor how long it took him.

'It *is* a Ken Follett,' Richard said, lifting up the jacket.

'A book can't really be described as Ken Follett-*esque* when it is actually Ken Follett.'

I saw something twitch in Janet's cheek and when she replied she made no effort to disguise the annoyance in her voice. 'Well, if *esque* means *in the style of* I suppose it would only be natural for Ken Follett to write in the style of Ken Follett. Anyway, I don't know why you read all that historical stuff.'

Richard snapped the book shut and got up.

'Where are you going?' Janet asked, looking flustered.

Richard didn't reply, but after he'd left the noise of his purposeful march upstairs filled the room.

'Honestly,' Janet said, rolling her eyes. 'It's enough having Jonathan and Mimi behaving like stroppy teenagers, but him too...' She trailed off, shaking her head.

'Has Mimi been stroppy today?' I asked, wondering if she'd spoken to her mother since our showdown earlier, fleeting though her head-start had been.

Janet let out an exasperated breath. 'Oh, she was in here a moment ago, flouncing about, looking for her phone charger and demanding imperiously we all stop what we were doing and come to her aid. She shouldn't be spending so much time glued to her iPhone. If she's going to get into Cambridge or Guildhall, that girl needs to buck her ideas up.'

Janet's words had built to something of a crescendo throughout her rant, and she closed her mouth suddenly, as if embarrassed with how candid she'd been about her frustrations with her daughter.

'I was probably the same at her age,' I said, trying to sound casual, then remembering my mood swings may have been down to other reasons: leaving home at seventeen, cutting off nearly all contact with my parents, becoming pregnant.

'Hmm,' Janet said, her mouth clenched as if saying, *I can well imagine it*.

The noise of someone thudding down the stairs once again filled the air. My stomach lurched, expecting it to be Mimi, but it was Richard coming back, looking more concerned than angry.

'One of the windows in the guest bedroom has smashed,' he said, a little out of breath. 'I don't know if it was... well, the explosion. Or the second one. Or if maybe a bird... A large pigeon perhaps?'

Janet just stared up at him as if he was completely insane. 'Richard, what do you expect me to do about it now? Start lugging up some plasterboard and hammering it in myself? We'll phone someone to come and fix it when the world isn't ending outside.' She flapped a hand towards the front window. 'We'll just have to wait until we know there aren't any more bangs.

Or overweight, nose-diving pigeons.' She let out a cold, over-the-top laugh as she said this.

Her husband made an expression as if he were chewing on a hornet, then said, 'It's going to cost a bit. I don't know if we can afford it. That window's a bit of an odd shape, and—'

'We can't do anything about it *now*,' Janet half shouted at him. She looked scandalised, her eyes darting between her husband and me. It took me a second to catch on, then I realised she very much didn't want her husband to start debating their finances in front of me.

Richard clenched his sharp jaw again, and then sat back down where he'd been minutes before. I stared at him, taking in his tall, thin frame, and the way his legs jutted out slightly like spider's legs – like they were too long for his body. And his hands, too. Big hands, like sinister crabs.

I've never felt good about myself after spending too long in Richard's company. All the guilt and regret doesn't remain at bay for long. But on this day, with all that guilt and regret, came another question – one which I'd failed to add to my list earlier when thinking about all the things I still didn't know. How had my son learned *my* secret? How did he know what I did nearly three years ago?

TWENTY-FIVE

Stephanie

THREE YEARS BEFORE THE EXPLOSION

After my odd introduction to the Franklins involving blood, grazes, and bandages, we first met them properly as a couple at someone else's home. We had been invited to a housewarming party at one of the new-builds towards the end of the road. It was an enormous, impressive, incongruously modern-looking building of the type people either love or hate. I got the sense there was a collective resentment, mingled with a sense of fascination, in the town towards the house, with all its glass and unusual angles. I'd gone on a stroll around the neighbourhood on the third day of living there and overheard two dog walkers moaning about them, wishing the developers had gone for something a bit more in keeping with the local style.

Pete had been hesitant when we were invited to the housewarming.

'We haven't even had a chance to do one ourselves yet,' he said, fingering the invitation between his large, firm hands. He did this when he wasn't sure about something. Fiddled with things. Rearranged items on the table. Checked his pockets for something or other, just to give his hands something to do.

'Would you actually want to do one?' I asked, looking at him a tad surprised.

'Well, no, probably not. But now it looks like we're unsociable if we don't.'

I knew what he meant but it wasn't going to bother me. 'If we go to this one, we won't be seen as unsociable.' I said, in a problem-solved kind of way.

'We'll have to get you a nice dress,' he replied, then swept me up off my feet and carried me to the bedroom. Our sheets still felt strange and new and, falling onto them, feeling them ripple under us, I wondered how long it would take until our new house felt like home.

We'd driven to Lakeside in Thurrock to go shopping for our clothes for the housewarming. Pete had grumbled about having to practically go past Bluewater to get there but I'd been insistent that I wanted to go into the Ikea near the shopping centre to get some final furnishings for the house. He had drawn in his breath through his nose in a martyred fashion but had accepted my request without complaint. He had never liked Ikea and didn't understand why I was content to buy a lamp for a tenner when we could get a very nice one in Selfridges for £300 – something of his old life he hadn't quite left behind. In London I'd been itching to start living a more 'normal' life in the suburbs, away from central London. I'd found moving into the flat on Warwick Square when I was just twenty-one, newly graduated with both a husband and baby, more than a little exciting. But as the years went by, I got tired of the weird in-between we found ourselves in. The area was more suited to MPs, film stars, businesspeople from places like Russia and the United Arab Emirates, and other members of the upper classes. Pete had been unwilling to mix within the posh circles he'd moved away from earlier in his twenties, yet still keen to live around streets he knew. He described the occasional invites we got to a summer evening drinks party in Eaton Square Gardens as a 'festival of snobbery', but then didn't understand when I picked up clothes for Danny in Sainsbury's.

'There's no point buying a boy Prada shirts,' I'd protested, when Pete had looked disapprovingly at some of the cheap sale-item buys.

'OK, maybe not Prada. But what's wrong with Ralph Lauren?' He had been genuinely puzzled.

In a way, that was the key difference between my husband's 'poshness' – for want of a better word – and the Franklins'. He wasn't pretending. He wasn't trying to cultivate a particular kind of lifestyle. He was actually, born and bred, one of the people that they wanted to be. So when we met them, after being shown into the dazzlingly bright hallway of Myanna and Jessica Thornton-Smythe's home at their housewarming party, I think that's what must have set their teeth on edge.

It had been Janet who had come over to us. We'd probably looked a bit lost and I had thought what a nice person she must be, saving us from being left wandering about the house without knowing anyone. 'Oh hello, you must be the Hadleys. Peter and Stephanie, isn't it? You've moved in just opposite us, haven't you? I think we exchanged waves the other day when I was helping supervise the Ocado delivery – so sorry I couldn't come over and introduce myself then and there.'

Exchanged waves. I replayed the phrase silently in my head, finding it funny.

'Anyway, it's lovely to meet you both. How was your move? Not too ghastly, was it? It must have been stressful.'

I'd been a bit taken aback by the way she had fitted so many questions into one burst of speech without waiting for replies to them, but I gave her the benefit of the doubt. Until, that is, I saw her raise her eyebrows at her husband when we had finished talking and move into the kitchen. It wasn't openly cruel, exactly, but there was something there that I didn't like. I knew then and there that Janet thought she was better than me, but I can't say it bothered me too much. Perhaps it hurt slightly – those sorts of things often do – but I wasn't about to run home crying.

The housewarming party started off awkward and got worse as it went on. Most people were kind and friendly, though I didn't get the feeling any of them would become great friends of ours. There were a number of promises made about 'meeting up for coffee' or 'getting together soon' or 'working something out'. Some people commented on my dress.

'It's a beautiful cut,' said one lady who simply introduced herself as Cynthia. 'May I ask where it's from?'

'It's from Topshop,' I said pleasantly.

The woman looked surprised. 'Oh, well, goodness! Of course, you've still got youth on your side, my dear.'

I couldn't work out if she was being patronising or trying to be kind, but it was the first of a number of digs about my age made by a variety of women in the town. As time moved on, however, I quickly began to associate this primarily with Janet.

During a particularly boring discussion about the competence of removal firms with a dull couple whose name left me as soon as they had uttered it, I was ushered away by one of the hosts, Myanna, who beamed at me as if we'd been friends for years and said, 'I must show you around!' I was grateful to be rescued but uneasy about being given a one-on-one tour by one of the house's owners. I had at first been vaguely intimidated by the sound of the Thornton-Smythes. They weren't the only ones with double-barrelled names in the street and I had always considered such people to be way out of my social reach. However, after a minute talking to Myanna I need not have worried. I couldn't believe how stupid I was for not working out that she and Jessica didn't have a double-barrelled name because they were posh, it was because, as lesbians, there wasn't a rule about which of their names they should take. So, naturally, they had used both of their surnames. Myanna took me into the garden, where heat lamps on stilts had been set up to provide both light and warmth.

'I needed a break and thought you looked as if you could do with one too,' she said, taking out a cigarette. 'Goodness, some of them are *unbearable*, aren't they!' She sounded like she'd been made to climb a mountain. Her accent was northern, with a soft, soothing quality to it.

I laughed. 'Yes, I know what you mean.'

Myanna puffed on her cigarette as if it was giving her energy to continue. 'Would you like one?' she said, conjuring a packet of them seemingly out of nowhere. She must have them hidden in her clothes somewhere. Most women were, like me, wearing dresses and the men had on smart shirts. Myanna, however, was wearing a cosy cardigan. It looked extremely comfortable and as if it would be wonderfully soft to the touch. Thanks to her natural good looks and blonde hair she still looked great, if a touch eccentric.

'I'm fine. Thanks though,' I said nervously, trying not to sound too disapproving.

'Don't smoke?'

'No. I tried it once, when I was at school.'

She smiled. 'Didn't last?'

'It didn't really begin,' I said, laughing awkwardly. I don't know why I was so keen for Myanna to like me, but I suspect it was because I didn't want the evening to feel like a failure. I hadn't made a single friend at the party at that point and I felt I was being offered one last chance to make a connection. 'I didn't like it much. Made me cough the first time. And my dad smoked and he coughed horrendously all the time and I thought if that's what it does then...' I let my sentence die limply, realising I was getting into difficult territory with a smoker.

'Probably best,' said Myanna, smiling, then she

changed the subject. 'How long have you been living here?'

'Just a week longer than you, actually.'

Myanna looked worried, 'Oh no, I do hope we haven't stolen your thunder!' She clasped my arm as if she'd suddenly had a fantastic idea. 'We should do a housewarming at your house, but not invite anyone else! Play loud music, make an obvious party of it, but bar all these horrendous uppity types from it. They'll go mad!'

I laughed at this, encouraged by her conspiratorial air and clearly wicked sense of humour. 'That does sound like an attractive option, I must admit!'

We chatted for a good half an hour, undisturbed, standing out there on the patio, her ultra-modern house shining behind us like some giant glass glow-fly. She told me about her engagement to Jessica. They were both investigative journalists, and had met when they were doing a piece for ITV five years ago on workplace bullying. I found this interesting and asked what else she'd done recently. 'Oh, well, I actually got a bit of a promotion after a story I did a couple of years ago, about all those MPs and businessmen involved in that terrible abusive sex ring.'

I nodded, to show I knew what she was talking about, but I didn't say anything. I was aware Pete had connections to, or even used to know, some of the people involved, back when he was growing up in London. I didn't like to think of our family having a link to things like that, no matter how tenuous.

'It was me who broke that story,' Myanna continued, taking another puff. 'So it's got me a lot of work, and I'm actually going to move into presenting work in front of the camera, not just the researching behind the scenes. That's how we could afford to buy this place, really – well, just about, with both our incomes. Coming up, I've got something about a *very* shady old bloke in the retail sector – shocking things going on there, although I can't really speak about it just yet.' She gave me a little wink. 'What do you do?'

I hesitated at first, then said, 'Well, I'm... unemployed.' I let out a little laugh, regretting my choice of word. I could have said 'stay-at-home mum' or 'I'm not working at present', but worried they'd sound like I was covering up or apologising. 'I think I might see if I can get a job nearby, now my son's getting older. Perhaps something in customer service... I've always fancied that.' I'd started to think aloud, although Myanna continued to smile and nod, encouraging me to go on. I gave her a heavily diluted account of how I met Pete, avoiding mentioning my age or that I'd still been at school, although Myanna herself didn't look that much older than me.

'Did you move out of London to be near family?' she asked. Perhaps she hadn't picked up on my slight Somerset accent, or maybe she thought Pete might have family in Kent.

'No,' I replied. 'My parents live just outside Taunton. Well, my dad does. I don't really see him… and my mum, well, she lives in the States, now. North Carolina.'

Myanna raised her eyebrows, 'Goodness, that's a bit of a move. Did she run off with an American?' She must have seen something in my face to suggest I found the subject troubling, because she instantly put a hand on my arm and said, 'Oh goodness, I'm so nosy. That's the journalist in me – I didn't mean to pry.'

'No, no, it's OK. I… My mother joined a cult.' I couldn't believe I was saying this to a woman I had only just met, but I felt some of the tightness that had started to spread across my chest ease slightly, as if a weight had been pulled off me. I closed my eyes for a few seconds, then opened them to see Myanna looking fascinated.

'*Really*? That's so interesting. What sort of cult? What do they do? How did she get into it?'

I gave her an abridged version of how my mother and a member of an eccentric club she had been part of in Somerset had made the pilgrimage over to the US, shortly after she and my Dad separated. She then sent two separate letters to me and my father two months later, explaining that she wouldn't be coming back. I don't know how she'd got all the visa stuff sorted or what actual employment she was going to take up while there. She didn't say. She simply said that since England no longer 'appealed to the energy of her spirit', she was better off staying put in America.

Myanna dialled down the oh-my-God-tell-me-more vibe she'd given out when I'd started speaking into something more considered and sensitive. She was kind and I found speaking to her both natural and comforting.

It's a shame that Myanna and her wife moved out of Kent relatively quickly. They were gone by the following Christmas. Jessica had been promoted to a management position at the Canadian branch of the production company she worked for and they had to move over there rather quickly. Although I wouldn't have said we became besties, Myanna did become a nice acquaintance; a friendly face in the town.

My conversation with her, on that first night we met, came to an end when Jessica walked up to us and apologised but needed Myanna in the kitchen as she couldn't find where they had put the unopened bags of Kettle Chips. Myanna made her apologies and said, 'Is there anything I can get you?' before she left.

'Er... actually, where are the toilets?'

Myanna leaned in close and whispered, 'If you go

round the side of the house to the right, there's some fire-exit stairs up to the balcony and the main bedroom. You can use the en suite in there if you don't want to battle through the crowds.'

I smiled. 'Thanks, that might be a better option.' She grinned back and disappeared off. I thought I should probably go and find Pete, who I'd last spotted being drawn into an animated conversation about business communication and logistics in the digital age with an overly posh middle-aged man in the house's dazzlingly white kitchen. I went back indoors and found him almost immediately, now talking to a woman. She was a little older than him and seemed to be getting a bit too tactile for my liking.

'Hi,' I said, walking up to them.

'Dearest, hi!' said Pete. I could tell he was slightly tipsy, though not flat-out drunk.

'Oh my, this can't be your daughter, can it?' The older lady descended into a fit of laughter. To my surprise and anger, Pete joined in with her, laughing along. I stared at him.

'I thought I should come and find you,' I said, 'in case you were worried.'

'I wasn't, don't worry,' he said, still trying not to chuckle.

That's nice to know, I thought, feeling crosser still.

Pete turned to the woman. 'This is my wife, Stephanie. Stephanie, this is Charlotte. She's in the same area of business as me.'

'Trying to get out of it!' She sounded drunker than he did and her exaggerated arm gestures whilst she talked were so animated I almost had to duck. 'Owning a company was once a dream of mine. Now it just seems to be an association of idiots.' More laughter from both her and Pete.

'What company do you own?' I asked, trying to sound less pissed off than I was.

'You wouldn't have heard of it,' Pete butted in.

'So what do you do, Miss Stephanie?' said Charlotte, the ghost of a smirk flitting around her mouth.

'Erm, well, I... I haven't started looking yet really. We've only just moved here. I was thinking of volunteering. Or perhaps doing a postgraduate degree, part time.'

I didn't mention anything about customer service, as I had to Myanna. I got the feeling this woman would turn her nose up at that. Regardless, Charlotte was obviously unimpressed. The ghost of a smirk on her face evolved into something more obvious and unkind.

'Well, well,' she said, slurring her words, 'you have found a good catch here, haven't you?' As she talked, Pete seated himself on the breakfast bar stool next to

Charlotte and she patted his thigh. On the second pat she got so close to his groin she must have touched the outline of something other than just leg and shrieked with laughter.

'Sorry! Hand slip!'

This sent them both shrieking off into near-hysterics.

'I'm going to the bathroom,' I said coldly and turned on my heel and walked back the way I'd come, out into the garden. I realised I was going the wrong way and couldn't bear the thought of going back inside and seeing her molest my husband once again whilst he laughed merrily along with her. I then remembered Myanna's offer to use the en suite in her bedroom via the fire escape. I decided to take her up on this, even though something about the idea of going into someone's private rooms at a party felt a little transgressive. I walked around to the side path to the right of the house, as she had described, and found a little winding staircase which did indeed lead to a small balcony. I looked out at the garden, careful to stand back so nobody saw me. Groups of people were drinking and laughing. The warm summer breeze brushed against me, causing the hairs on my arms to ripple.

I felt so alone, standing there, part of this neighbourhood but not quite part of it. I wanted to be at home with my boy; to rush home and hold him in my arms. *He* didn't judge me or look down on me or think of me as anything other than 'Mum'. I turned away and went through the French windows into the bedroom and found the en suite, towards the left of the room, admiring the sumptuous cream carpet and beautiful king-size bed as I went past. Whilst on the toilet I took out my phone to check there hadn't been any messages from Danny. No such luck. Of course I hadn't been hoping to read anything too worrying, I just wanted something – anything – to get me out of the house and make me start the short walk home, around the corner to my new house. I momentarily considered feigning a headache, but part of me didn't want to leave Pete when he was drunk and getting on a little too well with that Charlotte woman. I flushed the chain, washed my hands and opened the door.

I knew at once that I wasn't alone. A man sat on the bed, looking out of the French windows at the night sky. He turned as I walked out and I froze, wondering who he was.

'Oh, sorry. I didn't realise anyone was up here.' He moved more into the light, but I recognised him from his voice before I fully saw his face. It was Richard Franklin, one of the first people we had greeted when we arrived at the party. His deep, resonant tone was unmistakable. I looked at him, sitting there in the half-light flooding in from the bathroom. He was oddly attractive, something I only now appreciated when his wife wasn't hogging the limelight. He didn't stand up, just looked at me from the bed, not saying anything.

'Did... did you want to use the bathroom?' I said uncertainly, not knowing what to do or say or whether I should leave him to his pensive staring.

'It's amazing how quickly this type of event becomes a bore,' he said, ignoring my question. I realised he wasn't staring me in the eyes, but rather looking slightly behind me, as if seeing past me, searching for something else in the rush of light. 'I can't tell you how grim it all is. You're young; you probably still enjoy it. But for me it just gets all too much.'

I was seized with a sudden energy and marched forward and sat down on the bed next to him. I sat with him, side by side, staring out into the sky. It was completely clear, with stars twinkling at us from their place up in the heavens.

'To be completely honest, I'm getting really pissed off with everyone using my age as subject for conversation.' I was impressed with myself that I had the nerve to speak these words. He laughed – a big, deep laugh. I turned to look at him. 'No, it's true.' I tried to sound angry but couldn't help smiling. 'Nearly everyone I meet seems to mention how old I am. A woman downstairs practically accused me of being a teenager.' He stopped laughing and moved his gaze to my eyes.

'You do look young. But not *that* young. I'm sure it's just jealousy. Deep-rooted jealousy. Thinly disguised insecurity.'

He knew, I thought to myself. He understood. He is one of them but isn't blind to the ludicrousness of it. I had mistaken this man for just another pretentious idiot, but right then and there I liked him. More than that, I respected him. And all of a sudden, both of us leant towards each other, at exactly the same time.

I couldn't say that he had started it, or I had. We both met in the middle and started kissing. For weeks, months, afterwards I would examine that moment, millisecond by millisecond, trying to work out which of us was more guilty. I remembered being surprised by how easily I slipped into the activity, moving my tongue along his, the kissing enthusiastic though controlled. I barely had a chance to come up for air before he was pushing me down on my back and putting his weight on me, moving his hand along my dress and then under it, pulling down my kickers and unzipping his trousers. He pushed into me somewhat roughly, but I liked how desperate he felt. How strong and animalistic and unmistakably male. He wasn't the boyish young man who had made love to me on the front seat of a car. This was an experienced, world-weary man who knew what he wanted and had, for too long, been denied it: a young woman like me. And now he was taking it. And I, without hesitation, let him.

The sex didn't last long. His grunts got quicker and sharper and then he finished in a loud gasp and rolled off me. He was breathing loudly.

'I'm sorry. I shouldn't have done that,' he said straightaway. 'I... wasn't thinking.'

I hadn't been thinking either, if I was honest. Or maybe I had been thinking far too much and the collision of my thoughts had led me to that moment.

'We—we can't tell anyone about this... You do understand?' He was lying next to me, with his head turned to the side, staring at me. I refused to look at him. I just stared at the ceiling. 'I... You see, Janet... She would never... I just don't think it's worth the upset.'

There it was. The cliché. The cheating man suddenly worried about his wronged wife.

Best keep her in the dark.

Let's not ruin anyone's life.

We might be fucked up but why draw anyone else into our debauched little dalliance.

It hurt me at the time to accept it, but I knew he was right. I knew that I wouldn't say anything. I knew I would go back downstairs and tell my husband I was feeling a little unwell and I was going home. And I did just that – well, almost. I left Richard on the bed, doing up his trousers and walked back down the fire exit. I chickened out on the face-to-face with Pete; I just texted him my excuses and walked down the street towards our house. Once home, I went upstairs and knocked on Danny's door. He was awake, sitting in bed reading a Terry Pratchett novel.

'Hello, love,' I said. 'You enjoying your book?'

He smiled at me. 'Yes, it's good. Where's Dad?'

For a second I thought about telling him the truth: *your father is flirting with a woman ten years his senior whilst drinking too much wine and I'm feeling a bit tired after shagging one of our new neighbours, so I'm off to bed.*

But of course I didn't.

'He's still at the party. I had a bit of a headache so I came home.'

He nodded and looked at me, as if waiting for me to add something else. Instead of talking I just crossed the room, sat on his bed, and wrapped my arms around him. He returned the hug, but said in a puzzled voice, 'Mum, are you OK?'

I struggled to form a reply, the words getting stuck in my mouth. 'Yes, yes, I'm fine.' I was aware I was sounding strange, but couldn't help it.

'Are you crying?' Danny was sounding concerned

now and he withdrew from my embrace and looked at me searchingly. My eyes must have been shining with tears but I smiled and brushed them lightly. 'Yes, love, don't worry. I've just got a bit of a headache. I'll take a paracetamol and get off to bed. I just wanted to tell you I love you lots.' I gave his hand a final squeeze and got up and left.

I walked to my bedroom and threw myself down on the bed, not bothering to take off my dress. In retrospect, it would have been easier to think I had lain awake all night, wracked with guilt, waiting for my husband to return to tell him how much I loved him. But I didn't. I just slept. And the next morning I woke up beside Pete and went down to get breakfast as if nothing had happened.

We never spoke about the housewarming party again.

TWENTY-SIX

Stephanie

NOW

T hings are starting to come back to me. I manage to
sit up in my bed and have some food – a couple of
bites of toast, a sip of some hot tea. It makes me feel a
little better.

I even manage to start another conversation with the
woman in the bed next to me. She's had her curtains
drawn for a long time, but when I see her sitting up in
bed, I smile as best I can. She acknowledges me with a
nod. There's still something about her that's strangely
familiar, but even though I wrack my brains, I'm unable
to place her face.

'What are you in for, then?' She sounds surprisingly
brisk, and I can see she's tucking into what looks like a
chocolate yoghurt. Even from those brief words, I catch a

flavour of a West Country accent. It reminds me of my childhood.

'My head…' I say, pointing to the bandage. I realise it's not a very satisfactory response, but she doesn't ask for more information. She nods. Then she starts whistling very faintly, and I recognise it as the same tune she was humming earlier. And then it hits me – I know the song. It's a Christmas carol.

'What…' I say, and she stops as soon as I speak. 'What tune was that?' I ask, even though I know the answer. It's 'We Three Kings'.

'Sorry, dear? What tune?'

'I… You were… Nothing, sorry.' I rub at my head, wondering if I imagined it. Deciding to steer the conversation around to a more normal subject, I ask the question she put to me. 'What are you in here for?'

'I was attacked.' She says it so matter-of-factly that part of me wonders if I've misheard. Then she continues. 'My sister, she owed some people some money. Bad people.' She looks me in the eyes for a split second after these two words, as if they should mean something to me. Then she turns back to her dessert and says, 'She joined this group. Not a very nice group. But she didn't contribute to their way of life. Didn't follow their rules. She was, and remained, an outsider.'

Again, on this last word, she stares at me. And I

stare back. Desperate for something to say, and feeling very uneasy about the direction this conversation is taking, I ask: 'And why did they attack you?'

'Because I didn't give them what they wanted. They asked me if I would take my sister's place in the group. Asked if I would travel to America and continue the life she started there.'

My heart flutters a little. 'America?'

'Yes,' she says, her eyes now fixed upon me, not moving. 'And I was wrong to say no. So they came for me. And my family.'

'Who did?' I ask, my heart now pounding fast.

'The group. The leaders of the group.'

The room begins to tilt and sway. 'What... what group?'

'They came to my house. They poured petrol on the beds of my sleeping darlings. And then they hurt me outside the burning house with a hammer. A hammer to the back of the skull.'

I realise now that she has a bandage on her head, just like mine. 'A few taps. A few sharp taps. Then one big one. And then blackness.'

She's getting out of bed now, placing the empty yoghurt pot gently down on the bedside table. As she stands in front of me, I recognise her. She's older than I remember. Her hair is greyer, her skin more weathered. But it's her.

'Mum?' I say, staring up at her. And the hammer in her hand.

'This will hurt, my sweet one,' she says. 'But afterwards, all the pain will go away.'

Then she swings the hammer at my face.

My scream must have sounded out across the ward and beyond. I only realise how much I'm flailing when the hands start to hold me down and someone speaks in a loud, slow voice in my ear.

'Stephanie? Wake up, dear. Stop shouting now. Tell us where the pain is.'

I open my eyes and see two nurses peering over me, the one on my left trying to hold me still, the other brushing the hair out my face and looking into my eyes.

'Is she hallucinating?' one of the nurses says, her accent soft and Irish.

'No, no,' says the older English one. 'I think she's had a nightmare.'

I'm breathing heavily and try to get out some words, but they come in short, staccato bursts. 'I… was hit… on the head… with a hammer…'

But the nurse in front of me is shaking her head. 'Not with a hammer, my dear. That's not right at all. You fell when the debris was coming down from the explosion.

You were very lucky you weren't more hurt. Now come, try to sit up and we'll get you some fresh tea. If you get yourself sorted, hopefully you'll feel well enough to see your visitor when she returns.'

I stare between the two nurses in panic. 'Visitor? Was somebody here?'

They exchange a glance and the younger one says, 'Perhaps she's not in a fit state for visitors?'

'Well, we'll see,' the older one says. 'She said she'll be back to see if Stephanie's awake for this evening's visiting times.'

For a second, the dream lingers on and I imagine my mother turning up, all the way from North Carolina. But I know she can't be here. Whatever threat exists for me in reality, it's from someone far closer to home.

'She said her name was Janet,' the nurse said. 'Janet Franklin.'

TWENTY-SEVEN

Stephanie

THE DAY OF THE EXPLOSION

J anet went to see what she could find for lunch for us all around midday. She muttered something about some cold pesto pasta she might be able to serve with a salad as she went, leaving me in the lounge alone with her husband. Not a situation I would normally rush to be in.

I saw him examining me before he said anything. Richard has a way of doing this. I don't think he likes people to know where his attention is resting, so if you try and meet his gaze, he diverts his to something else in the room. Normally, I would put this down to typical Franklin superiority. His wife always did it in her own way through conversations – if she caught herself talking to someone about their subject of interest for too long, she would quickly swing the conversation back to either

her, her husband or her offspring's latest music recital. On this particular day, however, Richard seemed to be unusually nervous. He kept opening his mouth and then closing it again.

Eventually it got so annoying that I just hissed, 'What is it?' at him.

He seemed desperate to speak, but at the same time unwilling, constantly stealing glances over at the archway leading through to the kitchen. As soon as the gush of the taps sounded from the kitchen he moved off this place on the sofa, around the coffee table, and over to my side.

'Stephanie,' he said, quietly but urgently, casting another glance towards the kitchen. 'I need to speak to you. I know we haven't... for a while... since...'

'Since my family was killed,' I said, deliberately bluntly. I was in no mood to make his little speech easier. Let him suffer, I thought.

'Ah... yes. Terrible, terrible.'

'Terrible. Yes, that's exactly what it was.' I stared at him, refusing to blink. 'And it was also nothing to do with you.' I'm not quite sure why I said that. Part of me just wanted to point out that he wasn't an important person in my life. What had occurred between us nearly three years ago hadn't particularly shaken my world or changed it irrevocably. That the actual irrevocable thing in my life that really had shaken my world had absolutely nothing to do with him at all.

'I wanted… wanted to talk to you at the… well, the funeral. To tell you how much you've been in my thoughts… how much you are *always* in my thoughts. But that wouldn't have been the right moment.'

I stared back at him, trying to stop my eyes widening with amazement.

'Oh, you mean when they brought in the coffins of my family? Or afterwards, when I was so upset I could barely stand? Or when I was trying to talk to my in-laws who I barely know and who clearly had little interest in getting to know me? Yes, you're right, it would have been the wrong fucking moment.' I kept my voice steady, but I had to fight not to scream the words. He really was a tragic wreck of a man. And what did he mean 'always in my thoughts'? We made one mistake, years ago – did he have to go bringing it up? Placing so much importance on it? I'd done my very best over these past years *not* to place any importance on what we did.

'You've given me the suggestion, whenever we've met before, that you don't want to talk about what… what happened.'

I took a deep breath and clenched my teeth. 'No. No, I don't.'

'But, you see, the thing is… I *need* to talk about it.

You... we... what we did that night changed my life, Stephanie. I cannot overstate how massive the effect was on me. Afterwards I wanted to go and do things I hadn't done since my twenties. Paragliding, rock climbing, cliff jumping... I wanted to be free and feel that rush of adrenaline.'

I wasn't quite sure what to make of all this, but I didn't like the sound of it. 'Well, I'm glad I helped reawaken your love of adventure sports.'

He tutted. 'I'm serious. I've been going mad, all this time. All these long years. You showed me what life could be like. You raised everything above the... I don't know, the grey mundane of the day-to-day.'

I looked over towards the kitchen. Janet had the (presumably battery-powered) radio on, and I occasionally heard the odd word that made it clear it was a report about the explosions nearby. Still, this was a dangerous conversation to be having with her in such close proximity.

'I would like to make a suggestion,' Richard said hurriedly, grabbing my arm. I looked down at his hand and then, with my spare arm, gently but firmly lifted it off. He ignored this rejection and pressed on: 'I think we should see each other. I think I should message you whenever Janet goes out and you could come over. We could spend time together. I could help you... help you get back into the swing of things. It can't be good for you to be stuck inside that large house all on your own, day after day, month after month. Nobody would want that.'

'I think it's called grief,' I said blandly.

'What I'm saying is I could help you lift yourself out of it. Provide distraction, a way back to normality.'

I frowned at him. 'You're suggesting I come over here a few times a week so you can shag me when your wife's out, to distract me from the fact my husband and child are dead… and you think that sounds like *normality*?'

Even though I'd kept my voice quiet, he made a batting movement with his hand, signalling that I should keep it down, and threw another terrified look towards the kitchen. 'Maybe I didn't word it particularly well,' he conceded, looking pained.

A creak came from upstairs and then a thud, as if someone had put something heavy down on the floor. 'Have you seen Mimi recently?' I asked, trying to make it sound casual.

Richard shook his head, distractedly. 'No, why? I mean, I've seen her *today*; she was here earlier… What—?'

'It's nothing,' I said, wishing I hadn't asked. I moved a little away from him, making it clear our conversation was over. He seemed to get the message and edged back round the coffee table over to his seat opposite. But once he'd sat down, I decided to hazard another question. And I kept a close watch on his face as I asked it. 'Do you know anything about what was going on between Jonathan and Danny before his death?'

'Here we are!' Janet announced her return in a falsely cheery, sing-songy voice, putting down a large bowl of pesto pasta on the table, followed by a smaller bowl of what looked like a Caesar salad. 'I'll go and get some plates and we can tuck in – unless we'd prefer to go to the dinner table and eat it properly?'

A moment's silence greeted her question until eventually both Richard and I muttered something along the lines of 'No, it's OK.' Janet exited again to get plates and cutlery. I sat there, not daring to bring up my question again, but triumphant at the effect it had had on the man sitting opposite me.

Richard Franklin knew something. Because as soon as I'd asked him about Jonathan and Danny, the blood had drained from his face.

TWENTY-EIGHT

Stephanie

THREE YEARS BEFORE THE EXPLOSION

Not long after I had met her at the housewarming do, Myanna had asked me out for a coffee. I was delighted to be asked. I'd been thinking of contacting her throughout the days after the party. I'd even researched her a bit online and watched a few clips from her television programmes on YouTube. The big, famous one she'd done about the VIP sex ring was the most easily available, and it was clearly important work and very slickly done, but it was just one of many. I'd got completely immersed in a documentary she'd helmed about ADHD. I felt like I had a new celebrity friend – someone with a much more interesting life than mine. Part of me wondered if I'd be better off pretending that whole night when I'd met Myanna had never happened.

But no, I thought, this was an opportunity to make a good, proper friend. I'd be stupid to turn it down.

The guilt of my adultery, upstairs in the bedroom in Myanna's house, weighed heavy on me at times, and then alleviated, as if it had never happened. It was like a radio station going in and out of signal, and I was worried meeting up with Myanna would lock the guilt dial onto full beam. But I was surprised how easy and comfortable her company was, and for a lot of the time during our meet-up I didn't think once about Richard Franklin or the terrible thing we'd done.

We had initially arranged to meet at the Costa in the high street nearby, but in the morning of the day before we were supposed to go she phoned my mobile saying she had to get a few bits for her wife's birthday and would I like to come to Bluewater instead? She was driving, so all I had to do was hop in her car. And it was great. Really great. We went round lots of nice stores, I helped Myanna pick out something for Jessica ('You have such great taste, Stephanie!'), and then we had a muffin and a warm drink in one of the ground floor cafés. Whilst we were sipping our beverages and I was polishing off the last of the blueberry cake I had chosen, Myanna brought up the subject of Richard. Actually, it was the Franklins as a whole she brought up, but Richard was where we landed.

Whether that was my doing or hers I can't remember, but all of a sudden she put her hand on my arm and said, 'Stephanie....I saw you.'

I didn't know quite what she meant at first and then, with a rush of nauseating horror, I got the gist. I came very close to knocking over my hot chocolate but managed to save it. I looked at Myanna's face, searching for some sign of what I could expect next: anger, disgust, mockery. None of these, as it turned out. She just looked concerned. She kept her hand on mine and said, 'Stephanie, I'm not cross, nor am I judging you. I just wanted you to know that, well, he has a reputation for... for this kind of thing.'

'What kind of thing?' I was angry, for a moment, that our quiet little shag was part of a specific genre and that it constituted a *thing*, as if it were filed away somewhere in a library of shameful party shenanigans. It wasn't a *thing*. It was a mistake. Just something that happened that shouldn't have happened. Making it into a *thing* would give it a sense of importance and then it might evolve from a *thing* into a *problem*.

'Are you OK, Stephanie? It's just that I wanted to ask if it was... well, I'd hate to think... if something bad happened in my house... I just wanted to check...'

I took my arm away from her hand – not roughly, but

in a way that made me feel more in control of my own actions.

'It wasn't… No, it wasn't anything like that… I didn't try to stop him. In fact, at that moment, I wanted it.'

Myanna looked taken aback for a second, then let a cautious smile spread across her face. 'Oh… Oh, that's… well, that's a much better scenario in any case.'

The whole thing was very awkward. I told her I didn't make a habit of having sex in other people's bedrooms and that I was very sorry it had happened at her party, but all through this I wanted to discover what she meant about Richard having a 'reputation'. How on earth would Myanna know about his reputation? She'd barely been in the town five minutes and already she seemed to know more about my neighbours than I did.

Eventually I asked her and she shifted on her seat nervously then started stirring her drink with a spoon, turning her gaze to the swirling liquid. 'Pauline Warbeck, do you know her? Does curtains – we're having her design some for us. Lives nearby. Well, she told me he had a reputation for… well, for trying to talk young women into sex. Apparently there was some problem with a student at his last university. A little while ago now, lucky for him of course. These days he'd have been thoroughly named and shamed. He had to leave.

Nothing official, but I was told there was quite a bit of upset. From what she told me I'm amazed he managed to get another job so easily.' I hadn't heard any of this but it didn't exactly surprise me.

'What happened?' I asked cautiously.

'Well, it was all a bit ambiguous. Apparently the girl never made a formal complaint but there were whispers. And when I heard all this I remembered what I had seen, with you and him, and, well... I just wanted to check.'

I assured her again that it was not an attack, that I had willingly taken part. She just nodded and I decided it was time to change the subject. Straying into such awkward, personal territory had made me feel prickly and exposed. I'd thought talking about the situation with someone would have felt like having a weight taken off my shoulders, even just a tiny bit, but it didn't feel like that at all, and I was keen not to go further down the rabbit hole of Richard Franklin's past affairs.

'What are you working on at the moment?' I asked, smiling, probably sounding a little too enthusiastic.

Myanna looked a little taken aback.

'Oh, well, right now I'm just finishing up a project that's taken a while to get off the ground, to do with police inflating charge numbers in order to creatively embroider their clear-up rates. A lot of paperwork research on that one. Important but not that exciting. And my team and I are about to start on a rather interesting story, actually, about this author who novelised some childhood trauma of hers – there was some press about it when it all came out. She effectively blamed her parents for another child's death – one that she may have had a hand in. It all happened in Northumberland in the 80s. I'm actually from near there, originally – although the accent's nearly gone now – and it will be nice to go back up and do some digging around. So yes, a lot on right now. You know how it is.'

I nodded, even though I didn't. I didn't know what it was like to have a rich and varied career. I'd never regarded that as a failing – I'd always fiercely defend someone's right to make their own decisions in life. If I wanted to stay home because we didn't need two incomes, that was my choice and my business. But I'd be lying if I said there wasn't a part of me that envied Myanna.

I hadn't expected the topic of my moment with Richard to come up again, but it did, quite unexpectedly in the car on the way home, just before she dropped me off at my house.

'Are you not happy, Stephanie? With your marriage, that is? I'm sorry, I don't mean to pry, I just… well, I think I just wondered why you would risk it all?'

It was a very good question. And she'd managed to articulate it in such a clear way that I was completely flummoxed. I let too many beats of silence go by, so that it became awkward and Myanna began apologising.

'No, no, it's fine,' I hastened to reassure her. 'I just... I don't have an easy answer, other than that it was because he laughed at me.' Myanna looked confused, so I clarified: 'My husband, sorry. Not Richard. Pete did, that night. He laughed at me. It's funny, what you were saying earlier about your accent and how you've lost it, but it's the same with me. I used to have a really strong West Country accent and when I was at uni, I heard a friend of one of my classmates refer to me as 'the girl who talks like a farmer'. It was silly stuff, but it got a bit nasty at times, so I deliberately flattened out my voice. I watched videos online; listened to a lot of classic novels on CD, read by actors who'd been to RADA. I didn't want to became *posh* posh, just... I don't know, less likely to stand out. But I did all that for other people. Never for Pete. He never commented on the accent change. Whether he noticed it or not – and it wasn't an overnight thing; I did it over the course of years – I was pleased he didn't try to intervene; to persuade or dissuade.

'But that night, at the party, when he was drunk and flirting with that other woman... he just became one of them. I couldn't tell him apart from the rest. He was one of the people who looked down on me. It bothered me. It wasn't because of the flirting – or at least, not totally – it was that at that moment he treated me like I was stupid or thick or common. It was worse than if he'd cheated on me. But, as it turned out, I ended up cheating on him. I don't know deep down why I did it, or why I went so extreme so quickly instead of just having a go at him when we got home. Maybe that's the worst thing. The fact I chose the betrayal, rather than, I don't know, the moral high ground.'

The car had come to a stop outside my house as I finished and a light shower of rain was speckling the car windscreen. I looked over at Myanna and she turned to me and smiled.

'I'm not judging you, Stephanie. We all do things; we're all human. I think we probably spend so long pretending to be normal people we forget to be *real* people.'

I wasn't sure how to respond, so I just apologised again and she told me not to worry.

'I'm not trying to make you feel bad, Stephanie. Just… be yourself. Don't take things to heart. I'm sure you'll be fine.'

After that we parted, with her driving off round the corner towards her house and me going inside to get the boys' tea on and tidy up a bit before Pete got home from work. Everything just went on as normal. Pete and I carried on, nothing cataclysmic happened and Myanna, the only person who knew about my transgression, moved out of the street not long after.

TWENTY-NINE

Stephanie

THE DAY OF THE EXPLOSION

When Janet re-entered the lounge, I thought I saw a flicker of something on her face. Suspicion, maybe? Had she seen her husband dive back to his place opposite? Or, worse, had she heard anything of what had been said? I presumed the latter was unlikely – she'd settled herself down and was now tucking in to some of the food, her plate balanced on her knees, and looking quite comfortable. I doubted she'd have had much of an appetite if she'd just discovered her husband had shagged her much younger neighbour from across the street.

Once she'd finished her mouthful, Janet asked a question that I didn't welcome. She wanted to know about my parents. 'Did they offer to come and... well, come and be with you through this, um, this difficult time?'

I took longer to chew my food than I needed, thinking about how much to tell her. 'My parents live abroad.' I said it simply, wondering if it would be enough, but I should have known it wouldn't be.

'Yes, of course, I remember you saying before about that,' Janet said, dabbing at her mouth with a napkin, and pausing to pile some more salad onto her plate. To her left, Richard picked about a few pieces of pasta with a fork, frowning, as if he wasn't sure they were safe. 'I just wondered if they'd considered flying back to be with you. To be with and... support you.'

I knew what she was getting at and it was a natural question. I probed how I felt about it in my mind, to see if it was possible for me to talk without getting emotional. I decided to try it out.

'I didn't have much contact with them before... what happened... before the accident, and I still don't now. My dad retrained as a skiing instructor. He lives out in Norway now. He went out there on building work when he divorced my mum and never came back. And the skiing replaced the building. My mum moved to the United States. She joined... a group, some people who are... well, they're religious, I suppose. In a way. She didn't seem to think it was worth coming back for the funeral.'

I felt a hardness grow in my throat, so I stopped speaking. I couldn't stop my mind reeling back, as if I were being forced to watch a film, filled with flashes from both my childhood and my past months of grief-stricken isolation. The day when, as a pregnant teenager, my mother told me she was going to America. That she needed to find her true spirit and that the mundane life she'd been living in Taunton was suffocating her. The fact that her only daughter was about to give birth to her first grandson didn't seem to register. Apparently that was all part of the 'mundane' fabric of her life.

To be honest, I wasn't that surprised that the death of their son-in-law and grandchild hadn't really mobilised either of my parents. But in spite of that, a small sliver of hope had remained that somehow it would jolt them into action. I actually had a dream about it, on one of the first painful nights alone in the big house with nobody there. I dreamt the doorbell had rung in the middle of the night and I had crept downstairs and opened the door and there they were, together again and smiling. They came in and made me some hot chocolate and my mum put a blanket around me and sang me one of the songs she had used to sing when I was a child and my dad told me it was all going to be OK. I cried into her arms and was still crying when I woke up, alone in the big king-size bed, with nobody there to comfort me. I had hated them at that point. Hated that they couldn't swallow their pride, put aside their differences with each other and with me and travel to Kent to stay with me.

I told my dad about the accident on the phone. The first attempt didn't go very well; I kept sobbing and he couldn't understand what I was saying. He was desperate to get off the line as soon as he knew it was me, but I could tell he was unnerved by my sounds of distress.

'Stephanie, what's wrong?' he asked, sounding mildly worried.

I told him I was alone, that Pete had gone.

'You've broken up? Divorced? Well, we didn't think it would last, I have to say.'

I shrieked at him when he said that: 'He's fucking dead! He's dead! And my boy. My beautiful boy...'

I'd killed the call then, hoping he would ring back. But he didn't. He didn't ring back for another two days and even then it was to see 'if I'd managed to get myself together.' I hung up the phone. I was hurt. As hurt as it is possible to be.

My mother thought she had more of an excuse not visiting. Living in America, according to her philosophy, is like living on the moon. It's so far away and life is so different that she seemed to think no sensible person would ever presume she would come back to England. That would be 'an unreasonable request'. That was how she worded it when I'd emailed her on a happier occasion: to ask if she'd like to come to my wedding. An unreasonable request. Based on this experience, when I sat down to email her about the death of my family, I hadn't hoped for much. But part of me did hope.

Her reply could have finished me off. It could have led me straight to the cabinet of paracetamol and ibuprofen and aspirin and sleeping tablets. But it didn't. When I read it I simply closed down my laptop and went and buried myself under my duvet, every word of the email ringing through my head.

Dear Stephanie,

I'm sorry to hear about what's happening at the moment. The break-up of a family is a horrid thing and I wouldn't want anyone to experience it. I know this because it happened to me. Perhaps you now know the pain I felt when I realised we couldn't live comfortably together in one house anymore. You had your new man, your father never really cared about me, and I had nothing. That was when I realised I needed to make my journey across the ocean to find a better world. But I don't want to stir all that up again, not at this sad time for you, and I am truly very sorry that I am not able to be there with you now. I'm not going to lie, I think it might make it worse for you if I was to come. We are making great progress here in the group, finding our inner selves and I have just found an equilibrium that suits my human spirit-level of life. I don't want to upset that and I don't think your pain would be good for me right now. I also don't think I'd be good for you. It breaks my heart to think of you in so much pain, but life is at times full of pain. I pray you find a way through it.

We should stay in touch. I think email is probably the best way to do it at the moment.

From

Mum

I winced at the fact she'd referred to her freakish little cult as 'the group', as if it was something simple, non-threatening, supportive, like a book club or the Women's Institute. But it was nothing of the sort.

Of course, it had been Argento who had poisoned her against us. His strange, faux-accented whispers seeping into her ear as they painted sheets with purple and green swirls in the garden on a summer's day. Him telling her she'd never be happy here in England with her husband

and daughter. That they'd be better off leaving. He put together this weird handmade brochure – I remember it clearly when Mum used it to explain to me and Dad where she was going. It was like an unsettling little school art project, filled with tea-dyed pages and annotations in black pen, made around photos that had been stuck in with glue and bits of ancient tape. It apparently charted the journey of this group. I told mum the whole thing was ridiculous, which earned me a frown as she turned the pages, explaining how the photographs detailed the different rituals they did. The group had started up in the late 70s or early 80s, she said. They'd camp out at empty manor houses or country retreats. Get in touch with their 'inner spirits'. Then the 'elders' decided America was destined to be their new home – they'd received funding from some rich old lady over there, and they bought premises and grounds and wanted to recruit new members. My mother said all this to me and my dad as if she expected us to understand. We didn't. I told her the photos – some of which showed unclothed people standing in circles around trees – were disturbing and the leaders clearly even more insane than her group of local church friends. Dad didn't say anything at all. He just closed the large volume with a thud, dropped it on the kitchen table and walked out of the room.

She had been with them for well over a decade now. And according to that email she sent earlier this year, she was only just finding her 'human spirit-level'. That wasn't exactly great progress. Even if she had wanted to come and see me it wouldn't have surprised me if one of the 'elders' had persuaded her not to. I had been rather surprised they had even let her email, to be honest. They were funny about computers there, only letting their members use ones in the nearby local library once a fortnight. After all, they wouldn't want to disrupt their human-spirit levels, would they? I'd never really used the word *abandoned* before but that was the word that came into my head, as I thought about all this. Abandoned. It was like I was a child again, only this time an orphan, struggling to make sense of life with no prism to look through.

I became dimly aware of Janet seated in front of me, peering at me. She looked sad and her eyes were wide, as if she were seeing me for the first time. She put down her plate and rubbed her hands on her knees.

'I'm very sorry to hear that, Stephanie. I... I can't even begin to comprehend how hard all this must be, and with no support.' She opened her mouth, then paused, as if unsure whether to say something. At last, she said, 'I have a difficult relationship with my mother too.' She let the sentence hang there, not elaborating any further. Her husband stirred uncomfortably, shifting in his seat and looking awkwardly at the floor.

'Did you... did you have a falling out?' I asked tentatively.

Janet pulled in a deep breath, giving her time to collect her thoughts.

'Yes, sort of. Well, she was a dancer. Ballet. Quite a good one and, you see, I think my brother and I always got in the way. I don't think she was ever really meant to be a parent. I'm not saying we were unhappy all the time but, well, when her career started to wane, as it does with ballet dancers when they reach a certain age, she didn't quite know how to cope with us. I was in my late teens and my brother was in his twenties. And it all just fell apart, really. She started drinking and, not wanting to witness that, we drifted away.' As if carried off by those last three words, Janet too seemed to have floated off to somewhere else. She snapped back into the present within seconds, though, blinking away the distant look in her eyes. 'These days, it's all fine of course. We moved her into her place around the corner a few years ago, and we get along just fine, don't we, Richard?' She didn't wait for her husband to concur. 'We just muddle along and don't talk about the past.'

I nodded. I wondered if that would have worked for me, after all this time. If my mother moved back to

England, would I encourage her to live out her old age in the neighbourhood near me? Or would I tell her she'd made her bed and she had better live with it?

That was when I started to feel the desperate need to be alone. I rose to my feet and Janet looked panicked. 'Are you OK, Stephanie?'

I nodded, hurriedly. 'Yes, I...'

'You're not going to faint again, are you?' she asked, sounding a little like the old Janet – the one who regards fainting neighbours as a hassle rather than an emergency.

'No, I'm fine, I'm just...'

'Why don't we go and do the washing-up together,' Janet said, like an adult trying to talk a child down from an imminent tantrum. 'Richard's finished, haven't you, Richard?' She swiped the plate, still containing a notable amount of food, from her husband's hands, and piled it on top of mine and hers. 'Come on, Stephanie, you can carry the salad bowl.'

I didn't know what else to do other than obey, so I picked up the large wooden bowl and followed Janet through into the kitchen. I was a bit redundant when I got there, with Janet just loading things into a dishwasher she currently couldn't turn on as I stared out onto the bleak garden. I thought I could see the sky becoming brighter from behind the tall trees. Perhaps the situation at the power plant was getting under control.

Janet talked away to me and I only gave her half of my attention. The other half was elsewhere, still thinking about my parents. Imagining, as I did sometimes, what my mum's living quarters would look like in the group's accommodation. Would they have cells? En suites? Hammocks?

Janet's monologue next to me had drifted around various subjects: Mimi's music studies, the emergency happening outside the house, whether *Woman's Hour* has been the same since Jenni Murray left. None of it seemed important, but I presumed she was trying to be nice and distract me after my emotional moment earlier. After a short while, though, she raised a hand to her temple and I heard her say something about her head hurting.

'I think I've got a migraine coming,' she said. She flitted around the kitchen, opening cupboards and drawers, muttering furiously about her tablets being moved by someone, then said, 'They might be upstairs. I'm so sorry, Stephanie, would you forgive me if I had a lie down?'

I was a little taken aback – I had become so used to Janet's seemingly endless flow of words that this question momentarily threw me. But I told her it was fine and I'd carry on putting the plates away.

'Oh, you don't have to do that,' she said, waving her had distractedly, as if vaguely irritated by the thought. She disappeared off through the lounge and towards the stairs. No sooner had the creak of floorboards sounded from above than further movement in the lounge signalled that I was now alone with Richard – and the expression on his face suggested he wasn't going to let this opportunity slip by. He had a determined, almost fevered glint in his eyes that made him look quite desperate. Perhaps it was this resolve that gave him the bravery to be so bold, as he didn't just come into the kitchen to talk. He strode up to me and before I could say anything had angled his tall frame down to try and plant a kiss on my mouth. His lips had barely touched mine before I sprang back. 'What the—! Don't!' I spluttered as I dodged out of his way. 'For fuck's sake! Your *wife* is upstairs.'

'And your husband was downstairs the first time we made love, over at number 27. I'll never forget it.' He was trembling, his hand reaching out for me juddering, like an old video tape on pause.

'Don't... don't you *dare* mention Pete!' I could feel the white-hot anger starting to rise within me. Who the hell did this guy think he was? Did he think this was the way to my heart, to my affection? Reminding me that I'd screwed my neighbour while my now-deceased husband remained happy, chatting, joking, and very much *alive* downstairs? 'If only you knew how much I regretted that day,' I said. 'It's a moment that will *haunt* me, you understand. It wasn't "making love". It was a stupid moment… a stupid mistake.'

'Don't belittle it, please, Stephanie. I… I promise you, this isn't some sad old man sort of crush. I've felt this way for a long time. Every day, every moment…'

I couldn't stand here and listen to this near-sixty-year-old man talk to me like a love-struck teenager. I went to leave the kitchen, but he grabbed me with a surprisingly firm grip.

'I promise you, what I'm saying is real. And I know you feel the same way. I know you feel it the same way I do.' His earnest, pleading eyes were holding my gaze with such intensity that I didn't realise they were coming closer, and once again he was pressing his lips to mine and with the other hand pushing me back so I was leaning up against the kitchen sink. I tried to let out a muffled swear word, but his hand was now in place over my jaw and my neck and then—

'What the *actual* fuck?'

The exclamation came from the archway into the lounge. Richard jerked around and when he saw who was standing there he leaped back from me as if I were a live wire.

His daughter's expression was a carbon copy of the

look of astonishment she'd displayed when finding me in her brother's bedroom.

'Mimi... I... we... don't...' Richard seemed incapable of explaining himself and she didn't give him much of a chance.

'You're sick. Both of you. Mum's upstairs. How... how could... And YOU!' She pointed at me, her mouth curling in disgust. 'What are you, some sort of sex maniac? Shagging teenage boys and then having a go with their fathers hours later. Is that what you go in for?'

'No!' I gasped, stepping towards Mimi, but she backed away as if I were brandishing a weapon. 'Please, Mimi, let me explain about Jonathan. I wasn't—'

'*What* about Jonathan?' Richard said sharply.

'She's... She was...' Mimi seemed to be working herself up into a state, still pointing at me dramatically, reminding me of someone in an over-the-top play accusing the villain of murder.

Richard's face went from horror to annoyance very quickly.

'Mimi, stop raving and stop using language like that.'

Her eyes flared. 'Language? I'll give you fucking language, you sick fuck! How can you? With her? What are you doing?'

Her tears, which had already seemed not far off, started to arrive in large drops, falling across her face.

She looked distressed and confused and much younger than the aloof, beautiful young woman who had swanned around the lounge that morning.

'Mimi!' Richard made a move to grab her arm but she stepped back into the lounge.

'Don't you fucking touch me!' She was becoming more and more hysterical.

Richard's breathing was shallow but he managed to make his words sound firm.

'Mimi, can we just sit down and—'

'And talk about it? What is there to fucking talk about? You're a cheating prick and she's some crazy nympho bitch who is so desperate she has to fuck both teenagers and pensioners! It's MESSED UP!' She screamed the last two words and then stormed out of the lounge.

'Oh God,' Richard said. 'Janet.' He followed Mimi, and I heard him racing up the stairs seconds later.

I turned back to the plates on the drying board and absentmindedly picked one up, as if I were going to carry on tidying away after lunch, as if nothing had happened. There was something in the idea that felt quite comforting, but I didn't have the energy. Instead, I sat down at the kitchen table. I was still shaking and felt light-headed but the immense, crushing tiredness overrode everything else. Physically I had not exerted myself as much for many weeks as I had that day. Emotionally, I felt on the verge of a second crisis. Things were falling down around me, buildings in my head were imploding and crashing into each other. I was losing my grip on why I was there. I was crying, tears just falling without sobs. And even through my upset, I could hear the sound of someone – or many people – approaching.

I looked up and, distorted through my blurred, teary vision, a shape exploded into the space around me. I made out Mimi's face before a sharp pain shot through my scalp. She had grabbed my hair. She had great handfuls of it and she was dragging me off the chair. My legs gave way and I fell and there was a horrible ripping sound. I hit the floor, though I managed to save myself with my hands before my head reached the cold stone. I looked up and saw Mimi standing above me clutching something in her hand. I realised with horror that it was some of my hair. The girl had ripped out some of my bloody hair. I remained on the ground, unable to speak, and then hands were closing around my shoulders.

'Help me get her up, Richard.'

That was Janet's voice. Mimi had brought her mother down from her peaceful nap.

Regret spread through me, quicker and more powerful than the pain in my scalp. This had all been one terrible mistake. I should have left this house as soon as this all started to get out of control. But control wasn't something I could rely on anymore. I allowed myself to be hoisted up by both Janet and Richard onto the chair, then they both stood there, looking at me. Mimi was now the one on the floor, crouched in the corner looking truly wild. Her mascara had been smudged from her tears and her hair, which usually fell in an artfully dishevelled way, now looked wildly dishevelled. Tears were still making their way down the make-up stained tracks on her face and she was looking straight at me, almost unblinking.

'Why are you helping her? Mum, what are you doing?' She was sobbing rather than shouting now and Janet turned round to face her.

'I know you're upset, Mimi, but please calm yourself down. This isn't going to get any better with hysterics.'

Mimi continued to mutter something about 'I know what this is'. These words seemed strange and ominous to me, but Janet didn't seem to think they were worth much attention.

She turned back to face me and said, 'Stephanie, are you OK? Do you need me to get you a bandage for your head?'

What did she mean? I reached up and touched my head and felt a patch that was slightly sticky. I looked at my fingers and there was a small trace of blood on them.

Mimi's hair-ripping had made my scalp bleed. I shook my head slowly. 'I'll be OK.'

'Good,' said Janet calmly. 'Now maybe you'd like to tell me your side of what's been going on.' She was standing, with her arms folded, looking straight at me.

'I… which bit?' I was confused about what she knew already and didn't want to tell her any more than I had to. My head was starting to hurt now; the patch where I imagined the clump of hair used to be was stinging and the tiredness was once again threatening to take over.

'The part about you having an affair with my husband.'

I was both relieved and horrified. It was like a weight lifting off me, the truth coming out at last like tearing off a plaster. Having said that, the word *affair* hit me like a brick in the face. I had never classed our quick shag as an *affair*. It was like Myanna calling it a *thing*. It wasn't anything. Although explaining that to Janet without sounding like a clichéd 'other woman' was going to be tricky.

'I… er… we haven't been having an affair.'

Janet's expression didn't change. 'OK, so why is Mimi upset. What did she see that upset her?'

Mimi started to spit the words out in a furious hiss from her huddle on the floor.

'They were kissing! And she… He—'

'Be quiet, Mimi!' Janet interrupted her sharply, although when she turned back to me her voice was still strangely neutral. 'So, once again Stephanie, I invite you to tell me your side of the story. Leave nothing out. I want to hear it.'

I glanced around the kitchen, wondering dully if there was some room for escape. I wasn't sure if they'd stop me. Maybe I was their prisoner now. An image swam into my head: me kept in a dark room, next to old Christmas decorations and boxes containing backdated issues of *Country Living*. They'd feed me hummus and nettle-infused herbal tea and jeer at me as I spat at them. I laughed at that. A short chirrup of a laugh that escaped involuntarily, like an unfortunate sneeze at a funeral. Janet's lips drew together into a dangerously thin line.

'If you cannot answer my question, perhaps you could tell me what you find so funny?'

I found my voice. 'No, no, it's not funny. I'm so sorry. I didn't mean to laugh. It wasn't about any of this. My mind was... I'm sorry – I'm not doing very well.'

'She's fucking INSANE!'

Mimi was sounding hysterical again, and I felt irritated that this weird confession had to take place in her hearing. Janet said nothing to her daughter this time, just continued to stare at me. Richard was leaning up against the sink looking at his shoes. He looked old, broken, resigned. The only person who seemed to be holding it together was Janet.

'I had sex with Richard at the Thornton-Smythes' housewarming party a few years ago.'

Janet took in a slow, deep breath. 'I see. And since then?'

'Nothing. I promise you. Never once since. I wouldn't—'

'Yet you somehow managed to at the party?'

'Yes, I know, but that was different. I...' I was struggling to describe it, to put into words why I did what I did. 'I was upset. I wasn't thinking.'

'But there has been nothing since then?'

'Nothing. I swear it.' I tried to keep my breathing slow, to match Janet's calmness in order to prove to her my sincerity.

'She is LYING! And he's not even telling you half of it. He's obsessed with her – dirty fucking old man!'

'Mimi, do not talk about your father like that!' Janet snapped.

'*And* she's only giving you selected highlights,' Mimi said, pointing at me again. 'You tell her what you did! She hasn't told you everything, Mum. She's a fucking LIAR!'

Janet turned around to her. 'Mimi, you are going to

have to leave the room. I need to talk to Stephanie and you are not making this easy.'

I thought the girl was going to argue but instead she got up. 'Fine!' she shouted and ran out of the kitchen into the lounge. I could then hear her running up the stairs. She sounded like she was on a mission.

'So, now we have some quiet at last, perhaps you could explain what Mimi saw that made her run into my room screaming blue murder.'

Richard stirred behind her. 'It was my fault.'

'That I don't doubt,' Janet said whilst still looking at me, 'but I want to hear it from Stephanie.'

'Richard tried to kiss me and Mimi saw. That's all.'

Janet let out a sigh. 'Well, to be entirely honest, that's a lot better than it could have been. This isn't exactly ideal, of course. Richard will have to talk to Mimi, although she more or less told him she hates him already so I doubt there's much that will change there. But I have to say you've been lucky, Stephanie. My husband rarely lets his obsessions go quite so easily.'

Richard protested. 'Janet, please, I-I don't think you should—'

'I shouldn't do what, Richard? What shouldn't I do?' She was sounding angry now.

Richard recoiled back, as if stung.

'Right, if this is all settled,' Janet said, running a hand

over her forehead, 'I think the best thing we can do is decide to never speak of it again. We've all been a bit upset; we've all got our stresses. I know you've been through the very worst ordeal, Stephanie, and I don't want to be responsible for you experiencing more pain.'

So that was it? That was the showdown? I couldn't help feeling like it had all been a bit of an anti-climax. Apparently Janet wasn't going to lock me in the cellar. She hadn't even shouted at me. If anything, she was being kinder and more understanding than she had ever been before. I didn't understand, but I wasn't about to argue. I put my weight on the side of the table and went to heave myself up out of the chair, though I wasn't exactly sure where I was going to go.

But then I heard a commotion. From the landing above us and then the stairs, the sound of someone – or more than just someone – getting nearer. It only took a couple of seconds, then Mimi re-entered the kitchen, pulling her brother with her by the arm.

He stared around at all of us – at Richard by the sink, at Janet standing with her arms folded, and at me sitting at the table. We all stared back at him.

Looking terrified, he opened his mouth.

'What's going on?'

THIRTY

Stephanie

THE DAY OF THE EXPLOSION

'Mimi, let go of your brother. What on earth are you doing?' Janet's stern voice cut through the silence that followed her son's question.

'What am *I* doing? Ask him! Ask her!' She was still sounding close to madness, and struggling to hold on to coherent speech altogether.

'What's got into you today?' Janet was shouting now, sounding exasperated. 'I know you like every little drama to have the widest possible audience but this is really making everything a thousand times more difficult.'

Mimi half sobbed, half laughed. 'Your little boy isn't a spectator in all of this, *Mummy*.' She said the last word as if it revolted her, then pointed at me with vigour once more. 'SHE knows why I've brought him down here.'

Something seemed to have clicked in Janet's mind. Details of what Mimi was saying were starting to sink in. She turned her face to me, looking puzzled and a little scared, clearly willing me to take over and explain. I couldn't speak. No words would come.

'If you don't fucking tell her, I will!' Mimi shouted.

'Mimi, don't.' Jonathan looked as if he was about to be sick, but he managed to croak out a few words. 'I told you, it isn't what you think.'

I saw the boy look pleadingly first at me and then over to his father, as if trying to tell him wordlessly that we were heading into dangerous territory.

'Come on. Both of you. Give me an explanation.' Janet folded her arms again in a businesslike fashion, perhaps trying to claw back some sense of control.

There was a tightness inside my throat that felt like it would never go away. I tried to breathe calmly through my nose, wondering who would be next to speak, because it certainly wouldn't be me.

'I caught them at it!'

Janet looked horrified. 'What? What on earth are you talking about?' She glanced between Mimi, Jonathan, and me, and then to Richard. 'Caught who?'

'Her, of course! HER! And HIM!' She pointed at her brother. 'They were going at it on his bed, her on top of him.'

'We weren't. I told you,' Jonathan insisted, although his voice was weak and had barely an ounce of the conviction his sister had.

Janet gave a nervous little laugh, like someone unsure if they're part of a joke or something much more serious. 'I… don't think…' She looked at Jonathan. 'What is she talking about?'

'For fuck's sake, Mum! Why are you always so slow? She's been shagging both your men behind your back.'

The words 'your men' sounded like a strange way to refer to Richard and Jonathan, although they seemed to have hit home for Janet. She stared at me, then back at her daughter, then at me again. 'No… No, she hasn't. She…' Then once her words had died out, she uttered a simple question. 'Is it true?'

At last I found my voice. 'No.' I said it as firmly as I could. 'I was just trying to find out why he was blackmailing my son.'

I became aware of Jonathan shaking his head at this point. He'd transferred his gaze to me and was turning his head in small, sharp jerks, his eyes pleading, trying to stop me saying what I was about to say. But I'd well and truly had it with all of them. I wasn't going to stand here and be accused of something so ludicrous by a woman I'd never liked or respected. A woman who'd looked down on me from the moment I'd set foot in the town.

'*Blackmail?*' Janet repeated the word back to me as if she'd never heard it before.

'Jonathan and my... Danny, they were involved. Jonathan has pictures on his phone. Explicit pictures taken of the two of them together, taken by another boy at a party before Christmas. Intimate photos, and a video.'

I saw all the eyes in the room move towards the teenage boy, standing there, as if frozen with shock and fear. I was surprised he didn't just bolt for the door right then and there, but he seemed incapable of moving.

Eventually someone spoke, and to my surprise it was Richard. 'I think we should leave this here,' he said, straightening up.

'No, I don't think so,' said Janet, holding out a hand towards him, telling him to shut up and back down. 'I want to know what the hell she's talking about.' Her gaze was fixed on Jonathan, whose eyes were darting around the room like a cornered mouse.

'I said we should leave it,' Richard said, sounding more insistent now and making a move towards his two children.

'No!' Jonathan shouted. I wouldn't have thought he was capable of such a sound, but he managed to command the room in an instant. 'You're not doing this.'

It took me a moment to realise he was talking to his

father. The boy was staring at his dad with such a furious look on his face it could only be described as pure, unadulterated hatred. 'It was him. He made me... made me blackmail Danny. I kept the video on my laptop and he saw it when he was snooping at my homework, probably looking for some examples of me screwing up somewhere. And he really hit the fucking jackpot. He used it against me. Taunted me with it. What kind of fucking father does that to his own son?'

Janet looked over at her husband. 'What on earth? Is this true?'

Richard stayed silent, but panic was starting to flood his thin, strained face. It was dawning on him that there was no escaping this now. It was all coming out. Every secret. Every unanswered question that had been gnawing away at our families in one form or another for years.

'He made me ask Danny for clothes.'

It wasn't just me who seemed baffled by this sentence. Janet was still moving her head like she was at a tennis match, although her husband showed no sign of offering up any answers. All he did was shift his head so he was looking at the floor and raise a hand to rub his face.

'Clothes?' Both Janet and I said it at the same time, looking at Jonathan in our shared bewilderment. But before either of them could respond, Mimi shifted from her position on the floor and pulled herself up, her tearstained eyes wide. I wondered if she'd worked something out, or guessed what was going on.

'What bloody clothes?' I said, taking a step towards Jonathan. 'You were blackmailing Danny to get his *clothes*? Why?'

'Not Danny's clothes,' Jonathan said. 'Yours.'

I let that sink in for a second. Images flickered across my mind. Danny handing Jonathan a bag. His tense, pale face. And one of me, searching for a missing dress in my wardrobe. Blaming Pete for its absence.

I became dimly aware of Mimi next to me shaking her head and muttering 'God, this… this is so fucking sick.'

Janet turned around to look at her husband fully, her attention now entirely on him. 'Please tell me he's making it up.' She said it slowly, in almost a whisper. Richard didn't answer. He seemed to have been rendered speechless.

'I'm not making it up,' Jonathan said, looking scared but determined. 'It's… it's all to do with what he keeps in the attic.'

THIRTY-ONE

Stephanie

THE DAY OF THE EXPLOSION

Whatever I had been expecting to come out of Jonathan's mouth, this wasn't it, and after a day of weird revelations, this surpassed everything else.

'The *attic*?' Janet repeated back.

Jonathan nodded. 'I saw what he has in there. In his study.'

There was silence as everyone stared at Richard, wondering how he was going to respond to this. And he stared back at his wife, a mixture of anxiety and resignation on his face. Then she drew in a breath.

'My God…'

I was feeling very strange now and had an odd sense of things closing in around me. 'Please can someone tell me what he means. What's in the attic?'

Janet was still staring at her husband. 'Richard, you didn't...?'

He remained silent, then eventually looked away from his wife as though he couldn't cope with her unrelenting gaze for any longer. Something odd seemed to be happening to Janet. It was clear from her face that she had an idea where all this was leading and she really didn't like it.

I stepped forward so that I was standing in the space between Janet and Richard. 'What's going on?' I asked. But I got the feeling that no matter what I said, there was no penetrating whatever shared horror was going on between them – some awful realisation that made me feel redundant.

'I think,' Janet said, speaking slowly, as if she was still making up her mind about something, 'that we should do as Richard suggests, and leave all this alone.'

I wasn't going to have that. Not after all this. 'Tell me what's in the attic,' I demanded of Janet.

'It isn't important.' Janet stiffened, the shutters obviously going up. She wasn't going to let me in on this. I saw the resolve settling in her face.

'Well, it obviously is—'

'No, really, Stephanie, it doesn't concern you.' Janet still wasn't looking at me, and for some reason this enraged me more.

'It concerns me and it concerns my boy. My son.'

Silence roared through the kitchen, louder than any of the explosions we'd heard outside earlier. It was deafening. Unbearable.

'Well, I want to see what it is,' I said.

It wasn't a request or a question, but Janet still replied with a firm, 'No.'

'I do too,' Mimi piped up from behind me.

'No!' It was Richard's turn to object this time. He was looking horrified and took a step forward, perhaps to apprehend his daughter. She was too quick for him. Mimi had darted out of the kitchen in the direction of the hallway and I didn't wait around to see her parents' reaction. I bolted after her, racing as fast as I could through the lounge and after her up the stairs. I found her on the landing, fiddling with a cord that trailed down the wall from what appeared to be a trap door in the ceiling, pulling it hard.

'It's stuck,' Mimi said, trying to tug it downwards.

'Let me help,' I said, and the two of us took hold of it, jerking it sharply towards the floor as the sound of the other Franklins became louder as they began to dash after us, pushing each other out the way, scrambling to get up the stairs.

'Mimi, stop it! If you don't—' I heard Janet shout, but her words were drowned out by a metallic screech and then a clang as a miniature ladder-cum-staircase fell into view. I didn't wait for Mimi to let me go first, I just leaped at the rickety steps, which swayed a little as I climbed, heaving myself up into the darkness above.

The attic was very gloomy, with only a small amount of daylight coming in from a circular window to my left. I felt around on the wall for a switch and turned it on. A dim light flickered into life on the far right-hand corner of the narrow room, although it didn't travel very far. In the eerie yellowish glow, I stepped forward, around the neatly stacked boxes and a few suitcases. I wouldn't have time to look through those – I could already hear someone trying to climb up the staircase to join me, with a voice – almost definitely Mimi's – shouting, 'Fuck off, I'm going up there!'

At the far side of the wall, near the tiny window, I saw a dark-brown wooden desk with a MacBook open on its surface, its screen blank. Then something caught my attention at the back of the room. Something pale, poking out from what looked like a sleeping bag that covered a far corner of the attic like a duvet.

I reached for my phone in my pocket and switched on the torch function.

The thing that had caught my attention was a foot.

I froze, not knowing what to do. Part of me wanted to get out of there – to run away from this terrible house and never come back. But a louder voice in my head told me that I would never be able to rest until I knew what – or who – was under that sleeping bag. And I'd come this far.

I had hesitated for too long. The sound of someone pulling themselves up through the trap door filled the air around me and seconds later I was joined by Mimi, standing at my side, staring in the direction of the sharp beam of light from my phone.

'Oh shit. *Shit*,' she said and walked forward.

'Mimi, get away from there!' Janet shouted from the door in the floor. She was part of the way through it, although she seemed to be having more trouble heaving herself up than her nimble daughter had.

Mimi ignored her. She walked towards the sleeping bag, took hold of the corner flap just above the foot, and pulled.

A woman's frame came into view. It was obviously a woman from the shape of the chest and clothes – a full-length, short-sleeved dress with deep-pink flowers on it. Identical to the one that had gone missing from my wardrobe last year.

He made me ask Danny for clothes… Your clothes.

Jonathan's words seemed to echo around me as I moved closer, terrified of what else I might see. Who was this woman?

And then Mimi said something that made no sense.

'Fuck, this must have cost a fortune.' She bent down and took hold of the body and heaved it up, so the face came into view. And I saw what it was.

It wasn't a real body. It was a dolly, or a dummy, or some weird mixture of the two, with a blank, emotionless face, and arms and legs of a realistic but still fake material.

'Mimi, put it down,' Janet said breathlessly, pulling herself to her feet.

'Ahhh, fuck!' Mimi shouted, in apparent disgust. I looked down and saw her foot had knocked over a stack of little boxes.

Boxes of condoms and a small bottle.

'Put it down!' shrieked Janet.

'That's *my* dress it's wearing,' I said, leaning forward to grab at it, but Janet dived forward and pulled me back.

'It's nothing,' she said. 'It's… it's…'

'Perverted, that's what!' Mimi yelled. 'Wake up, Mum. You've married some sick fuck who dresses up human-sized dolls in the attic and—'

'Stop it!' Janet screamed.

The seconds that followed became a jagged confusion in my brain.

Only later would I be able to put some order to them. But at that moment, there was such an intense rush to the whole situation – with my grabbing at the dress, the one I'd accused my now dead husband of losing, and Janet screaming at me and her daughter – that my brain seemed to stop processing things properly. Which is probably why I didn't realise fully where the pain was coming from in my arm, and then my shoulder, and then, finally, as I hit the floor, my head.

Then everything shut off, like a television that had lost power, and things were quiet at last.

THIRTY-TWO

Stephanie

NOW

I think I came to briefly in the ambulance, but I can't remember much about it, other than someone saying, 'You hit your head.' Even though I was almost entirely out of it, I remember feeling a little irritated by the patronising tone of voice, like I was a patient with memory loss who didn't know what year we were in or who the prime minister was.

Funnily enough, back when I first arrived at the hospital, they did actually ask me all those questions to check my cognitive skills and general recall were still functioning without issue. I could give them the answers they wanted to the basic stuff – I even told them I thought the prime minister was a bit of a prick. None of that mattered much to me though, because something about the whole situation was very, very wrong.

I knew it as soon as the nurse told me that I'd been taken to hospital after falling over in the street just outside my home. Neighbours had supposedly seen me fall and taken me into their house, and when I'd passed out completely they'd phoned an ambulance, worried about concussion or a brain injury.

'The good news is that surgery wasn't necessary, although the arm and shoulder fracture will be a bit painful while it heals,' the nurse said, giving my uninjured arm a squeeze. 'You're just so lucky you have such *nice* neighbours.'

Sitting here now, a day later, I mull the story over in my head as the TV by the bed of the person next to me plays out a news report on its weak, tinny speakers.

The explosion at the power station. The massive clear-up operation is now underway.

Memories float in and out of clarity in my mind.

Me, stepping out of my house and the sky dark with smoke.

Some rubble on the road.

Had I tripped over then and banged my head?

Memories of waking up on the Franklins' sofa do seem real to me.

Trying to make sense of them feels like trying to catch fog in my hands. My head aches so I stop and just lie still.

The rest of the late afternoon of that second day is filled with dizziness and sleep. Nightmares cloud my spinning mind. I even tell a doctor about them. 'Like hallucinations, they are,' I say to him, while he peruses some papers about my head injury. I get the feeling the whole thing bores him a bit. Not life-threatening enough to be of interest, perhaps. He tells me I'll feel better soon and then wanders away.

As the light outside dims into an unusually beautiful sunset, bathing the ward in a soothing yellow glow, I begin to think of my boy, and of Pete. And how there won't be anyone to visit me or take me home. I'll have to get a taxi, when the time comes. I'll have to put myself to bed and wake up stiff and aching the next morning, in need of painkillers, with nobody there to bring me a hot drink or tell me everything is going to be OK.

It's while I'm thinking about the boys that something sounds in my head, like a little alarm bell.

Danny.

Something about Danny.

It's the same feeling I used to get when I was a teenager if I'd forgotten to do a bit of schoolwork or left my pencil case at home. The feeling of something incomplete, forgotten, not finished. A task left undone. And another image floats into my mind then too. An image of another boy, sitting on his bed, crying.

It's Jonathan Franklin.

And Mimi, too, crying in the kitchen.

And the words… chilling words.

It's about what he keeps in the attic.

Like a key, those words unlock a different sensation. The feeling of hands on me. The pressure of them. Pushing me. And then falling. Falling.

I sit up, causing a sharp pain in my arm and making me gasp.

'You shouldn't move too quickly, you know,' a nurse says to me as if I'm three years old. 'And your visitor is back. Now you're awake…' She turns to talk to someone just out of my field of view. 'She's woken up now. Just here.'

I hear footsteps, and then she comes into view.

Janet Franklin.

She's even brought grapes.

'Stephanie, how are you feeling?' she says, in a not dissimilar voice to the nurse who's just left us. 'Are you in pain?'

I look up at her, struggling to speak. While she waits, Janet takes the plastic wrapper off the grapes and lays the box down on the table near my bed. 'You gave us such a fright,' she says, still in her smooth, slightly patronising tone. 'You had a bump on the head, outside in the street. Do you remember?'

I open my mouth and close it again. Was she really doing this? I feel a creeping wave of disbelief and revulsion spread through me. She couldn't... She wouldn't...

'I see you're still a bit confused,' she says, smiling and shaking her head.

'I'm not confused.' I say the words very quietly, but even amidst the bustle of the hospital ward, she can hear them. And I see her face harden.

'It's only natural,' she says, her eyes now fixed on mine, 'to feel a little bit overwhelmed when you've had such an ordeal. I couldn't bear you being alone, so I just had to come and see you. Check you're remembering everything clearly.'

I take a deep breath. 'I wasn't in the street. I was in the attic. We were in there. Me, you, and Mimi. And we'd found—'

'In the attic?' she says, cutting across me, a frown now troubling her face, the smile replaced with a look of apparent concern. 'No, no, Stephanie, you've got the whole thing very muddled in your head. Nobody's been in the attic in our house for years.'

'But,' I splutter, 'Richard's study is in there. It's where he works.'

She's still shaking her head. 'We don't really use it much. Anyway, you didn't even go upstairs. We'd only just helped you into the house after your fall when you collapsed and we had to phone 999.'

I can feel my breathing starting to quicken. She isn't going to do this. I'm not going to let her do this. 'Did you push me?' I keep the words quiet but emphatic, determined that she hear them clearly. I don't want to sound hysterical or confused. I want her to know I am giving her this chance to explain properly what happened.

It doesn't surprise me when she opts not to take it.

'*Push* you? My dear, I was inside the house when you fell. And you were across the street. Nobody pushed you. You fell and hurt yourself. We've all been so worried about you.' Her voice stays sweet and smooth, but there's something else buried within it. Something hard and cold, like she's embedded ice inside each word.

Then a memory arrives in my mind without warning, like a vivid scene being replayed before my eyes. And suddenly I know what to say.

'Who are Alexa and Logan?'

It gets a reaction. Her eyes, which had been cool and steady, now widen quickly, then narrow.

I carry on, before she can speak.

'I saw a note you wrote to them. Or one of your practice attempts. I suppose you thought you'd binned it? Kept it out of sight? Why did you need to go to stay with them? Why did you need time to heal?'

She takes a deep breath and says, 'I don't know where you're getting all this from, Stephanie, but I'm not ashamed to say that I was... well, I needed a small operation last year and I stayed with them. Some friends. I didn't want to bother my husband and children. Didn't want to worry them. So I just said I was staying with them for a week, just to... um... see the sights around... um... Berwick-upon-Tweed. Not that much to see, but they do have an Elizabethan Wall, which is worth a look, I suppose...'

She seems to have drifted off in her mind a little because her expression is now glazed. Then it snaps back to me, full of a fierce, precise attention, as if a switch had just re-activated her.

'So what did you expect to be able to do with this knowledge, Stephanie? Talk me round to believing your bizarre fantasies? Or perhaps even blackmail me? Threaten to tell my husband secrets you suppose you have about my health? What a troubled person you are. I really do feel sorry for you.'

She stares at me. I stare at her. We stay like that, looking at each other for what feels like an eternity. Her eyes never leave mine and mine never leave hers. Eventually I can't bear the idea of being in her company for a single second longer. 'You're monsters,' I say through clenched teeth. 'You and your husband. And I pity your children.'

Her face twitches ever so slightly when I say those final words. For a moment, I think she's going to say something. A cruel retort, perhaps, or further feigned concern. But she doesn't. She just clutches her handbag to her side, walks around the bed and out of sight, leaving me alone.

I wait until she's definitely gone. I couldn't bear a forceful confrontation – not now. And besides, Janet won't run off anywhere. She'll try to keep up the front, go back to normal. Once I'm sure she's safely down the corridor and out of earshot, I catch the eye of a nurse walking down the ward with a water jug.

'Excuse me,' I say, as loudly as I can manage.

She looks over to me and offers a kind smile. 'Can I get you anything?'

'Yes,' I say, giving a small nod. 'I want to speak to the police.'

THIRTY-THREE

Stephanie

A FEW WEEKS LATER

Detective Constable Rebecca Abbott sits at my kitchen countertop, sipping a mug of coffee. She's surprisingly young – about my age, perhaps even younger – but has an air of authority about her that I find reassuring.

'I know this isn't the news you want to hear,' she says, 'but I'm afraid my hands are tied. There isn't enough evidence in the medical reports on your injuries to go against what the Franklins – the only witnesses – are saying. It could all fit perfectly with what they're claiming.' I open my mouth to object, but she raises a hand to stop me. 'I know your views on their story. And between you and me, I think they do show signs of, well, lying, but there just isn't enough proof to carry on looking into it. Trust me, I've made the case to my superiors, but after everything's taken into account, it comes down to a your-word-against-theirs situation.'

I'm trying to stop myself getting angry. After all, DC Abbott is only doing her job, but I can't help but feel furious that they're going to get off scot-free. 'Can't you get a warrant to search their attic? To find that weird sex doll Richard Franklin's keeping up there?'

With a grim, regretful smile, DC Abbott shakes her head. 'Stephanie, we don't need to get a search warrant. They volunteered to show us around. If there was anything to see, they would have cleared it out and disposed of it long before we got there, and we don't have the resources to go through dump sites or dig things up or track their movements to see where it could be. There's just not enough evidence that a crime has been committed. And I hate to say it, but even if it all happened the way you said, the Franklins could easily just say you fell down the attic doorway yourself, without any foul play.'

'If there wasn't any foul play, why would they all be lying? Re-interview the kids. Mimi and Jonathan hate their parents; it's obvious. They'd crack, I *know* it. They're sick of being controlled. I'm amazed Mimi hasn't already.'

DC Abbott is doing her sad nothing-is-going-to-change face. 'This is the end of the road. I'm sorry. If there was some new compelling evidence, then we could take another look at it all. But for now, we're a bit stuck.'

She finishes her coffee and leaves soon after.

I spend the rest of the afternoon cleaning the kitchen, even though it's already close to spotless. Then I take my iPad from the countertop where it's been charging and go to sit in the lounge. Settling down on the sofa, I tap onto the currently open tab and scroll down, glancing at my Facebook Messenger conversation with Myanna. Even though I haven't spoken to her for a while, I've decided it could be good to have an investigative journalist as a friend at the moment. Especially if the police can't help me. I switch over to my web browser which is open at a property website for a house in New Zealand. It's a bit too big for me, I think, even bigger than this place. But it's a potential, so I bookmark it and go back to the search results.

It's time to leave Kent. Leave England. Start again somewhere else. Everything that has happened over the past year has stained it for me. It was a place of happy memories, wonderful memories, but they've all mixed in with the bad to the point where I struggle to see through it all. I need space. Distance. A chance to hit reset, without constant reminders of times past – and reminders of what could have been – waiting at every turn.

I'm about to look at a smaller property for sale in St Mary's Bay, Auckland when an email notification pops up at the top of the screen. And the sender's address causes a jolt within me. I quickly navigate to the mail app, tap on the new arrival, and begin to read.

Hi Stephanie.

I got your email address from Mum's phone in her contact list marked 'Rugby club mums'. Hope it's OK to message you.

Basically, to cut a long story short, Mum and Dad paid me and Jonathan to keep quiet. They threatened us, and bribed us, and told us it would ruin all our lives if we told the truth about what happened that day. We went along with it. To tell you the truth, that whole day was so fucked up I didn't really have it in me to fight with them anymore so I just let them win. I'm really sorry for that, but I haven't been able to sleep or concentrate since, so I wanted to send you a message to say you're not mad. It did all happen, no matter what Mum says.

I saw what she did. I saw her push you. I didn't want to believe it at first. I tried to convince myself I hadn't seen it, but I've hated Mum for ages and now that she's made me lie to the police, she's gone too far. She must have realised what was up there just before you discovered it. I heard her and Dad arguing later that day about how she'd found history on his computer of him looking at certain sex product websites online, and how he'd promised her he'd stumbled on to it. It's all pretty sick, really, the thought of him buying that doll and dressing it up to look like you. You must have been freaked when you saw it. Jonathan knew about it already, of course. He'd seen Dad coming down from the attic and locking it behind him on a day he'd thought we were all out, so he stole the key and went to look. He should have been a bit smarter with the whole blackmail thing. Realised what Dad said were empty threats and just threatened to tell Mum everything. I've told him this but I don't want to be too hard on him. I don't think I've been that nice to him for a while and didn't realise how much he was grieving after Danny's death.

The two of us have been speaking about what happened and we've both agreed that we'll back you up. We'll say whatever you want us to. No matter what they do to us. For Danny.

I'm not sure if anything will come of it or if it's enough to put Mum and Dad in prison. It probably isn't. But the fuss of the whole thing will serve them right. Show them their fucked-up attempts to have the perfect family are well and truly over.

Oh, and Jonathan says he's so sorry about what happened between him and Danny, and that he told him about you and my Dad. He says he hates himself that Danny died before he could make things better between them. And he's truly sorry. And so am I, for everything that's happened.

Best,

Mimi.

I reread the email three times. Then I go and make myself some tea before returning to the lounge. Choosing my words carefully, I write a concise but heartfelt reply to Mimi, thanking her for being so honest and apologising to her for how the day I visited turned out.

Then I click the forward button on the email and enter the address for Detective Constable Rebecca Abbott.

I will make my move to New Zealand eventually. But I think I can stay in Kent a little while longer. I have a few things to settle before I go.

Danny

I wake up about 2am, lying on my bed, shivering from the cold. The duvet isn't on me, so I pull myself out of bed to sort out the covers and get in properly. I notice Mum has left something in a mug on my desk near my bed – probably hot chocolate, I think, nudging it away from the edge, but it's lost its heat so I don't drink any. Everything seems to be very still and quiet in the house and in the street outside, the golden fairy lights on the Franklins' house opposite are twinkling through the branches of the trees. It feels a bit like I've missed Christmas. Missed all the fun and the excitement. The whole world just seemed to be filled with pain and worry, all of it flowing out of a terrible wound-like fear inside me.

And then my phone buzzes from inside my trousers

on the floor and I see the screen light up. I bend down and pull it out, noticing that there are seven WhatsApp messages. All from Jonathan.

Hey, I need to speak to you. It's important.

I just saw you all arrive home. Can I come over? I really need to speak, don't want to message, just tell me when I can see you.

Please, can you just sneak out for a walk or something, I need to talk to you, it's good news.

Message me when you see this in the morning.

The last message has only just arrived. Does that mean Jonathan is about to go to sleep? If I want to reply, to find out what he's talking about, I have to be quick. I start to type:

I was asleep. Awake now. But I don't think you should come over. Parents might hear.

I see his status switch to 'Online' and he starts to type. His reply says:

I'll be really quiet. I can climb up the balcony to your window.

I think about it for a second. 'Good news' he had said in his message. I can't bear the idea of going to sleep and not finding out what has got him so excited. I type back:

OK

He manages it as quietly as he said, climbing up onto the balcony and up to my window with only a slight rustle of leaves. There he stands, looking in at me. And me at him.

'Come in,' I whisper, motioning to him. He moves forwards and enters my room properly, taking care to open the doors carefully and not make unnecessary noise.

'What's going on?' I ask, sitting on the side of my bed as he sits down on my desk chair.

'It's about... everything.'

I get worried then. 'You're not going to ask me to steal anything else of my mum's, because I—'

He cuts me off. 'No, no, it's something good. I think. The other day me, Mum, and Mimi were going to go out for a look in the shops. January sales and stuff, you know. Mimi was keen, but I wasn't really bothered. We were leaving Dad in the house alone.'

He pauses and takes in a breath, then bites his lip. He does this when he's nervous about saying something. I'm starting to notice things about him I never did before. His little ticks, his habits. Things that piss me off. And things that make me want to give him a hug.

'Anyway,' he carries on, 'Dad thought he was home by himself. I think Mum and Mimi just forgot to tell him I'd bailed on the shopping trip. I had a bit of a headache and didn't feel like being shoved around by idiots in Bluewater. I was in my room when I heard a creak on the landing. Dad had gone up into the attic. He was in there for quite a while, nearly an hour. Then he came back down. A bit later he went off to a squash game with one of his friends and I was home alone. I—'

I feel my eyes widen. 'You went up into the attic? What was up there?'

He seems to be deciding something, now biting at his lips so hard I'm surprised they didn't bleed. 'Don't worry about that – nothing really terrible or illegal. I don't think you should know. I don't think you'd *want* to know if I told you, but that's not the point: the point is, there's *no way* he's going to blackmail me or you about anything ever again. I now know something he's never going to want anyone to find out, especially Mum.'

I frown and think about this for a moment. 'So what are you saying is...'

He leans forward and takes hold of my hands. 'I'm saying you need to stop worrying. Stop looking like the whole world is going to collapse in on you at any moment. *Everything's* fine.'

I stay quiet for a moment, then say, 'It's really shit what your dad did. You telling him what was bothering you and him using it against you like that.'

Jonathan nods slowly. 'I know. But my dad's never going to do anything with those pics or videos – I don't think he really would have done anyway. He'd find it too embarrassing to show anyone. I'm sorry I gave in to him so easily and I'm sorry I... I wasn't strong enough... for you. I shouldn't have put you through all this.'

I look down at his hands on mine. They seem to glow a little from the pale light coming in from the balcony. I feel the cold breeze flow in and I shiver a little. I move back onto the bed and pull up the covers over my legs and say to him, 'Do you want to get in?'

His eyebrows go up. Surprised. Hopeful. 'You'd still want to? You don't... you don't hate me?'

I shake my head. 'No. I'd never hate you. I...' I find I can't get out the rest of the sentence. But Jonathan seems to understand. He gets up from the chair. 'I don't think I should stay. We're going to see family friends in Fulham tomorrow morning, leaving early.'

I nod and smile at him. He stays still for a moment, his body turned towards the balcony doors, but his face still on me, as if he can't make up his mind whether to say something. Eventually he says, 'Was it real? What we did. I know... I know you said we couldn't ever really be properly... I know you're not... But at the party, when we were, you know... kissing and, well, it felt real to me. Or was it all just, I don't know, in my head?'

I know what he's asking me. I know what he wants to hear. And it surprises me when I realise I want to hear the same thing too. It's strange but, realising that fact finally helps me make sense of why I've felt so awful all these past months. It isn't the fear of discovery or being embarrassed by whatever hold Richard Franklin has over us both. It's the thought of losing Jonathan as a friend.

I get up out of bed, walk straight over to where he stands and hug him. He hugs me back. And suddenly, it's like everything's right in the world once again.

'It was real,' I say quietly, pulling away from him and staring into his eyes. 'But we need to talk about things. We never got a chance to, but I think we should. Because it's important I don't lead you on with you thinking that we could—'

'I get it, honestly,' he says, smiling. 'I get that it was a one-off. I get that you'll never feel the same. And it's OK. It really is.'

'But that doesn't mean it wasn't... important,' I say, choosing my words as carefully as I can. 'And that doesn't mean I don't love you. In my own way.'

He smiles at me again, and I know he understands. And instead of feeling disappointment, or that I've let him down, it's like we're on the verge of a new phase, a new time together, one where we figure out where we stand as friends. Because we will always be friends, regardless of what happened in the past. And this unlocks a feeling of excitement within me. The feeling you get when you wake up and you realise it's the Christmas break, or you're about to go to the airport for a holiday. That feeling of infinite possibilities, suddenly stretching before you. The gift of time.

'I need to go but I really want to stay,' he says, and I laugh quietly.

'There'll be other nights,' I say, 'and other days. And weeks. And months. And years. But we can start with just tomorrow night. You can stay over properly.'

He seems to like this plan, and gives my shoulder a little squeeze before saying, 'Are you going round Scotty's for band practice? I know we've kind of, well, stopped, but he's been on at me to start again. Please come.'

I think about tomorrow, a day that seems strangely far away, even though, at 2.30am, we're practically there already. 'My dad said he wants to take me for dinner and the cinema. So I could go for a bit and leave early. Then when we get back you can come round.'

'That sounds like a plan,' he says.

Then he disappears off, back the way he came, climbing nimbly down to the ground. When he reaches the pavement he waves. And I wave at him. Then I go back to bed, feeling as if I've been transformed into someone new, like suddenly everything has turned from darkness to brilliant gold.

There's so much to look forward to now.

Acknowledgments

I'd like to thank all the readers who picked up my four previous books and took time to recommend them to friends and leave reviews online. I'm enormously grateful.

Special thanks to my family: Leno, for such wonderful kindness and encouragement, my parents, sisters Molly and Amy, granny and uncle, and to Rebecca and Tom and all my close friends. All your support is more wonderful than I can put into words. Also, I'd like to add that *The Locked Attic* features some parents who aren't great examples of how to raise teenagers and luckily I have a mum and dad who are the complete opposite of this and always encouraged me to follow my dreams.

I would like to thank my wonderful agent Joanna Swainson and everyone at Hardman & Swainson for being such a brilliant team. Huge thanks to Bethan Morgan, Charlotte Ledger, Sara Roberts, Emma Petfield, Lucy Bennett, Claire Fenby and everyone at One More Chapter and HarperCollins. I consider myself incredibly lucky to be included in such an amazing publisher family.

Many thanks to Dr. Veronica Spencer at the University of Southampton for reading a very early draft of this novel and for being so generous with time, thoughts and feedback.

A massive thank you to all my former colleagues at Waterstones and to all the booksellers across the world who have been so amazing at pressing my novels into the hands of readers and to the authors who so generously read early proofs of The Locked Attic. The journey to this book being on the shelf has been a long one (I started its initial drafting in 2014) and it's so exciting to see it go out into the world and with such amazing support behind it. I'm extremely grateful.

Now read on for an exclusive bonus chapter telling the story of what happened when Danny met Titus at Marwood Manor...

You can learn more about the secret history of Titus in *The Dinner Guest*...

Danny

I don't want to go to Dad's friends' house in the country, but Mum puts her foot down when I tell her I want to stay in my room at home.

'No,' she says, simply, 'you're not staying here alone,' and then goes off to have one of her hushed-voices conversations with Dad. They've been doing that a lot lately. And to be honest I can't blame them.

I bring my AirPods with me, planning to listen to music on the drive from Kent to Oxford, but I end up putting on a *Harry Potter* audiobook and listening to it quietly in the back of the car. It feels comforting, familiar, like I'm ten years old again, when I used to listen to each book over and over before I went to sleep.

I end up pausing the book when the car starts to turn up the long driveway of the house. Mum and Dad have

343

been here without me and apparently I came here once when I was very young, but I hardly remember it.

As Dad parks the car and we step out into the cold December air, I look up at the vast shape of the mansion towering above us and wonder why the family don't rent it out for horror movies. It would be the perfect setting for some haunted house story.

Once we're inside, Mum and Dad get talking to a bunch of people I have no interest in speaking to, then introduce me to a boy called Titus – a guy of about my age, with short blonde hair and dressed in a white open-collar shirt and skinny black trousers. I wasn't listening when they explained who he was or how he is related to our hosts Lord and Lady Ashton or Dad's friend Rupert, so I feel a bit taken aback when it was suggested he take me on a tour of the house.

'Righty-ho, come on Daniel!' he says, practically gathering me up in his arms like I'm a nervous child and he a kindly teacher.

I'm steered away from the main gaggle of guests and out into the entrance hall we'd come through. It's quieter in here, now most of the guests have gone through into the library or what appears to be a main lounge or dining area.

'Everything down here is a bit boring,' Titus says, 'so

I'll show you the upper levels and some of the secret passageways. They're always fun.'

He makes it sound as if we're in The Famous Five or something and I'm about to nod, just to be polite, when someone calls over to us from the large staircase. A very attractive girl wearing a tight-fitting deep-purple dress is making her way down. I get the feeling she is a year or two older than I am, or maybe that's just down to the confident way she holds herself.

'Disaster averted!' she says, beaming over at us. 'I had another pair in my bag.'

'Pippa lost an earring and the world was about to end,' Titus explains to me, rolling his eyes and grinning. 'Pippa, this is Daniel, son of Rupert's old friend Pete and... I'm so sorry, your mother's name...?'

It's impossible for me not to be distracted by the new arrival's beauty and for a moment I'm not sure what Titus is asking me, then things click into place and I stammer, 'Oh... err... Stephanie.'

Whether Pippa knows who my parents are or not, she doesn't give anything away – she just smiles and does a half-embrace-half-kiss-on-the-cheek thing I find quietly mortifying.

'Pippa's my girlfriend,' Titus says. He doesn't exactly say it as code for *so back the fuck off* but there is an underlying hardness to his words, almost implying a degree of ownership. I'm not sure I like it.

'So you're... Lord and Lady Ashton's granddaughter, is that right?' I ask, feeling like I should contribute something to this awkward little meeting.

'Yes, Daddy's gone and Mummy's in America, so I spend most of my time here these days. Although I do pop back and forth to the States for work when my studies allow. All a bit of a bore, but it's important to make one's mark now, isn't it? When you're still young. '

I nod, as if I know what she means.

We eventually end up going upstairs, as Titus had suggested, and he shows me into a room on one of the gallery landings that looks like a kind-of upstairs lounge.

'This used to be a bedroom,' he explains, 'but my dad allowed me to get the bed taken out and convert it into a cinema and games room.'

A large cream sofa is situated along one of the walls facing an extremely large television mounted on the other.

'Do sit down,' Titus says, gesturing to the sofa.

'Gosh, I'm gasping,' Pippa says, and wanders over to a small table in the corner by some bookshelves where a collection of bottles are gathered. 'Daniel, you haven't got a drink? That's terribly slipshod of you, Titus? Here we go, have some wine.'

'There's champagne,' Titus mutters, sitting down and turning to look at me.

'Titus, literally *nobody* drinks champagne these days,' Pippa says with theatrical disdain.

'Err, I think you'll find literally *everybody* downstairs is doing just that,' Titus responds.

'Nonsense,' Pippa says, then winks at me, smiling a little. She offers me a large glass of what appears to be red wine.

I sip at it and say, 'Great, thanks,' and she looks satisfied. It tastes vile in my mouth and suddenly I'm wishing I'd faked flu or something just so I could have stayed home and not been in this strange place with this odd couple. It's like they are play-acting at being grown ups, as though they are in their thirties rather than their late teens.

'I shouldn't have too much, really,' Pippa says, dragging over a separate small chair and dropping herself into it. 'I should really get some work done tomorrow.'

'Pippa's a journalist,' Titus says. 'She writes for a US blogging site – gives them a British perspective on things.'

'Ah, nice,' I say. 'Err… what sort of stuff do you write about?' As soon as I say it, I worry the word 'stuff'

347

sounds a little immature or disrespectful, but Pippa doesn't seem to notice.

'Oh, lots of things,' she says, then launches into a lengthy description of some of her latest stories, rattling off the names of pieces she's recently authored and which ones had ended up 'trending' or 'going totally fucking viral'. 'It's mostly stuff about just the sheer fucking nonsense of our age,' she says, taking a healthy mouthful of her wine. 'As in our times. The world. Politics.'

She starts to give examples of why she thinks the world has 'turned literally upside-fucking-down' and I sit and nod while Titus murmurs 'hmm' and 'so true' every now and then from his seat next to me.

I don't exactly disagree with everything Pippa is saying – a lot of it is stuff I regard to be general common sense. But it is the *way* she is saying them I don't like. All posh and superior, as if every other person who might hold a different view to her is a total idiot and it is her job to show them how stupid they've been all their lives.

As the minutes tick by, she becomes less and less likeable.

'I get the feeling Pippa's going to be the celebrity in our marriage,' Titus says, grinning over at her.

'Marriage?' I ask, confused. 'Are you... you're not married, are you?'

Titus laughs. 'Not yet. But we're engaged. Sorry, I really should have said fiancée earlier rather than girlfriend.'

Pippa beams and holds out her hand.

For a moment I have no idea what she is doing, but then I notice the large ring on her finger. It looks sparkly and expensive. 'Oh... err... very nice.'

'I know, it is rather,' she says, smiling over at her husband-to-be. Titus grins back, his smug expression distorting his good looks. I suddenly feel the urge to hit him.

'Are you OK?' Pippa asks, staring at me as if concerned I'm ill.

'Oh, yeah, sorry,' I say, realising I may have allowed my emotions to show too visibly. 'So... err... you're Rupert's stepson?' I ask, hoping to get the topic back onto the family tree, presuming it will be more neutral territory and I can semi-zone out if it gets too dull. But to my surprise, I seem to have hit upon a controversial subject.

I see Titus and Pippa exchange looks and then Titus says, 'I suppose you could say that, yes. My family situation is... difficult.' There are a few moments of silence, then Titus says, slowly, 'I don't know if your parents have told you, or if you saw it in the papers, but a little while ago there was a murder in a house in Chelsea. Carlyle Square.'

I frown. 'I think… yeah, I think I remember my dad mentioning that at one point and that he knew… oh fuck, I'm sorry, was that your…'

'My adopted father who died, yes,' Titus says, nodding. His eyes are focused on the drink in his hand. I feel the atmosphere in the room has suddenly changed. I wish I'd never brought up the subject – wish I'd left them chatting about their wedding plans. 'It's tainted so many things. Impossible to get the stain of it off. Pippa and I first got together properly at a party here. Gorgeous summer evening, it was. But of course, our delightful meeting was soon overshadowed by bloodshed.'

I get the feeling he is rather enjoying this little monologue and he says the final word with emphasis, almost revelling in it. The effect is unsettling.

'It was a tragic ordeal,' Titus says, his finger now tracing the rim of his wine glass. Then he turns his head, his eyes looking straight into mine. His voice becomes quieter, and I feel a prickle of nerves at the back of my neck. 'Do you know,' he says, 'I could tell you things about that night… *such* things… that could bring this whole party, this whole house, tumbling down around us…'

'Titus,' Pippa says. I can see that she's gone tense, her

relaxed posture now replaced with alertness. Her tone is unmistakable. It's clearly supposed to be a warning. A warning to stop there. Not say too much. Not bring this stranger – me – any further into their web of secrets.

A loud bang suddenly breaks the tension in the room. I jump and look around to see a shower of sparks outside the window.

'Oh fuck, is it midnight already?' Pippa says, looking at her phone. 'No… they're early.'

'I think it's just a few tester ones to keep the guests on their toes,' Titus says, his eyes off me now, his voice full of the casual good humour he'd had previously. He gets up, stretches a little and wanders over to the window.

A rap on the door then makes us all start.

'Titus, mate, you there?' The door opens and a guy of around Titus's age comes in, although he's much taller and has darker hair.

'Fuck off, Ambrose,' Pippa says, although her tone is playful rather than harsh. 'We're not in the mood to play today.'

I don't know what she means by 'play' and I'm not sure I want to.

I notice Ambrose smirking in response. 'I see you found a fresh new conquest for the evening,' he nods over at me. 'I must say I'm rather offended you didn't come and find *me*.'

'You had your fun last time,' Titus says. 'And Daniel here is having a drink with us. Nothing else. Well, not unless he wants anything else.' Titus flicks his eyebrows at me.

'I don't... think...' I stammer, looking at him, and then Pippa.

'Oh, ignore him, he's only playing with you,' Pippa says. 'We'll get to know you a bit more first, don't worry.'

'Danny, what my lovely fiancée is trying to say, oh-so-politely, is that... well, if you'd like to join us in a... err... little New Year treat later, we'd be very open to your company.'

I have no idea what to say to this and a pin-drop silence follows.

'I apologise for my manners.' The new arrival holds out his hand. I get the feeling he's coming to my rescue. 'I'm Ambrose, one of Titus's school friends.'

I can't work out what's happening. I don't know if Titus and Pippa are being serious – if they actually are asking if I want to get into bed with them or something like that – or if this is an awful practical joke and I'm a figure of fun to them.

From these thoughts, others spiral.

Feelings of humiliation.

Blood-chilling embarrassment.

It's like everything inside my mind is shifting, edging

to the left, making the room sway. The guilt that I've been carrying around in me is now building to something resembling dread, fear, and panic.

I look up at Ambrose's face and for a second I'm convinced I see Scotty's stupid grin, his mischievous eyes, his hands clasped around an iPhone as he aims it at me. And then, worse than this, I feel Jonathan is here, somewhere in the shadows, watching me, with these strange, shallow, people, in a house I don't know. And I feel like I'm hurting him all over again.

'Err, mate,' Ambrose is saying, his outstretched hand still in front of me. 'Hello? Are you still with us?'

'Are you sure you're OK, Daniel?' Pippa's voice says from next to me.

'Yeah…' I say quickly, 'I'm fine… I need to go…' I stand up, stumbling a little, feeling dizzy.

'Are you sure everything's fine, mate?' Ambrose asks.

'Yeah, sure, I just… need to find my parents.'

'We should probably be heading down too,' Titus says, yawning, coming over towards us. 'We'll have to rain-check our little bit of naughtiness, my love,' he says to Pippa, then turns to his friend. 'We'll have to see if Ambrose is around later and still awake enough.'

'You haven't got long until the midnight countdown,' Ambrose says, ignoring the barely-veiled invitation and looking at his watch.

'I'll see you guys later,' I mutter, and turn to leave.

'Titus, show Daniel out,' Pippa says from the chair, making no effort to move herself.

'I'll come with you,' Ambrose says. 'Come on Daniel, let's go back to the fray and leave these two bohemians to their deadly sins.'

I go out onto the landing with Ambrose, who lays a hand on my shoulder as soon as we've closed the door behind us.

'Mate, you've honestly gone as white as a sheet. Are you sure you're OK?' I'm not sure how to answer this, and leave the gap a little too long, as Ambrose hurriedly says, 'Let's get you some water and a sit down.'

He seems to know the house well and leads me down some corridors away from the well-lit landing area through to a very grand looking bathroom, complete with both a walk-in shower and an enormous bath with gold taps.

'Take a seat on there,' Ambrose says, steering me towards a bench-like seat along the side of the wall, with a pile of clean towels neatly folded and stacked at the end of it.

Ambrose takes up a glass from the side of the sink, remarking that it looks clean as he fills it with tap water.

'Drink some of this,' he says. 'Now, do you want to talk about what's wrong?'

I do as I am told with the water, but shake my head.

'I can't,' I say, 'It's too... too weird. And I don't know you... I'm sorry, that sounded rude.'

Ambrose lets out a short laugh. 'I can do weird. As you can probably tell from what you just heard, I'm no stranger to the odd dalliance with those two. So go on, shoot.'

So I start talking.

And I talk and talk and suddenly it's all pouring out of me and I'm telling this complete stranger everything that's been happening over the past months. Everything about me kissing Jonathan and then doing more than that, then it all going wrong with Scotty and the photos and all the fucked up stuff with Jonathan's dad and my mum. I find myself starting to cry as I get to that part.

Ambrose doesn't interrupt, but when I become properly upset he just lays a hand on my arm. It feels nice, and I'm glad when he keeps it there as I finish my story, telling him how what had just happened with Titus and Pippa had brought it all back.

'Well,' Ambrose says, once I've got to the end and there's nothing more to tell, 'goodness me, that's a lot.'

'I'm sorry,' I say, instantly feeling embarrassed for sharing so much with him.

'No, no, not at all, I didn't mean that,' he says, 'I just... well, first and foremost, you shouldn't let yourself or your friend be blackmailed. That needs to be sorted. If I were you, just tell your mum everything. She'll figure it out. It might be embarrassing and bloody awkward, but it's better than letting it torture you like this.'

I nod, knowing what he says is true.

'And second, you need to tell your friend that you're heterosexual. It's fine you've experimented a bit and that doesn't take away from the importance of that. But I can tell you from experience that the novelty and excitement of experimentation can wear off. In the end, it's not about novelty and excitement, it's about being comfortable with the person you're sharing a bed with. And if that person needs to be a girl, not a boy, you need to be honest with your mate about that. If he loves you like he says he does, he will understand.'

I nod again. There's something in Ambrose's calm but firm tone that's soothing and reassuring.

'Give me your phone for a sec,' he says. 'Unlock it first.' I take it out of my pocket and do as he instructs. He takes it and taps away for a moment, then hands it back. 'Here you go. That's my number. I'm sure you've got other friends you can talk to, but if you ever want to message or chat with someone a bit removed from your every day life, I'm your man. Message whenever you want.'

'Thank you,' I say, pocketing the phone and wiping

my eyes. 'Thank you for being so nice to me.' I worry it sounds pathetic to say it, like something a little child would say, but Ambrose smiles in response.

'I hate seeing someone looking all at sea and confused. And... well, Rupert – he's my older cousin – he once told me about a time when he was having a Christmas party here, back when he was a uni student on winter break. He says he realised one of his guests, who had been brought along by others, was very much out of her depth and needed someone to be on her side and come to her rescue. Her friends had all gone off and left her. So he decided to be that person. I've never forgotten that. And... well... I hope I've been that person for you today.'

I give him a weak smile. 'You have. You really have. And I've only met your cousin for a second or two downstairs, but he seems like a really nice bloke.'

'He is,' Ambrose says, straightening up. 'It's remarkable how normal he is considering his weird upbringing. As a child, his parents kept him trapped away in one of the top-most rooms upstairs, apparently, convinced he had some terrible light sensitivity problem. A misdiagnosis, thankfully. But he lives a perfectly normal life now and seems really happy with Charles, his new husband.'

'I'm glad,' I say. And I mean it.

'Well, I'm so sorry, but we're very close to midnight, and I really should—'

'Sorry, yeah, sure, go,' I say, standing up as well. 'I might not... I might stay here. Or wander about the house, if that's OK. I don't feel like seeing everyone downstairs at the moment.'

'Do whatever you please,' Ambrose says. 'It's not my house, of course, but I doubt anyone would mind you exploring. Although, if you could bear me offering you one last piece of advice. Tread carefully when it comes to Titus. He's... not the guy he used to be. Pippa's all right, and Titus is still a friend, but... just be careful about him. He's changed in recent years, and I'm not entirely sure I like what I've seen. I know, for my sins, how fun they can be. Do yourself a favour and chalk it up to experience and just leave it there. Your life will be much simpler without those two in it.'

A slight chill runs down the back of my head as I listen to Ambrose's words.

'He... he said some things to me... things I didn't quite... things about his father... adopted father... about his murder...'

Ambrose's eyes lock with mine then and he holds my gaze for a few seconds before blinking.

Then he says, 'Yes. He's said some things to me too.

Take my advice. Just don't go there. It seems you have enough in your own life to be going on with.'

And with that, he turns on his heel and walks out the door.

Don't forget to pick up your copy of *The Dinner Guest* to find out more about Titus and a past steeped in blood and secrets...

**Four people walked into the dining room that night.
One would never leave.**

Matthew: the perfect husband.
Titus: the perfect son.
Charlie: the perfect illusion.
Rachel: the perfect stranger.

Charlie didn't want her at the book club. Matthew
wouldn't listen. And that's how Charlie finds himself
slumped beside his husband's body, their son sitting
silently at the dinner table, while Rachel calls 999, the
bloody knife still gripped in her hand.

**Two strangers meet on the pier
Only one walks away...**

Screenwriter Caroline Byrne is desperate to know why
her daughter Jessica died, murdered in Stratford when
she was supposed to be at a friend's in Somerset.

When Caroline discovers the messages Jessica had been
sending a boy named Michael, she realises it's because of
him. Because he failed to meet her that day. He's the
reason why her daughter is dead. And so she makes a
choice. He's the one who's going to pay.
That is her promise. Her price.

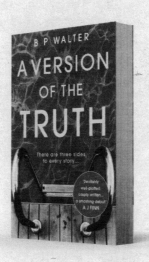

We all see what we want to see…

2019: Julianne is preparing a family dinner when her son comes to show her something on his iPad – something that will make her question everything about her marriage and turn her husband into a stranger.

1990: A fresher student at Oxford, Holly is well out of her depth when she falls into an uneasy friendship with a group of older students and begins to develop feelings for one in particular. He's confident, quiet, attractive, and seems to like her too. But she soon begins to realise she might just be a disposable pawn in a very sinister game.

If you go down to the woods today,
you're in for a big surprise…

Kitty Marchland has always known that her family aren't like others. But when her father uproots them to a remote cottage in the woods, she realises that her parents are keeping secrets from her – secrets that could unravel everything.

Years later, Kitty starts to question what really happened out in the forest. When the police revisit a suspicious death, she must examine her most painful memories – and this time, there's nowhere to hide…

ONE MORE CHAPTER

YOUR NUMBER ONE STOP
FOR PAGETURNING BOOKS

The author and One More Chapter would like to thank everyone who contributed to the publication of this story...

With special thanks to Bethan Morgan.

Analytics
Emma Harvey
Connor Hayes
Maria Osa

Audio
Charlotte Brown

Contracts
Georgina Hoffman
Florence Shepherd

Design
Lucy Bennett
Fiona Greenway
Holly Macdonald
Liane Payne
Dean Russell
Caroline Young

Digital Sales
Michael Davies
Hannah Lismore
Fliss Porter
Georgina Ugen
Kelly Webster

Editorial
Charlotte Ledger
Lydia Mason
Rebecca Millar
Bethan Morgan
Jennie Rothwell
Tony Russell
Kimberley Young

Harper360
Emily Gerbner
Jean Marie Kelly
Juliette Pasquini
emma sullivan
Sophia Wilhelm

HarperCollins Canada
Peter Borcsok

International Sales
Hannah Avery
Alice Gomer
Phillipa Walker

Marketing & Publicity
Emma Petfield
Sara Roberts

Operations
Melissa Okusanya
Hannah Stamp

Production
Emily Chan
Denis Manson
Sophie Waeland

Rights
Lana Beckwith
Samuel Birkett
Rachel McCarron
Agnes Rigou
Zoe Shine
Aisling Smyth

The HarperCollins Distribution Team

The HarperCollins Finance & Royalties Team

The HarperCollins Legal Team

The HarperCollins Technology Team

Trade Marketing
Ben Hurd

UK Sales
Yazmeen Akhtar
Laura Carpenter
Isabel Coburn
Jay Cochrane
Sarah Munro
Gemma Rayner
Erin White
Leah Woods

And every other essential link in the chain from delivery drivers to booksellers to librarians and beyond!

ONE MORE CHAPTER

YOUR NUMBER ONE STOP

FOR PAGETURNING BOOKS

One More Chapter is an
award-winning global
division of HarperCollins.

Subscribe to our newsletter to get our
latest eBook deals and stay up to date
with all our new releases!

signup.harpercollins.co.uk/
join/signup-omc

Meet the team at
www.onemorechapter.com

Follow us!
@OneMoreChapter_
@OneMoreChapter
@onemorechapterhc

Do you write unputdownable fiction?
We love to hear from new voices.
Find out how to submit your novel at
www.onemorechapter.com/submissions